# MURDER ON
# SUGAR STREET

# MURDER ON SUGAR STREET

## JEAN HARRINGTON

**W❂RLDWIDE**

TORONTO • NEW YORK • LONDON
AMSTERDAM • PARIS • SYDNEY • HAMBURG
STOCKHOLM • ATHENS • TOKYO • MILAN
MADRID • WARSAW • BUDAPEST • AUCKLAND

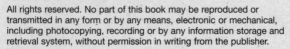

**W♦RLDWIDE**™

ISBN-13: 978-1-335-73642-0

Murder on Sugar Street

First published in 2020 by Camel Press,
an imprint of Epicentre Press, Inc.
This edition published in 2021.

Recycling programs
for this product may
not exist in your area.

For questions and comments about the quality of this book,
please contact us at CustomerService@Harlequin.com.

Harlequin Enterprises ULC
22 Adelaide St. West, 40th Floor
Toronto, Ontario M5H 4E3, Canada
www.ReaderService.com

**Printed in U.S.A.**

# ONE

A GOOD OL' BOY named Carl Huggins came to me a while back with big news. He wanted to sell the Chocolate Moose, a former bordello he inherited from his daddy's side of the family.

"It's been boarded up for fifteen years now, and that's a mighty long time," Carl said, laying a key attached to a heart-shaped ring on my desk. "Another year or two and the place'll be beyond repair. That would be a cryin' shame, seeing as how it's a beloved landmark and all. So I'm set on selling and won't let nobody but Winthrop Realty handle the sale."

"Well, you're mighty flattering, Mr. Huggins," I began, "but—"

"It's only as it should be, Honey. After all, Saxby Winthrop's great-granddaddy founded this here realty office, and he was the Moose's biggest customer."

I didn't ask what he meant by biggest but took him at his word and then gave him the bad news. "Before I try to sell the property, Mr. Huggins, you need to understand one thing."

"Oh?" His left eyebrow quirked up as if there wasn't a thing in the world he needed help in understanding. "What might that be?"

I suspected he wouldn't take kindly to what I had

to say, so to ease my tension, I leaned back in Saxby's well-worn chair and swiveled up a storm. "The fact is, due to the house's reputation, finding a buyer might be well nigh impossible."

With his forefinger, he stabbed the air in front of my nose. "Hmph. For your information, missy, everybody here in Eureka Falls loved the Moose."

"Not everybody," I countered, bringing the chair to a full stop.

"You mean the womenfolk?"

*Bingo.* "And, Mr. Huggins, let's not disremember one very important fact."

"What's that?"

"When it comes to buying a family home, the woman is pretty much the decider. A house is not a home, if you know what I'm getting at."

Of course, he did. I could see it in his eyes, but not ready to give up being ornery, he said, "Meaning?"

"A lot of potential buyers won't have anything to do with an old cat house. Not even if you set the price real low. Which I think you'll have to do."

"You do, huh?" He perched on the edge of his chair and leaned over my desk so far, his Confederate belt buckle scraped the edge. "What's the top selling price of other houses on Sugar?"

"If you give me a minute, I'll check my Multiple Listing stats."

"You go right ahead and do that, young lady. With that long blond hair and them big gray eyes, you're mighty pretty, but that don't mean diddly when it comes to strikin' a deal. What I want is for you to get the highest price possible for the Moose."

He squashed his John Deere back onto his head,

gave the brim a yank and stomped out of my office. Too bad. I hadn't had time to tell him the agency was no longer Winthrop's. It was Ingersoll Realty now, with the name written in gold on the front window for all the world to see.

Ingersoll happens to be my name. Honey Ingersoll, thank you very kindly. I'm twenty-five, going on twenty-six, living the single life and determined to run the most successful realty business Eureka Falls, Arkansas, ever did see. That meant I had to beat out my competitor, Sam Ridley. Sam was my former boss and the man I once loved for three fruitless years. If he had loved me back I wouldn't still be in the single state today, but all the heartbreak's behind me now. The future is what matters, and to make it blossom like a prize-wining rose, I had to keep on selling every house I could. Even, if need be, a cat house.

# TWO

---

AFTER CARL LEFT, I sat for a spell, thinking about his offer and what it meant to Ingersoll Realty. Though beloved by some, in general the Moose had a shady reputation around town, and I couldn't let my business be tarred with that brush. I was struggling to establish myself as an honorable, above-board Realtor, someone you could trust with the most important purchase of a lifetime.

On the other hand, any house, even one with a bad name, didn't have a soul. Like any other listing, it was made up of brick and mortar, wood and plaster. At least that's what I told myself. What had gone on at the Moose ended years ago. People forget. I swiveled a while longer, letting all these thoughts swirl around in my head, then muttering a word not fit for mixed company, I brought the chair to a stop and strode out to Mindy, my receptionist. After taking over from Saxby Winthrop, I'd moved her desk by the front window so she could greet people as soon as they stepped inside. The arrangement mostly worked out fine except when, like now, she filed her nails for everyone on Main Street to see.

"Plum Wicked, today?" I asked, pointing to her finished right hand.

She turned red in the cheeks. "Only five more to go and I'll put the polish away."

"Good. When you do, will you look up ML sales figures for properties on Sugar Street. Go back four or five years. I need a long view of the street's price range."

"Will do."

That done, I grabbed my purse and Carl's heart-shaped key ring and lit out for the Moose.

RIGHT OFF MAIN STREET, Sugar Street was one of the oldest in town. It was also one of the quirkiest, anchored by Grace Church in limestone and granite on one side of Sugar and Main and the Toole Shed Sports Bar on the other. God and mammon cohabiting side-by-side, an example folks always mentioned when they wanted tighter zoning laws.

But what made the street wonderful was that all along it a double row of ancient elms reached for the sky. The branches were bare naked now but come summer, they would shade the roofs, the lawns and all of Sugar's front verandahs, a real nice feature, one I've always admired.

I liked the way the road curved, too, drifting left, then right, making you feel you were meandering, even when you had a purpose in mind. Then when you least expected it, the curve ended in a cul-de-sac, and snugged in that dead end stood the Chocolate Moose.

*Oh my.* I peered through the windshield, searching for traces of former glory and found a few: stately columns holding up the verandah, a carved front door with a stained glass inset, and wooden shutters at the windows, though one hung loose from a single hinge.

In a high wind, it would bang against the wall like a scary scene in *The Chainsaw Massacre.*

Carl Huggins had been correct. From all outward signs, the Moose was in tough shape. Even the chocolate brown paint that gave the house its name was flaking off, leaving the shingles bare in places.

I stepped out of the car and strolled up the uneven brick walk studded with tufts of frozen grass. Come spring, someone would have a major weeding job on their hands, but at least the verandah stairs felt sturdy underfoot. No crashing through loose floorboards.

With the key at the lock, I was about to open the front door when a "Yoohoo, hello, there!" stopped my hand in midair. I whirled around.

An elderly woman, a sweater tossed over the shoulders of her cotton dress came hurrying across the street in bedroom slippers. She was a heavy-set, fleshy person, and the effort cost her. But finally, all huffy and puffy, she joined me on the verandah and stuck out a hand. "I'm Verna Ledbetter," she said. "And you are?"

A chilly breeze was blowing through her permed hair, and I'd warrant through her dress too. But she didn't seem to feel the cold as she waited for my answer.

Something about her was familiar. "Do I know you, ma'am?"

"Well, most folks in town do. My husband was pastor of Grace Church for years." Her eyes clouded over. "Until he passed."

"I'm sorry for your loss, Mrs. Ledbetter," I said, shaking her hand. "I must have seen your picture in the *Star*. No wonder I feel like we've met."

Craning her neck, she peered up at me—and I'm

only five-six, well, five-nine in my red open-toe stilettos.

"I don't recall seeing you in church, that's why I came over." She half-turned to point to a well-kept bungalow diagonally across the street. "I live there now. After Roger passed, I had to move out of the parsonage. It nearly killed me, so full of memories you know, but God's will be done."

"Amen." *What on earth did this woman want?*

"You still haven't told me your name."

"Oh, sorry. I'm Honey Ingersoll of Ingersoll Realty." I rummaged in my purse for a business card.

She read it and frowned. "Does this mean the *house*," she spat out the word, "has been sold?"

"Not yet, but it's about to go on the market."

"Oh my God." A hand flew up to her mouth. "My deepest fear's been realized. I begged Roger Junior, he's my son, not to buy that house across the way for me, but he never did listen." She glanced over her shoulders, and though there was no one to hear, she hushed her voice. "Are you aware of what this property was used for?"

"Yes, ma'am, I am."

"A whorehouse. Right on the same street as a house of God."

"A sorry business, I agree, but those days are long gone, and well, as the Bible tells us, Jesus hung with prostitutes."

"Don't you quote the Bible to me, young woman." She looked me over carefully, as if taking in my red heels and matching bag for the first time. "You're not planning to reopen this abomination, are you? 'Cause if you are—"

I threw up my hands. "No, no, no! Have no fear on that score, Mrs. Ledbetter."

"Good. If I had the money, I'd buy the place and tear it to the ground. But," she shrugged, "a minister works for the Lord not for filthy lucre." Her voice hardened. "Be careful who you sell this abomination to, Miss Ingersoll." She snatched at the sweater that was about to fly off her shoulders. "Or you might find it'll meet with an accident."

# THREE

As Verna Ledbetter slipper-shuffled across the street for home, I told myself bullies came in all shapes and sizes. I'd learned that in grade school, so no surprise there. I guess as a minister's widow she felt honor-bound to keep Sugar Street free of sinners. Well, I wished her luck and, turning back to the Moose's front door, I twisted the key in the squeaky lock. It turned easily enough, and I stepped inside.

I have to admit my pulse revved a bit, what with the house's reputation and all, but no need for that. It was as sedate as a tomb and just as cold. No dull-eyed women, no laughter, no eager good ol' boys. Those days were over forever, and good riddance.

I shivered. If there was a furnace in the basement, I doubted it had been turned on all winter. Or maybe not for years. I sniffed and tried not to inhale the damp, musty air that hinted of dead mice, or worse, live ones.

In the dim half light, I could tell that the rooms on either side of the front hall were empty of furnishings but couldn't make out much more than that. I flipped the light switch by the front door. Nothing. Of course, the electricity had been turned off. Carl Huggins sure had some work to do if he wanted top dollar on this property.

I strode over to one of the front windows and yanked on the dark green shade that had been pulled down to the sill. It fell off the roller and clattered to the floor.

That should scare the mice. I glanced around at the now bright, sunlit room, the old dining room maybe, and let out a whistle. The temperature in here might be frigid, but the walls were hot as Hades, painted the same shocking pink as that stomach preparation some folks favored. Even the radiator and the bricks around the mantel were pink. I wandered back out to the center hall. Cabbage roses everywhere, big fat ones in deep red. In the parlor on the other side of the hall, I raised another shade, more carefully this time, and groaned. The walls were a shiny gold with the fireplace mantel sprayed to match. Was the rest of the house as bad?

Worse.

A drab, gray shell, the kitchen had outdated cabinets, a linoleum floor and thirty-year-old appliances. I sighed. Understandable. No one had come to the Moose for a nice, home-cooked meal.

Now for the bedrooms.

Telling myself not to be silly, still I crept up the stairs like a person heading into Sodom and Gomorrah. I didn't get too far when Grandma Ingersoll spoke up. Though she passed ten years ago, she still talked to me from time to time.

"Are you pure as the driven snow, Honey? A while back, didn't you live with Saxby Winthrop for two whole years even though you had no love for the man? We both know that's the God's honest truth, so don't go judging folks because they sin different than you do."

By the time Grandma finished setting me straight, I'd reached the landing, took a deep breath and pushed open the first door. A big square room, it had been emptied of everything, even sin.

The same for the second room in front and a third in the back. As for the bathroom, everything in there was what you might call pure antique—including a claw-foot tub and a tank toilet with a chain for flushing. I closed the door and opened the one to the last bedroom, figuring it would be the same as the others, a square empty box with hideous, flowered wallpaper.

Wrong.

A double bed with an old iron frame stood in the center of the room, its lumpy mattress topped with a pile of faded throw pillows and a homey-looking quilt pieced in what appeared to be the log cabin pattern. Imagine that. A log cabin quilt. My momma had one years ago. To get a better look at the stitching, I raised the cracked window shade before turning back to the bed. The mattress must have had a lot of hard use; it was uneven as all get out.

Sure enough, the quilt had been pieced in pink, green and blue, a pretty combination much like my momma's. I picked up a corner to have a look at the backing and let out a scream. Staring up at me, grinning from ear to ear, was a human skull.

# FOUR

LIKE THE QUILT had caught fire, I dropped it. Still screaming my head off, I ran down the stairs as fast as those killer heels would let me, flung open the front door and high-tailed down the brick path that sure hadn't led to Oz.

Locked in the Lincoln, with my hands trembling so bad they were useless as cooked spaghetti, I fumbled in my purse for the cell. After two tries, I finally hit Sheriff Matt's number. He picked up on the first ring, and I heaved a sigh of relief. I could always depend on Matt Rameros. He was my go-to person—in more ways than one.

"Matt, I just found a dead body. Oh God, it's awful. All the flesh is eaten away. It's nothing but bones. I'm so upset I can't think, I can't talk straight, I can't—"

"Whoa, Honey, whoa. Slow down. Where are you?"

"On Sugar Street, outside the Chocolate Moose."

A pause on the other end of the line. "What are you doing there?"

"Looking it over. Carl Huggins is putting it up for sale."

"You're safe?"

"I guess. I'm locked in my car."

"Sit tight. I'll be right there. Keep your engine running, and if anybody approaches, drive off immediately. Understand?"

I nodded—that's how far gone I was—and hung up.

In a few minutes, a siren wailed in the distance, came closer and, with blue lights blazing, a cruiser screeched to a halt in back of my car. That's one good thing about a small town. Nothing is too far away, including the cops.

Matt, short, solid and forever dependable strode over to me followed by lanky deputy, Zach Johnson. At the sight of them, all the tension whooshed out of me. Had Verna Ledbetter heard the sirens? I glanced across the street. Yup. The lace curtains at her front window had been snatched aside, and a woman stood there peering out.

Looking anxious, Matt opened my driver's side door. "You all right?"

I nodded and pointed at the Moose. "But whoever's upstairs on that bed hasn't been right for a long time. Who would do that, Matt? Leave a body to rot until all the flesh dropped away." The mousy odor of the house came rushing back to me. "Or was eaten away." I shuddered.

"Keep the car locked and sit tight. We'll be back." He upped his chin at Zach. "Let's go."

Hands on holsters, they hurried up the brick walk and disappeared into the Moose.

Before leaning back on the headrest and closing my eyes, I risked another peek across the street. The shadowy figure still stood at the window, figuring, I guess, that whatever was going on outside beat the soaps.

In no time flat, both men came stomping down the verandah steps. My eyes snapped open, and at the sight of Matt striding toward me with a big smile on his face, I flung open the car door and jumped out. "What's so funny?"

"Nothing really, Honey. Actually, it's kind of sad."

*"What?"*

"That body up there?"

*"Yes?"*

"It's a plant. A practical joke. Or somebody's idea of one. Look at this."

He handed me a slip of paper. Letters in different sizes and colors had been cut out of a magazine and pasted together to form words:

*Carl Huggins,*
*You got skeletons in your closet, boy.*

I lowered the paper. "What about the body?"

"It's a lab specimen. The kind they use in anatomy classes."

"Really?" Though I'd graduated from Davis County High School, my daddy had told me to take business courses and skip all the folderol—like science. The only skeletons I'd seen before today were Halloween fakes.

Matt pocketed the note. "There's an implied threat here that isn't good. As long as you're okay, I think Zach and I will pay a little call on Mr. Huggins. See if he has any idea who might have done this. Another thing, was the house locked up when you got here?"

"I think so. The front door, anyway."

Matt turned to his deputy. "Before we leave, want to check around?"

Zach, silent as usual, nodded and took off.

Matt swiveled his attention back to me. "When you got here, did you see anyone around the property?"

"Only Reverend Ledbetter's widow. She's pretty upset the Moose is going on the market. She'd like to see it torn down instead."

"Yeah? Where does she live?"

"Over there." I pointed to her bungalow.

As we both glanced across the street, the lace curtains in Verna's front window twitched closed and then lay still.

The excitement over, Matt went back to the station, and wasting no time, I hightailed it for work right after him. I had a phone call to make.

# FIVE

"CARL, WE'RE HAVING an open house at the Moose this weekend. Saturday and Sunday from one to five."

"You mean you're invitin' everybody in Eureka Falls to traipse through the place?"

"If we're lucky," I said, sensing resistance in the voice booming through the line.

"What good'll that do? Every snoopy Sally for twenty miles around will be comin' in to gawk. Nothing more, either, mark my words."

"You could be right. But an open house won't cost anything except my time. It's the fastest way to get the property seen by the greatest number of people. And we need to cast a wide net. The truth is, Carl," I paused, knowing he'd take my words as an insult and not as an appraisal, "the Moose is in bad shape."

"Well, a coat of paint'll do wonders."

"True, that will help. So will new wiring, new plumbing and a new roof." I took a deep breath and let the list sink in. "What's the furnace like?"

"That all you got to say?"

"No, the house has good bones—big rooms, high ceilings and moldings like you don't see everyday, but—"

"You saying the Moose is a dump?"

*Bingo.* "It could be a showplace, but not without a total facelift, if you take my meaning."

A deep, put-upon sigh chuffed into my ear. "Daddy paid taxes on the place all these years and for no good reason I can think of. I was aiming to get back the money he's put out, but from what you're saying, I can't expect no more than ten cents on the dollar."

"The market's tight, Carl, and the history of the house, plus its condition—"

"Say no more, missy. First, I got the sheriff talking about a skeleton and asking if I got enemies. Which I ain't. Now I got you telling me the Moose is a dump. That's enough grief. So, let's give that there open house a shot. See what happens."

He hung up.

KELSEY DAVIS, EDITOR of the *Eureka Falls Star* peered at the photograph, the address, and then glanced up at me real fast. "If I'm not mistaken, this is that old…the, ah…the Chocolate Moose."

"Correct, Kelsey, it is."

"Well, I'll be hornswoggled. This is the most interesting piece of local news since Josie at the diner married her short order cook." He threw back his head and broke into a belly laugh. He took a while getting over it, too, before saying, "You can count on me being at your open house. Wouldn't miss it, in fact. The Moose up for sale will make a great feature article." His voice had gone a little high with excitement. "No charge, of course. Not for the article. Now as to the ad, how big do you want it?"

We settled on a quarter page, right side placement. That and an announcement in the agency's front window near Mindy's desk ought to cause a buzz. Maybe even turn a curiosity seeker into a buyer. It only took one to make a sale.

Saturday morning dawned bright, clear and cold. The day before, I raised all the shades in the Moose to let in as much sunshine and warmth as possible and had Eureka Falls Fuel Service take a look at the furnace, which they declared hopeless.

Four hours in an unheated house in the middle of January called for guerilla clothes—shit-kicker boots from my high school days, long johns, wool pants, two sweaters and a knitted muffler in bright purple wrapped around my neck three or four times. Gloves, too, just in case. Plus, a thermos of coffee.

Stowing the gloves in my pockets, I stood by the entrance, waiting for the first visitor. I didn't have long to wait. At one on the dot, Kelsey Davis bounced up the steps toting his fancy camera like he was about to photograph a party.

"Welcome," I said. "You're the first one to come calling."

"Couldn't wait to see the place. I've heard so much about it."

I pointed to a notebook I'd set out on a card table along with some business cards and a stack of flyers praising the property—its high ceilings, fancy moldings, fireplaces, the quiet location near churches, shopping, restaurants. And at the bottom of the page in big bold letters: "Priced To Sell."

"Will you sign the guest book for me, Kelsey, and include your phone number, please?"

"Sure." He did, then raised his camera. "Mind if I take a few pictures? Might use one or two in the article."

"Why that would be grand, if you can get a good

one." I waved my arms around at the empty rooms. "It might not be easy what with the wallpaper and all."

"I'll do my best." He headed upstairs as a pair of giggling women strolled in. My Realtor's warning flag told me they were here for entertainment only, but I greeted them with a warm, country smile anyway. A serious-looking couple followed them then an elderly gentleman who needed a cane to manage the verandah steps. A former client of the Moose?

"Just wanted to see the ol' place one last time," he said heading into the parlor. *Yup, a former customer and not ashamed to admit it.*

By one thirty, the rooms were buzzing. By two, despite a light snowfall, a line had formed at the foot of the stairs. It was so long you'd think this was the opening of a new movie or something. Everyone wanted to see the bedrooms, but nobody would get a skeleton scare up there like I'd had. As evidence of the prank, Matt kept the skeleton at the station. But since no one had been hurt and nothing stolen, the investigation had ended there. As for the rickety iron bed, Joe's Junque carted it off to the dump.

By three o'clock, Kelsey had photographed every room and was busy interviewing visitors who weren't too shy to admit their curiosity, and the guest book was filled through page four. Though I'd lost track of how many people had come and gone, I'd greeted a lot of folks, done a lot of smiling, and shaken a lot of hands. But nobody had said a single word about bidding on the Moose. So maybe Carl had been right; the open house was a waste of time.

And then it wasn't.

From behind me, a deep voice murmured, "Long time, no see."

*Andy Ballou.* As I turned to look at him, he stepped around to face me. Nothing had changed. He was as tall as I remembered, his hair as dark, and his eyes still seemed to peer into your secret wishes. And he still smiled like he was glad to see me. I guess that was good, but I hoped he wasn't about to start something with me again. For all his height and elegance and his law degree from Vanderbilt University, the truth is I just didn't trust him.

"It's my fault we haven't met these past months. I'm afraid I've been remiss."

"Does that mean neglectful?" I asked.

"It does," he said, not looking at me now but staring at the ugly gold wallpaper like it was the best thing he'd ever met up with.

Though Andy used to be my lawyer, I hadn't seen him for six months, not since the murderer of Carmen DeLuca, his client and lover, was sent to jail. Long over Sam Ridley by then, I might have fallen for Andy, but he was too slick talking for a plain-spoken girl like me. Besides, when I first met him, he was in love with a dead woman. When I realized that, I didn't return his calls, and after a while they stopped.

I managed a smile, wondering why he was here and what he wanted from me.

An elderly man, this one without a cane but with a drift of musky Old Spice aftershave, was about to leave. He nodded as he went by. "Thank you, ma'am, for the trip down memory lane."

I offered him a flyer. He refused it with a shake of his head. "No thank you. It wouldn't do to bring that home. Give myself away, don't you know."

"So you're not interested in the asking price either."

"Not any more, my dear."

*Oh.*

As he made his way out the door, I glanced over at Andy who looked like he was about to bust a gut.

I pointed to the elderly gentleman's retreating back. "He just out-foxed me. Guess I have a lot to learn."

"Don't worry about it, Honey. In the things that matter, you're sharp as a tack."

I shook my head. "Country smarts ain't...aren't what I mean. I grew up in a double-wide at the end of a dirt road. Unfinished edges stick out all over me. And you, well, you're a smooth-taking lawyer."

It was after five now, starting to get dark. No footsteps echoed on the bare hardwood floors. We were alone. The open house was over. I grabbed the flyers and guest book, stuffed them in an envelope and set them on the parlor mantel.

"Let me help," Andy said, taking the card table and upending it. My, he sure was trying to be nice. What was that all about? While he folded the table legs, I went upstairs to check for stragglers, but the rooms were empty.

"I'll put the table out by your car," Andy called over a shoulder as I came downstairs and hurried out to the kitchen to make sure the back door was locked.

Though I could no longer feel my feet, and my fingers were stiff as a box of pencils, the frigid air in the kitchen took my breath away.

Good Lord, the rear door to the mudroom was open and rocking back and forth on its rusty hinges. I hurried out to grab it before it banged against the wall, in my haste nearly tripping over something in the gloom. What the heck was that?

I glanced down. A man with his legs drawn up under him, lay huddled on the floor. In the dim light, I couldn't tell who it was and bent over him. He didn't move. Had he fainted? Was he dead? As if in answer, he moaned and rolled onto his side. I gasped. "Kelsey, what happened? Are you sick?"

"No. Mugged." With a groan, he sat up and, propping himself against the wall, he fingered his head. "It's sticky. I think I'm bleeding." He shivered. "It's freezing in here."

*The door.* As I hurried over to slam it shut, a single, bare patch of brown on the snow-covered yard caught my eye. What could that be? Curious, I leaned over the porch railing.

*Omigod.* A woman in a brown parka lay on the ground. She was stretched out on her back, and beneath her, a streak of what looked like blood had gouged a little river in the snow.

I screamed, and Andy came running around the side of the house.

"My God, what's the—"

"There, down there," I yelled, pointing.

He raced to the woman, knelt beside her and put his fingers on her throat. "I can't get a pulse," he said. "I think she's gone. Call 911." He glanced up and, as if hating to admit it, added, "It's Darlene Petty, a client of mine."

# SIX

Outside the Moose, an ambulance and Matt's cruiser screeched to a halt at about the same time. While one medic tended to Kelsey who, shoulders hunched, hadn't moved from the mudroom floor, Sheriff Matt, Deputy Zach and the other medic hurried to the woman who lay unmoving on the snow.

The medic knelt by her side, stripped open her jacket and examined her for signs of life. After a long, tense moment, he shook his head then gently closed her coat and her eyes. "We're too late," he said to Matt. He pointed to a rip in the front of her parka. "She was stabbed. Looks like she bled out."

"We need the coroner." Grim-faced, Matt took out his cell, called State Police and asked for Detective Bradshaw in the homicide division.

The kitchen door opened and aided by the medic, Kelsey Davis, his face nearly as white as the bandage on his head, stumbled down the back stairs to the yard.

"He may have a concussion," the medic told Matt. "We'll take him in for an MRI."

"My wife's going to be upset. And what about my car?"

"If you give us your keys," Matt said, "my deputy will drive it to your home and notify your wife as well.

Before you leave, do you have anything to tell us? Anything you might have seen or heard?"

"Yeah. My camera. It's gone. It was a Leica. I paid five thousand dollars for that baby. Used it nearly every day, and I can't afford to replace it. Now what?"

"You didn't see who hit you?"

Kelsey shook his head and winced again. "The back door was open. I went to shut it and the next thing you know I'm on the floor."

Mad as a swarm of hornets, and who could blame him? Kelsey let himself be helped into the ambulance.

I blew out a breath. He'd get a story all right, but not the one he'd planned on.

To escape the cold and put some feeling back into our fingers and toes, Andy and I sat in the backseat of Matt's cruiser with the car heater going full blast and waited for Detective Bradshaw and the medical examiner.

His phone calls finished, Matt got in behind the wheel and half-turned to us. "Deputy Zach's out back with the body. I'll spell him in a few minutes, but first I want to get a heads up before Bradshaw arrives. While the open house was going on, Honey, did you see anyone or anything that seemed suspicious?"

"No, nothing. Everyone acted very mannerly, though most of the folks were just curiosity seekers. No one offered to bid on the house." I couldn't hold back a sigh. "Not even the ones who signed the guest book."

Matt's eyes sparked with interest. "Everybody had to sign in?"

I shook my head. "No. Some folks walked on by. Then it got so busy I lost track. But quite a few pages are filled."

"Bradshaw will want to take a look at that." Matt paused, made a note in his smart phone then upped his chin at Andy. "When did you get here?"

"Around quarter to five, just before closing time. Only a few stragglers were left. I didn't notice anything unusual."

"You interested in buying the Moose?" A testy edge in Matt's voice.

"No, I'm interested in..." *Honey? I think he was going to say my name but caught himself in time.* "...in, let's say, historic preservation."

"That so?" Matt frowned. "Did either of you know the deceased?"

I shook my head.

"She was Darlene Petty, a client of mine," Andy said.

"Did you know she'd be here today?"

"Not at all. Though I'm not surprised."

"Explain."

I'd seldom known Matt to be so short with his words but forgot all about that when Andy said, "Darlene had a personal interest in the Moose."

"What kind of interest?" Matt asked, his tone frosty.

Andy leaned forward and stretched his hands over his knees. "Lawyer-client confidentiality doesn't terminate with death, so I'm not free to reveal the nature of our discussion. Not without a court order."

"That'll be up to the man," Matt said. "And here he is."

Holding his back stiff as a plank, Matt climbed out of the cruiser and slammed the door. Detective Bradshaw from the Arkansas State Police had just rolled up in his big, black SUV.

# SEVEN

ALONE IN THE CRUISER, Andy and I sat side-by-side in an awkward silence. I was about to crack and mention something, anything, even the snow when he pulled off his gloves then tugged off mine. He took one of my hands. "I've missed you, Honey. Have you—"

Before I could pull my hand back, Matt opened the cruiser door. As he peered in, he turned red in the face, though that could have been due to the cold. "Detective Bradshaw will take your statements in his vehicle. It's roomier."

Frowning, like he'd never gotten the hang of smiling, he held the cruiser door open for us. Our gloves back on, Andy and I trudged through the deepening snow to the SUV where we repeated what we'd told Matt earlier.

When we were through, Detective Bradshaw, tall, lean and poker-faced, said, "That's all for now. Try to get to the station tomorrow to sign your witness statements. If we need you later in the week, we'll be in touch." He snapped his notebook closed and turned on the wipers. A few swipes of the blades cleared the windshield, but not for long. "Looks like the storm's getting worse."

The snow, falling soft and slow most of the afternoon, had picked up speed and, whipped by the wind, began pelting the car. Bradshaw glanced up at the sky then back at Andy and me. "I believe the efficiency of our state snow removal system is about to be tested. I suggest we all hit the road ASAP. If you wish to leave your vehicles here overnight, we'd be happy to escort you both safely home."

Smooth as silk, Andy hauled out his lawyerly language. "I appreciate the courtesy, detective, but I'll be glad to see to Miss Ingersoll's safety."

Andy sure had an elegant way of speaking, but talk is cheap. He had most likely come to the Moose today because of his client, Darlene Petty, not because of me.

So, keeping my voice cool as the temperature, I said, "Thank you, Mr. Ballou, but Sheriff Rameros has offered to see me home." A lie white as the snow falling all around us.

WITH THE SNOW so thick, I couldn't tell if Verna Ledbetter was still peering through her lace curtains. If so, she had a lot to tsk-tsk over, but the excitement was about to die. The ambulance carrying Kelsey Davis had already left for the Yarborough County Hospital. Darlene Petty's remains had been lifted into the coroner's panel truck and transported to the morgue. And a few minutes later, the medical examiner left, too, followed by Detective Bradshaw. With a regretful little smile, Andy whispered in my ear, "I'll be in touch," and drove off.

I asked Matt for a ride home and gave Zach the heart-shaped key ring so he could lock up the Moose. When he returned with the keys, Matt said," Get Kelsey's car over to his wife. I'll bring Honey home and pick you up at the Davis house as soon as I can."

With a great spinning of tire wheels, Zach took

off. Still looking out of sorts, Matt helped me into the cruiser, got in and turned on the ignition.

"The weather's taken a bad turn," I said, hoping to start him talking.

"I have eyes to see." His voice was as cold as the ice filming the road.

"Oh, really?" Heat rushed through my veins. "That tone, sheriff, is not…not acceptable. When you speak to me, keep a polite tongue in your head. You hear?"

He touched two fingers to his uniform hat. "Yes, ma'am. And when you're in my cruiser, don't play patty cake. I'm not running a dating service."

"He was keeping my hands warm."

"Tell me something I don't know."

"You jealous?"

"Damn right," he said, stomping out of the car to clear off the windshield and free the wipers from the frozen glass.

The frown still in place, he knocked snow off his uniform hat before slouching back behind the wheel.

"There's something you might like to know, sheriff," I said as polite as if he'd just stopped me for running a red light. He didn't ask, "What?" but I plunged on anyway. "I think Attorney Ballou came to the open house to see Darlene Petty. Not to see me."

"That your theory?" Setting the wipers on top speed, he put the cruiser in gear. I was sorry Matt was upset, but this had been a long disaster of a day, and I felt as frozen as the world outside the cruiser, too cold and frozen to bother sparring with him any more.

We coasted along Sugar just fine, at least most of the way. A few feet shy of Grace Church on the corner of Main, the front wheels seized up on a patch of ice.

The car swerved out of control and slid off the road, straight into a wind-whipped drift.

"Damn." Matt revved the engine, keeping his foot on the gas pedal so long a cloud of black smoke spewed out of the exhaust, but the cruiser didn't budge. "No traction," he muttered. "I'll have to get the shovel from the trunk and dig us free."

Despite our predicament, the silent, falling snow was a picture to behold, turning the veiled lights of nearby houses into soft, glowing stars.

"Looks like we're having a white Christmas," I said.

"Christmas is over. This is just a mean-hearted storm." Matt flung opened the driver's side door, stepped out and nearly fell on his rear, grabbing the door edge in the nick of time. "It's glare ice. Stay where you are."

He inched along the front of the cruiser to my door, opened it and offered me a hand. "Come on, it's not as slippery here. I'll help you over to the Toole Shed. You can wait in there while I dig out."

"Why don't I stay and help you? Once the front end is clear, I can get behind the wheel and rock the car back and forth while—"

To my relief, for the first time in over an hour, he smiled. "There's probably a law against that. I'll be just fine, knowing you're warm."

And I did feel warm just then, for more reasons than one, as I trudged, with Matt's arm around me, over to the bar and grill.

# EIGHT

THOUGH NEARLY DESERTED TONIGHT, the Toole Shed Sports Bar was a Eureka Falls institution. Tim O'Toole and his daddy before him had run the place since the Chocolate Moose's so-called glory days. Rumor had it that the Shed's two original owners, Carl Huggins' daddy and Tim O'Toole's, were silent partners. If not in crime, in shabby dealings.

But that was then, and this was now, and Tim was known for running a clean, well-tended business. In any event, I was grateful to get out of the cold and step into the Shed's warm, steamy air.

Except for a couple of men perched on barstools, their eyes focused on a big screen TV, the place was empty. No wonder Tim greeted me like a long-lost friend and beckoned me over to the bar. A big man with long bones and short hair that made him look like he'd just been released from military service—or prison—he flashed a smile as he ran a rag over the bar top. "What's a pretty girl like you doing out on a night like this?"

"I'm waiting on the sheriff. We got stuck across the street, and he's digging out." I glanced over at the two customers who were listening in. "He sure could use a helping hand."

They went back to their beers.

"Why the sheriff? You in trouble?" Tim laughed at his own joke, showing off a set of big, yellow molars. His laugh set my teeth on edge. Nothing about today had been funny, not a single thing.

"No, I'm not in trouble, but somebody is."

The two customers looked over, and Tim stopped swiping at the bar top. "You don't say?"

"Afraid so. A woman was found murdered this afternoon. Right here on Sugar Street."

Picking up their beers, the men moved in closer.

"You hear that?" Tim asked them. "A murder, right up the street." He switched his attention back to me. "You know who was killed?"

I shook my head, unwilling to give him Darlene's name before her family could be notified. "I never saw her before in my life."

"Well, that's what I call a darn shame, a crime like that in our own backyard. Makes a body wonder who the poor soul was, don't it?"

"Yes, it does."

"I suppose we'll know soon enough. As soon as the *Star* gets a hold of the particulars."

With Kelsey in the shape he left in, I doubted the bad news would hit the press very fast, but I nodded anyway.

"That's quite a story, Miss…ah, Miss…"

I held out a hand. "Honey Ingersoll's the name. I run Ingersoll Realty over on Main." I plucked a business card out of my purse and set it on the bar. "If you know of anyone interested in buying a house on Sugar Street, would you let me know?"

"Sure thing." He picked up the card and slid it into his pants pocket. "Which one you selling?"

"The big one in the cul-de-sac."

His jaw dropped, and he forgot about ragging the bar. "Well, I'll be damned. You hear that, fellas? The Moose is up for grabs."

After they got through whistling, Tim leaned over to me and rested his elbows on the bar. "Honey, that house has got a bad history. You better be careful. A lot of folks hereabouts won't take kindly to having the Moose occupied again, and I'm one of them. If you know what I mean."

"Your warning's a little late, Tim. I've already been threatened."

I flung my purse over a shoulder and slid off the barstool.

"Where you going? You haven't had a drink yet."

Without bothering to answer him, I marched across the room and yanked open the door.

"Hey, tell the sheriff, I'd be happy to do some shoveling," he called, "but I'm short-handed. My bar girl, couldn't make it in tonight."

"That's too bad. Anybody I know?"

I don't know what inspired me to ask, but I'm glad I did.

"Joanne Petty," he said.

# NINE

"MATT, STOP SHOVELING for a minute."

He peered around the cruiser's front end, face red with effort, bare hands white-knuckled from cold. Pushing the shovel upright into a drift, he straightened and caught a deep breath. "Almost through. Why aren't you inside, keeping warm?"

"Couldn't abide any more of Tim O'Toole's blather."

He laughed and yanked the business end of the shovel out of the snow.

"Tim told me something you ought to hear."

"What's that?" A shovelful hit the sidewalk.

"His bar girl is someone named Joanne Petty."

"Petty, huh? Interesting, but that's a fairly common name in these parts. This Joanne might not be kin to the victim you found, might not even know her."

I stomped my feet, and not just to keep them warm. "On the other hand, she might."

"Correct." Matt opened the trunk and tossed in the shovel. "Why don't you wait in the cruiser out of the cold while I go have a little chat with Tim?"

"THEY'RE RELATED, ALL RIGHT," Matt said ten minutes later as he slid behind the wheel. "According to Tim, she's Darlene's daughter and lives at the same address,

here in town. At least on weekends while she's work-
ing at the Shed. Monday through Friday she lives in
Fayetteville. In the Kappa Kappa Gamma sorority at
U of A."

"Oh my, good for her." I tamped down a twinge of
regret at never having been to college. Never having
stepped foot in a sorority house. Never, when you came
right down to it, ever having had a head for book learning.

Matt put the cruiser in gear, inched forward and
eased onto a nearly deserted Main Street. The wind
buffeted the car, sending the overhead traffic signals
swaying over the road. We fishtailed on an icy patch
then steadied.

"Okay, this is a first," Matt said, running a red light.
"If we stop, we might get stuck again." He peered
through the hard-working wipers. "No sign of a plow.
Guess this one caught the highway crew with their
pants down."

"Well, high time they pulled up their britches and
got to work."

He laughed and yanked his attention from the road
for a second to glance across at me. "Funny thing about
Tim O'Toole. When I said I needed to get in touch with
his employee, he didn't ask why."

*Maybe he already knew the answer.*

Anyway, Matt dropped me off safe and sound but
without a goodbye kiss. Now what did that mean?
Mysteries, big and small, were piling up around me
like snow, and I didn't have an answer for a single
one of them.

# TEN

LATER THAN USUAL, but with its usual thud, the *Sunday Star* hit my front stoop. Risking an icy draft, I opened the door and grabbed the paper.

Despite the blow to his head, Kelsey had come through. In big, bold letters, his headline screamed: "Murder On Sugar Street." I sank onto the living room sofa and read his account. The *Star* was a family newspaper, so Kelsey had seen fit not to mention the house's bawdy history, only that it was a property well known to some of Eureka Falls' older citizens. How was that for saying something without saying it? Anyway, I was grateful for his careful wording, if not for his photographs showing the Moose all run down and shabby looking. Below those pictures he'd printed a snapshot of Darlene Petty looking years younger than the woman I found stabbed to death.

I padded over to the front window and peeked out. Traffic was moving along Hillside Avenue. The plows had been out during the night, then. So had Matt or Zach, or both, for brushed clean of snow, my Lincoln sat outside in my designated spot. And sure enough, when I checked the foyer floor, the keys had been dropped through the mail slot.

An hour later, in a black turtle neck, jeans and yes-

terday's boots that had dried stiffer than Verna Ledbetter's face, I slowly drove over the frozen roads to the
office. With the Moose a closed-off crime scene, there
would be no open house today and, after a quick call
to the station, I learned my witness statement wouldn't
be ready for signing until late afternoon. No need to
waste the day. I could set up appointments for the coming week, check my voice mail, and be ready to take
calls from folks interested in bidding on the Moose. A
long shot, as my gambler daddy used to say.

Hoping passersby would notice Ingersoll Realty was
open for business, I brought my laptop over to Mindy's
desk. The sunshine reflecting off the snow felt warm
and comforting, for yesterday's chill hadn't left my
bones, not completely. Though the cold I felt probably
had nothing to do with winter weather and a lot to do
with the image of Darlene Petty stretched out on the frozen ground with her life's blood draining into the snow.

Anyway, by forcing the sadness out of my mind and
concentrating on the tasks that needed doing, I finished
the desk work by three and arranged for two showings
later in the week. But even with Kelsey's story plastered
all over the *Star*—or maybe because of it—not a single
soul had called asking about the Sugar Street house.

I was about to leave for the day when the front door
opened, letting in a gust of bone-chilling air and a
young woman who stomped the snow off her boots
and swung a backpack off her shoulders. Straight, dark
hair fanned out from under a woolen ski cap pulled low
on her forehead. The scarf wrapped around her throat
matched her hat and a pair of cornflower blue eyes
that would have been mighty fetching if they weren't
so red and puffy.

"Welcome to Ingersoll's," I said. "How can I help you?"

I really wanted to know, for in a parka with a University of Arkansas crest next to the zipper, she sure didn't look like she wanted to buy an old whore house. Or any other house, for that matter.

"My name is—"

"Joanne Petty?"

Her stressed, pretty eyes widened. "How did you know?"

"A wild guess." I got up from Mindy's desk and went around it to shake her hand. "I'm so sorry about your momma."

Her chin quivered, and the tears hovering under her lids spilled over. Instead of shaking her hand, I hugged her, hard. She was soon sobbing so bad I helped her into the visitor's chair across from the desk.

"Is there anything, anything at all, I can do for you?"

"My…my momma," she began.

"Yes?" Softly.

"The police told me you found her."

"I did. I'm sorry to say."

Her lower lip trembled. "She was so wonderful. And…and now she's gone."

The tears were taking over her cheeks. I snatched some tissues out of the box Mindy kept on the desk and pressed them into Joanne's hand. She stared at them like she had no notion what they were for.

Helpless in the face of her grief, I patted her back and murmured little meaningless words. "There, there now. It'll be all right. Please don't cry." Words that aimed to be comforting but weren't. There were no words to ease such sorrow. And then, somehow, there were.

Still clutching the tissues, she glanced up from her hands. "You were there when my momma died."

"Well—"

"Before she passed, did she speak to you, say even a few words?" Letting the tissues fall to her lap, Joanne reached out to seize my hand. Then came the real question, the one I guessed had brought her here today. "At the end, did she mention my name, or ask for me?"

When I found her, Darlene's life had already bled into the snow. She had no message for anyone, not even her daughter. But as I watched this broken girl weep for what had been stolen from her, I knew what I had to do.

"Yes, your momma whispered in my ear. She said, 'Tell Joanne goodbye for me. Say I love her.' Those were her very last words. She loved you so much she couldn't leave this earth without telling you so." I knew I'd never told a truer lie.

While Darlene's message from the brink of the grave couldn't make Joanne happy, it did help dry her tears and put a wobbly smile on her face. "Thank you so much. When the detective let on that you'd found her, I knew there had to be more than he was saying. Momma would never leave me without a single word."

"No, she wasn't that kind of person."

"You knew her?"

*Uh-oh.* As Granny Ingersoll always said, one lie leads to another.

"Well, Eureka Falls isn't a real big town. Seems like everyone around here knows everyone else."

She nodded, but only slightly. Clearly, she wasn't convinced. "Sometimes people think they know others, but they don't. Not really." She bent down to pick up her backpack. "I'll always be grateful to you, Miss Ingersoll."

"Honey. Call me Honey. And please don't rush off. I made coffee a while ago, and the pot's still full. There's a box of jelly donuts too."

Though I couldn't have been but a few years older than Joanne, I felt motherly toward her just then, maybe because she needed mothering so bad.

Anyway, her chin firmed, and I thought she'd refuse, but she let the backpack slip out of her fingers and, reaching for some fresh tissues, dabbed at her eyes. "I'd like that, Honey."

And so we sat by the plate glass window for a while, sipping coffee and watching the traffic slowly ease past the snow piled up on both sides of Main Street.

To break the silence that had fallen between us, I said, "Tell me what you're studying at the university."

"I'm an anthropology major."

"Really? What *is* that?"

"The study of ancient civilizations."

"Well, I'll be darned. What kind of civilizations?"

"Any and every kind. We search for signs of human habitation, of lost cultures. In other words, we dig."

"Dig?"

"Into the site to learn what life was like centuries ago. Maybe thousands of years ago."

"Since Bible days?"

"Maybe older than that."

"*Why?* What do you hope to find?"

She shrugged. "It depends on the dig. Old bones, pottery shards, tools, that sort of thing."

Though I didn't say so, what a silly thing to fuss over. What good could it do to dig up old bones and stuff? Also, it was downright creepy to talk about such doings now, what with her momma about to be buried and all. The weather struck me as a lot safer, so I pointed out the window. "Look at all that snow piled around. Yesterday was really something. Worse storm in ten years, so they say."

"I know. I couldn't get in from Fayetteville. I waited too long, and the roads got all icy. Then a state policeman came to the sorority to tell me…"

Her voice trailed off into nothing.

"My momma passed too. I know how much it hurts. I really do." I reached across the desk to squeeze her hand then said the dumbest darn thing. "Have a jelly donut. It'll make you feel better."

As if anything could, but she attempted a smile and almost made it. "Maybe I should. I haven't eaten since yesterday, and I have to stay alert. Wouldn't do to fall asleep on Mr. Ballou."

That sure made me sit up and take notice. "Mr. Andarius Ballou, Esquire?"

She nodded, plucked a raspberry-filled donut from the box and set it on her paper napkin. "He was my momma's attorney. Now I'm fixing on making him mine."

"I know him" I said. *But not as well as I might have.*

She took a bite of her donut. "I'm meeting him later today to talk about my Aunt Juanita. My momma's sister." Joanne wiped her sticky fingers on the paper napkin, staring down at it as she spoke. "The truth is, well, Juanita used to work at the Moose."

"As a…?"

Joanne flushed pink all the way to her hairline. "I'm afraid so. But that's not why Momma called on Mr. Ballou."

"No?" I leaned in closer so as not to miss a word.

Joanne shook her head. "No, when their Aunt Louise passed away a month or so ago, Momma had to go through her papers and such. That's when she found an old letter from Juanita. It got her all upset."

"Why?"

"In the letter, Juanita said she was scared of someone."

"Did she say who?"

"No. Just that she was leaving Eureka Falls to hide out for a while and not to worry about her. Next thing you know, she commits suicide. Jumps off the Ames Bridge over the Arkansas. Her body was never found. Swept down river and was lost, or so the story goes."

"Story?" I felt one of my eyebrows quirk up. "Your momma didn't believe it?"

"For years she did. You see, at the time Juanita disappeared, she sent another letter. A suicide note, I guess you could call it, and everybody believed that one. Even Momma. But not since last month after she found the old letter Juanita had sent to Aunt Louise."

"Why not?"

"It's dated a week after Juanita's suicide."

*Ouch.* "So, she could have been alive when she was reported dead?"

"That's what Momma thought. She surely was hoping Juanita might still be alive."

"Or she could have died—somehow—some way—after sending the suicide note."

"Right. Either way, whether Juanita is dead or alive, I aim to find out. I stopped by Momma's apartment on my way here to get the letter to Aunt Louise. I'm bringing it to Mr. Ballou." Joanne wiped the sugar off her lips, crumpled her napkin and tossed it in the waste can. "Juanita's a stranger to me. I never knew her, never met her, never even saw her. But I have to learn what really happened to her for my momma's sake." She stood and picked up her backpack. "I think Momma was killed because she was looking for Juanita. Dead or alive, somebody doesn't want her found."

"What happened to that other letter, Juanita's suicide note?"

"I don't know. Momma went looking for it sometime ago, but she was told it had been destroyed."

"Who told her that?"

"The person Juanita sent the letter to. A clergyman she trusted. The pastor of Grace Church. Reverend Ledbetter."

# ELEVEN

I'D NEVER SLEPT with Andy Ballou, not once. I never trusted him enough for that and still didn't. What was I? Some kind of fiddle to be picked up, plucked, then tossed aside when the song ended? Anyway, as he stared at me across the waiting room outside Matt's office at the Eureka Falls Police Station, those were my thoughts. Maybe I should have been ashamed of them, but I wasn't. I was wary.

"Honey," he said, his eyes sparking. "Again. At last."

The man had no call speaking to me like that, but he didn't seem to know it. "I intended to call you yesterday, but something came up and I didn't have a chance to. Would you have hung up if I did?"

"Why would I do such a thing? You helped me real well when I took over the real estate agency."

"But that was business, what I had in—"

Matt Rameros suddenly opened his office door and poked his head out. "Honey, Ballou, come in, your statements are ready."

Andy and I followed him into his sorry, plywood box of an office. I sat on the one molded-plastic chair facing the desk, and Matt dragged in a second one for Andy.

As he waited, we read through our statements and

signed them without comment. Then Andy dropped a bombshell. "Joanne Petty still missing?" he asked Matt.

Matt nodded. "Far as I know. No one we contacted has been in touch with her. It's too soon to issue a missing person's report, but I think it would be prudent to enter her mother's apartment without further delay."

"You have a warrant?" Andy asked.

"It's in the works. My deputy's gone to pick it up." Matt turned our statements face down on his desk and stood.

"Would somebody tell me what's going on?" I asked, reaching for the purse I'd set on the floor by my chair.

"We don't know for certain," Andy said. "Joanne Petty was supposed to meet me yesterday afternoon but never arrived. Under the circumstances, I was worried and called the sheriff."

"So far, no one in town's seen her since her mother was murdered," Matt said.

"I did." Both men turned to me, their jaws gaping open. "She came to the office yesterday. We had a long chat about her momma. Afterwards she left to meet you, Andy."

"She never made it," he said, grim-faced.

My breath caught in my throat. Oh Lordy, had I been the last one to see Joanne alive? At the horrible notion, all heat drained from my face, turning my flushed cheeks icy cold.

Andy rose from his seat. "I'll follow you to her apartment," he said to Matt.

"I can't stop you from following me, but I go in alone," Matt said.

"As you wish."

"You got that right." Matt opened the door to his

office and ushered us out without another word or the faintest hint of a smile. Worse, when I passed him, his eyeball contact was steely as all get out. I heaved a mental sigh. Lately, I wasn't giving anybody what they wanted—definitely not Matt and not even Carl Huggins. And for sure not poor Joanne Petty, wherever she might be on this cold Monday morning.

As the two men drove off, Matt with just a farewell dip of his uniform hat, Andy with a murmured, "I'll call you," I piled into the Lincoln and eased over fresh patches of ice to my office, relieved to see the building manager had cleared the rear parking lot.

Mindy was already at her place by the front window, looking fetching in a tight, black turtle neck, boots to her knees, and a sliver of a black mini skirt. Thank the Lord somebody had invented tights. Otherwise, she'd be stopping traffic on Main Street.

She leaped out of her chair the minute I stepped inside. "Omigod, Honey. The whole town's talking. You found a dead woman *murdered*?"

"I'm afraid I did."

"My girlfriends are so scared. They've been calling and calling, but I told them all I knew was what was in the paper. Did you—"

"Later, okay?" To soften my words, I said, "You know something? Black is really good on you."

"On you, too." She eyed my pants suit. "Black is always good on blondes. After reading about the murder, I figured it was the right color for today." She brushed a fringe of bangs out of her eyes with a long, daggery nail. I pointed to it.

"That have a name?"

She held out her hand, fingers spread wide. "Black Widow."

I almost said, "perfect" but caught myself in time. There was nothing perfect about the weekend's events, but black, the color of burials, felt right even though nothing else did.

"Any calls?" I asked as she handed me the morning's mail.

"A few cranks rang up. One ol' lady said the Moose should be burned to the ground."

"Not surprising. Anything else?"

"Two folks asked for the sale price."

"Oh?" I glanced up from the mail.

"As soon as I axed—"

"Asked."

"Yeah, as soon as I axed for a number so you could call back with the price, they hung up. Both of them."

Okay, this probably wasn't a good time to start, but I was vexed enough in general to stir up a hornets' nest.

"Mindy, do you know who our biggest competitor is?"

She looked stunned, like I'd asked the dumbest question in the world. "Why Mr. Sam Ridley of Ridley's Real Estate. Everybody knows that."

"Right. And do you know where he went to school?"

She shook her head.

"Princeton University."

"Wow, I didn't know that."

"Well, now you do. Do you also know why I'm telling you this?"

"Haven't a clue."

"Because Mr. Ridley looks like he went to Princeton,

acts like he went to Princeton and talks like he went to Princeton. In other words, he's a mighty elegant man."

"Oh, I'll say. One of my girlfriends saw him at—"

I held up a hand, palm out. "You and I didn't go to college, never mind a fancy school like Princeton, so we have to work harder than Sam Ridley to be professional. To have people think we're as smart and capable as he is. Otherwise, why should they trust us to sell their houses? Or to steer them to a good buy?"

"I don't get your drift, Honey."

"When you answer our phone and you need to ask a body for a piece of information, what do you say?"

"I say, 'Can I ax you—'"

"Stop right there. Did you hear it? The 'x'?"

Mindy put her hands on her hips. "Honey, I don't understand a thing you're saying. Have you taken leave of your senses?"

"Maybe. I'm kind of half-crazed by what's gone down lately. But I'll tell you this: I struggle every day to use the right words, to sound like a professional woman, and one thing I've learned is that there is no x in asked. When you say it, try thinking of the Bible."

Her mouth rounded into one of those disbelieving O's.

"Try it. What's the beast of burden the Bible mentions over and over? The—"

"Ass?"

"Exactly. So, pretend a client is calling and you need to know something. What do you say?"

"I want to ax you a question."

"I want to kill myself."

"Well, my goodness."

"Don't worry, I won't. It's one of those figures of

speech Sheriff Rameros told me about. We can talk this over later, all right? Until then, if anyone calls sounding half way reasonable, send him on through to me."

"Will do."

Frazzled beyond belief, I brought the mail, all bills, into my office, ditched my down parka and sat swiveling for a spell.

The Moose wasn't the only house I had for sale. There was a bungalow on a neat street of look-a-likes that in my humble opinion was priced above fair market value, a condo two blocks from the office that was a steal, and a townhouse in a business block that was being remodeled as housing units. But truth be told, the Moose is what held my attention. The Moose and the tragic death of Darlene Petty and now the mysterious whereabouts of Joanne. Not to mention Kelsey Davis's mugging and the disappearance of his five-thousand-dollar camera.

In the outer office, the phone rang on and off all morning, but Mindy didn't forward any calls, so I figured they were all dead ends. Either that or her girlfriends were checking up to see how her weekend had gone. I tamped down my irritation. As friends, they had a right to their curiosity, didn't they?

And as a Realtor with a toxic house on the market, I had the same right, didn't I?

*Yes.*

I grabbed my cell and punched in Matt's number. "Any news for me?" I asked right off, knowing he'd recognize my voice.

"Nothing so far. Joanne's not in her mother's apartment. I'll keep you posted." The line went dead.

*Hmmph, still upset.*

While I tried to think things through, I set the swivel

back to doing what it was born for. Other than agreeing to meet Matt in front of a preacher, there wasn't much I could do to ease that situation. And if Joanne, God forbid, had come to harm, nothing I could do would help her, either. But I didn't want to go down that road. I wanted to believe she was alive and well and kicking up her heels somewhere. If so, where might she be?

*Think. Think.* I was trying, but the squeaky swivel didn't help. Those springs could use a drop of oil.

The one person on earth Joanne had loved the most was her momma. Until Darlene's body was released for burial, the closest Joanne could get to her would be the last place she had been on earth. The Moose. A long shot, but my appointment to show the bungalow wasn't until two. Plenty of time to get over to Sugar Street and look around.

Oh crap, I forgot about the crime tape. But there it was, a yellow plastic ribbon stretched across the steps to the verandah.

More than likely tape would block off the back porch too. After all, that was where… I stifled a sigh and climbed out of the Lincoln. The sun blazed away like it was July or something, the snow melting and running in rivulets along the street. Within seconds, the wet had seeped into my high-heeled suede boots, and by the time I tromped around to the side of the house, my feet were soaked. And darn it, the back porch *was* taped off.

I took a deep breath of winter air and watched a cardinal, a ruby jewel, flit from branch to branch. Who could blame him? I'd fly too if I could. This had been a fool's errand. And I was the fool to think Joanne would be hanging around this dismal, closed-up house even if her beloved momma had died here.

Now what? Break the tape and break the law? Or forget about inspecting the house and leave?

"Hello there. You don't give up, do you?"

Startled, I whirled around, stepped in a puddle and cussed.

In a pair of men's shoes and the same cotton dress I remembered, Verna Ledbetter said, "You know better than that, Miss Ingersoll."

"Indeed, I do, Mrs. Ledbetter. The devil made me do it."

She nodded. "He's a sly one, no doubt of that." She pointed to the tape across the back steps. "Isn't this God awful? I knew opening up this house meant nothing but evil." She sniffed like the clear, cold air offended her. "While I'm not one to praise myself, this time I'm justified. Why only last night I told Joanne if—"

I gasped. "By any chance would you be meaning Joanne Petty?"

"Why yes, the poor thing. Yesterday afternoon I happened to be looking out my front window, don't you know, and saw her wandering around over here. After all my years of ministry by Roger's side I know a lost soul when I see one, so I invited her in to sit for a spell."

Verna stepped out of some slush and moved onto a bit of dry turf. "When I spied you getting out of your car just now, I wondered if you had any news about, you know, the murder."

I shook my head. "All I can tell you is the police are searching for Joanne. Do you have any idea where she might be?"

"Why, of course, I do."

# TWELVE

VERNA REMOVED HER men's tie shoes at her kitchen door and scowled at my damp boots. After I wiped them good on a scrap of rug she kept in the entryway, she said, "Come in, then. The girl's in the kitchen."

And so she was. Joanne Petty in the flesh.

She looked up from the sink where she was drying a cup on a dish towel so smooth I'd lay odds it had been ironed. She turned to me with a little smile. "Honey, what a nice surprise."

"I'm sure glad to see you, too," I said, the air whooshing out of my lungs in relief. "Attorney Ballou's so worried he has the police out searching for you."

It's a good thing she had set the cup down by the sink, or it likely would have slipped out of her hand and smashed to smithereens all over Verna's shiny kitchen floor. That would have been a shame, seeing as the floor was so clean you could eat off it.

Before I could say any more, Joanne hid her face in her hands and burst into tears.

"Now see what you've gone and done." Verna whipped a crocheted handkerchief out of her skirt pocket and handed it to Joanne.

"Don't cry," I pleaded. "I'll call the lawyer and the sheriff. Tell them you're safe. I promise, it'll be all right."

She nodded and wiped her eyes. "Mr. Ballou shouldn't have bothered the police."

"But he—"

"Mrs. Ledbetter called him yesterday to say I was here and would see him today."

"Verna?" I asked.

She stood at the sink, peering out at the back yard. "Land's sake, if that cardinal isn't on my clothes line again. Why it's getting so a body can't hang out a decent wash these days."

"Verna? Did you call Joanne's attorney yesterday?"

She folded a dish cloth over the sink rim before turning to me slowly, like she was puzzling out the answer to a hard question. "I tried. The phone rang and rang but nobody picked up."

"You told me you called him," Joanne said.

"Well, for heaven's sake, girl, didn't you just hear me say I did?"

"But—"

"It don't...doesn't matter," I said to Joanne, though, of course it did. "What matters is that Verna kept you safe all night. But since the sheriff is looking for you, why don't I call him while you collect your things? Then I'll drive you over to Mr. Ballou's office if you like."

"Thanks, Honey, my car's parked down at the Toole Shed lot, but I'd rather ride with you. I didn't mean to cause so much trouble. I just wanted to see my momma's last resting place. Now everybody's all upset."

I shook my head. "No, we're not." My second lie in less than two minutes. "Are we, Verna?"

As Joanne hurried out of the kitchen, I shot Verna a steely glance. I must have been getting better at them, for she looked down, studying the linoleum pattern like she'd never seen it before.

"Sins of omission," I whispered, something from a long-ago Bible lesson I couldn't quite recollect but somehow remembered.

At my words, she pulled her attention from the floor to peer into my face. What I saw glittering in her eyes caused me to take a step backward. Though that wasn't the only thing that gave me a sudden chill. A well filled knife rack stood beside the sink, and I had a notion that if touched, the knives would be sharp as hog stickers.

JOANNE GAVE VERNA a good-bye hug—personally, I couldn't bring myself to touch her—and we left for Andy's office. Traffic was light, but with snow lingering in spots, the going was slow. "The sheriff said he'd let Mr. Ballou know you're on your way," I said, as we stopped at a traffic light.

Joanne glanced across the front seat. "I should never have broken that appointment yesterday, but Mrs. Ledbetter was so kind I hated to refuse her. She had cooked a big supper and all, so I…"

"Stayed. No harm done. You needed the company is all."

As miserable as a motherless puppy, she nodded. "Mr. Ballou wants to see that letter I told you about. The one where Juanita says she's scared of somebody. I have it in my backpack. Right inside this flap."

She lifted the bag to her lap, undid the Velcro opening and reached in. "Omigod." The pack slipped to the floor mat. "The letter's gone."

# THIRTEEN

ONE LOOK AT Joanne's crumpling face, I pulled over in front of Josie's Diner and killed the engine. "Why don't you take everything out of the pack and double check? It might be in a different pocket."

"No." She shook her head. "When I left Fayetteville, I put the letter in the outer flap and haven't touched it since."

"Check anyway."

With a sigh, she did as I asked. "Told you so," she said a few seconds later. Her chin and her voice wobbly, she stuffed everything back in. "Mr. Ballou will never believe there ever was a letter. Nobody will believe it. Nobody."

She half turned to me, her eyes a bitter blue. "You know something, Honey? I swear my momma died because of that letter." She choked up like going on was too painful, but then she coughed and cleared her throat. "The backpack was never out of my sight except last night while I was asleep. There's only one person who could have taken it."

We blurted out the same name. "Verna Ledbetter."

"But she's such a God-fearing person." Joanne clearly didn't want to believe bad about the woman.

"Maybe taking the letter was her idea of the right thing to do."

"But *why*?"

"I don't know. All I know is you need it to convince the police there might be a connection between Juanita's disappearance and your mother's death. It isn't much to go on, but it's all we have."

*We.* So maybe Joanne and me...I...weren't sisters, not even second cousins twice removed, but still I felt a kinship though we'd only met yesterday. Not so many years ago, I was alone and scared, too. I didn't have no...any...murder and suicide weighing me down, either. Just Billy Tubbs and his ready fists. He was my first boyfriend, and I'm ashamed to admit he gave me a black eye one day. But I'm proud to say I left him that very same day. Then Josie gave me a waitressing job in the diner and helped me put my life in order.

While my early troubles had been partly my own doing, Joanne's had been dumped on her by other people, and that was worse. Anyway, whatever the cause, the girl needed a helping hand. It was as simple as that.

I sucked in a breath of winter air. "We've got to get the letter back." *If it hasn't already been destroyed.* "So, you willing to break the law?"

"How?" Her eyes big.

"You get Verna out of the house while I go in and search it."

"You'd do that for me?" she asked, tears threatening to roll down her cheeks.

"To help catch your mother's killer? Yes."

I searched my purse for a tissue, found a wrinkled one and pressed it into her hand. "You keep on blubbering, you'll wash all the pretty blue color out of those eyes of yours." I turned on the engine and pulled into traffic. "Now before you call on Mr. Ballou, let's make us up a game plan for outfoxing Mrs. Ledbetter."

WHILE JOANNE DROVE up Sugar to get Verna and take her to Josie's Diner for lunch, I parked in the Toole Shed lot and waited. In no time flat, they sailed by in Joanne's Mini-Cooper. Verna staring straight ahead and Joanne, to her credit, not giving the Shed's lot a passing glance before turning onto Main Street.

As soon as they got through the stop light, I put on my shades, tied a scarf around my head and hopped out of the Lincoln. Five minutes later, I stood at Verna's front door, pretended to ring the bell and, with my heart in my mouth, tried the handle.

*Yes.* Joanne had left it unlocked. Clever girl. She'd make a good anthro, anthro—whatever.

Inside, the radiators hissed like snakes. I stayed still for a moment, breathing in air perfumed with cleaning solutions—lye, bleach and some kind of industrial strength soap. Now where to look? Verna was too neat a housekeeper to leave anything out of place. I had to search where a letter would look like it belonged. In the kitchen first. She might have messages and bills and such on a shelf, maybe near her cook books. Working fast, I riffled through some circulars and utility bills, but the letter wasn't there.

A desk then. Quick as a fox in a henhouse, I raced into the dining room and then into the front parlor but nothing in either room looked like a place to stash papers. I ran down the narrow hall to the bedrooms. In the second one, on top of an old kneehole desk, a letter holder was filled with neatly arranged envelopes. I lifted them out and sorted through the stack. *Ha.* Hidden in the middle I hit pay dirt—a yellowing envelope addressed in a bold hand to Miss Louise Nivens.

I dropped the rest of the stack onto the desktop, reached in the envelope and plucked out the letter.

Dear Aunt Louise,

I know you're worried about me, and I'm sorry
for all the grief I've caused. At heart, I'm a good
girl, please believe me.

   Also I'm scared right now. Somebody is
threatening me. I'm telling you this not to upset
you any more than I already have but to say if
anything happens to me, please call the police.
Kindly regards,

Your loving niece,
*Juanita*

*Wow.* This was everything Joanne had said it was
and more. Why Aunt Louise hadn't brought it to the
police years ago was anyone's guess, but Joanne was
right, they needed to see it now.

   As I stared at the letter, something about it seemed
familiar, something I'd seen before but couldn't quite
recollect for a second before it came back to me in a
flash. The paper had the same yellow cast as the hate
note I found in the Moose by the fake skeleton.

   I'd have to—*wait.* Except for the steamy radiators,
the house held a deadly silence. So what was that? A
click, a step, a door closing.

   *Omigod.*

   "Are you home, Mother? How about a sandwich?"

   *Verna's son. The one who never listened.*

   I stuffed the letter into its envelope and shoved it in
my coat pocket. The other letters I dropped back in the
desk top holder. Pulse pounding like some kind of jun-
gle drum, I looked frantically around for a place to hide.

   *Under the bed.*

"Mother, do you know you left your front door unlocked? How many times have I told you to be careful?"

I slid beneath the twin bed until my backside hit the wall. Trying to make myself small, I huddled in a ball, knees to chin. Heart hammering in my chest, I lay without moving or making a sound. Overhead, a few inches from my eyes, the springs sagged down, and to my left, a flowered bedspread hung to the floor.

"Hello, anybody home?"

Keeping still as a church mouse, I peered out from under the hem of the bedspread fringe. Verna's son, quiet in his sock feet, stepped into the room, checking to be sure his momma was okay. Despite all, I had to smile. To keep her floors clean, he'd taken off his snowy shoes. So he did listen.

He padded into the other bedroom. A minute later, the refrigerator door opened and quickly slammed shut.

"Nothing worth eating around here. I should've known."

A few quick footsteps—he'd likely put his shoes back on—and the house returned to its hissy silence. I stayed under the bed for a while until I was sure he was gone before crawling out. *Ha.* No need to even brush myself off. There were no dust bunnies in Verna Ledbetter's house.

A few moments later, I slipped away more than satisfied with my prize. What I'd found had been worth risking jail for. Suppose after all these years, the writer of the skeleton threat had used the same notepaper as the letter stashed in my coat pocket? What could that mean?

# FOURTEEN

LIKE BAD GUYS were hot on our trail, I drove to Andy's law office hunched over the wheel with one eye checking the rearview mirror while Joanne, peering out the passenger side window, rode shotgun. In both our minds, we carried the key to unlocking a murder mystery.

Andy Ballou thought otherwise. "Very interesting, ladies. But without a closer connection, I can't see how Juanita's letter will help prove your theory that there's been foul play."

"Theory?" Joanne leaped up, grabbed the letter off his desk and pulled it out of the envelope. "Look at the date. Look at the postmark on the envelope. This was written and mailed *after* the suicide."

He leaned back in his chair and laced his hands together over his nice, flat belly. "Suppose Juanita had the date wrong? Or suppose whoever wrote it hung onto it for a few days before dropping it in a mailbox?"

Joanne glanced over at me, her eyes dull. "He's right."

"We left out something, Andy," I said.

"Now what would that be?" The tone of his voice saying whatever it was, he doubted it would amount to any more than a hair on a flea-ridden dog.

I pointed to Juanita's letter. "I think this letter and

the hate note I found in the Moose last week were written on the same kind of paper."

"Proving?" One of his eyebrows arched up, daring me to go on.

"Proving that the same person could have written them both. Either Juanita or somebody who knows what happened to her."

"First of all, a handwriting expert would have to examine both documents."

*Uh-oh.* "The hate note didn't have any writing on it."

"It was typed?"

I shook my head. "No. The letters were cut out of a magazine and pasted on the page."

"Well, there goes a significant piece of your evidence."

"But what if the papers match?"

"Even if they do, I think what you'd have is nothing more than an interesting dead end, unless of course—"

I moved to the edge of my chair. "Yes?"

"You have both documents tested. It's doubtful they'd contain DNA evidence, but there might be fingerprints. Still, it's a long shot. How many people have handled these letters?"

"I don't know about the hate note Honey found," Joanne said, "but I'd venture to say Juanita's suicide letter to Aunt Louise has only been handled by her and my mom. And now you and me."

"Don't forget Verna Ledbetter," I added.

Joanne's shoulders slumped. "Right."

"There's also the person who wrote it in the first place," Andy added. "In light of what's happened to Darlene, my guess is the police will test the hate note for prints. Whether they'll share that information with you is another story." He tapped the Nivens envelope. "As far as this letter is concerned, see if the police will test it as well." Then he arched a brow and shot me a wicked grin. "Seems our town sheriff's in a tizzy over you. If you work your magic on him, he might fall over backward to help."

I felt my spine stiffen. Matt was too honorable to do anything he didn't think was in his department's best interest. "You don't know the sheriff, then."

"And you do?"

Somehow, the subject had gone down a slippery slope. Not wanting to slide along with it, I stood, buttoned my coat and smoothed on my gloves. What I knew about Matt was none of Andy's business, but this wasn't the time to tell him so. I was here to help Joanne and for no other reason.

Joanne plucked the letter off Andy's desk. "I'll be needing this."

He nodded. "If the police refuse to help, you can send it to a private lab, but that won't be free. Until your mother's estate goes through probate, money will be tight. So you might want to rethink your—"

She shook her head. "No. I've done my thinking. I'm on semester break, so I can work at the Toole Shed every night. I wasn't going to. It seems disrespectful to work in a bar right now but," her jaw firmed, "I'll do it. I'll do whatever it takes, Mr. Ballou. Whatever it takes."

She tucked the letter in her backpack and zipped the flap. Andy escorted us to his office door. "I'll be in touch, Joanne, as soon as I have your mother's affairs in order. Be careful, both of you."

As Joanne started down the stairs, he said, "Can I have a word with you, Honey?"

"Take your time," Joanne called over a shoulder. "I'll wait in the car."

Andy put his hands on my shoulders. To my relief, the down coat and the gloves, the scarf and the hat kept him from pulling me close. I didn't want him to, so I was glad for the heavy clothes. Though he was an attractive man and a good lawyer, he was just too slick, too well, Vanderbilt, for me to get up close and personal with. Still, he was helping Joanne, and for her sake, I smiled and made nice.

"What I told you the other day is true," he said. "I've wanted to call you. All these months. You don't know how many times I almost did but—"

"Didn't."

He touched his forehead to mine. "If you had hung up or told me not to call again, that would have been the end. Until that happened, I had hope." He stepped back a little to look into my eyes. "Am I allowed to hope?"

I couldn't believe my ears. Andy Ballou who stood up in courtrooms and pleaded big, important cases was standing there pleading with me—and waiting for an answer.

I was flabbergasted and pulled away.

"Will you have dinner with me? The Hickory Lounge? Saturday evening?" he asked, moving in closer again.

*The Hickory with its romantic little alcoves and dim lighting? No way!*

Since I had accompanied Joanne here today, he knew I was helping her search for her mother's killer. Going forward, Joanne might need his legal advice. Maybe I would too. It would be best not to refuse. So instead of, "No, sorry, I'm busy," I hesitated, struggling for a reply. Then, ah! "What about the Toole Shed instead?"

He reared back. "Really?"

"Um-hum. I heard tell they have great burgers."

He shrugged. "Not quite what I had in mind, but if that's what you'd like."

"I would." It was the least date-like place I could think of, and that's just what I wanted.

"I'll meet you there."

"Eight?"

"So late? I eat my burgers a lot earlier than that."

He laughed and I hurried down the stairs. Joanne was leaning against the Lincoln, shivering.

"Oh gosh. I'm sorry," I said, letting her in the car and turning on the heater.

She looked across the front seat with a little, knowing smile. "He ask you out?"

"Yup. The Toole Shed for burgers."

"Knew it. He's crazy about you. I could see that a mile away."

"You think?"

"Absolutely." Her smile fled like it had never been. "You're lucky. I wish I had someone to love."

She sounded so wistful, so lonely, I tried to lighten her mood. "Who said anything about *love*? We're just going out for burgers."

"There's burgers, and then there's burgers. They're not all created equal."

No, they weren't. Some weren't hardly fit to bite into, but not wanting to shake Joanne's confidence in Andy's legal ability, I held my tongue. A few minutes later at the police station, Joanne *did* get lucky. Sort of.

Matt listened to her story without interrupting then took a pair of cotton gloves from a desk drawer and examined the letter to Aunt Louise.

"Strictly speaking, this letter refers to a closed case that's almost twenty years old. Even with the anomaly in the dates, which could have several causes, we wouldn't take this any further. But," he picked up the hate note, "the paper used for both documents appears to be identical. In light of what happened on Sugar Street, I think the two letters should be dusted for prints."

Joanne beamed like morning sun.

"However," Matt folded the letters carefully and slipped them into a manila envelope, "unless the prints we find match others in our database, they'll be of limited value."

Her sunny glow dimming, Joanne moved to the edge of her chair. "You're saying we need a match to prove anything?"

"Exactly. Either that, or a lucky break."

She stood. "In other words, Sheriff, we need to dig."

# FIFTEEN

CRIME BUSTING DIDN'T earn my daily bread, so after dropping Joanne off to pick up her car, I took every short cut I knew to Robinwood Lane and the bungalow that was up for sale. Even so, I was seven minutes late, and the frowns on the faces of my clients didn't bode well. The Archers, Lenny and Mildred, were a fifty-something couple looking to downsize. The bungalow was probably perfect for them, except for one thing, the price.

Lenny heaved his bulk out of his pickup and made a heavy point of looking at his watch. "Took time off the job for this, so let's go."

"My, it's cold, isn't it?" Mildred said, giving me a little shudder to prove it.

*Not a good beginning.*

We strolled up the front walk to the narrow porch. "This will be a pretty place on summer evenings," I said.

"Well, it ain't summer now," Lenny replied.

*Actually, a bad beginning.*

Once inside, my spirits lifted. The homeowners, a young couple with a growing family who were getting cramped in the small rooms, had listened to my advice. The lamps were lit, filling the rooms with cozy pools of light. All the baby toys and pictures had been whisked away and, best of all, a delicious aroma—chocolate chip cookies?—wafted through the air.

"Oh, this is real homey," Mildred said. "Not big but the kitchen's a good size. And the appliances are fairly new. I like it, Lenny."

Music to my ears, until Lenny asked, "What's the price again?"

I told him what the owners wanted.

He snorted. "And pigs want to fly. Knock off ten grand, and we'll consider it."

"The owners might take five less, but I don't know about ten."

He shrugged. "That's my offer."

"You might want to remember this house has everything you asked for. It's all on one floor, handy to the grocery stores and on a quiet, residential street."

"Like I said, ten off. This one's not the only fish in the sea."

"True, but sometimes you drop in your pole and don't find what you're looking for." My retort struck some kind of chord in Lenny. He shot Mildred a piercing look that caused her to go all pink in the cheeks.

"You got anything else to show us?" he asked.

"Not that one on Sugar Street," Mildred said quickly, the pink intensifying.

"No, you want something smaller. It's too big," I said knowing right well that hadn't been her intent.

"Size means nothing when a place is tainted. Why, no decent woman in town would think of stepping foot in the place, never mind *living* in it. You ask me, it ought to be torn down."

"Before we leave, I think I'll take a look at the furnace," Lenny said.

*Ha. Despite the bluster, he was interested.*

I opened the basement door, and he scooted down the stairs for a look-see.

Mildred sank onto one of the living room chairs, settling into the cushions, making herself right to home. "A good friend of mine went to the open house you had last Saturday. Said that Chocolate Moose place is in terrible shape."

"Is she somebody I know?"

"Maybe, her name's Reba Knight. She's the County Clerk. Works in Records over at the courthouse. Has for years."

"I don't recall seeing her, but the house was pretty crowded."

Heavy footsteps came clomping up the stairs. "Ten grand off, or no deal."

Mildred sent a tinkling little chuckle into the sweet-smelling air. "No fooling Reba. She knows every single secret in Eureka Falls. She says all you have to do is look at the records."

# SIXTEEN

BETWEEN A BABY screaming in the background and a television going full blast, I could hardly hear a word the woman from Robinwood Lane had to say. A door slammed and the phone got so quiet I thought she'd hung up, but a moment later, her voice, vexed to the nines, huffed back on the line.

"If I don't get a bigger place soon, I'll go plumb crazy, so tell your client seventy-five hundred off, and the house is his." She lowered her voice. "I'll work on my husband on this end, and you work your end. Together we'll sell this place, and it can't happen soon enough. Let me know what the man says, okay?"

She must have opened the door—that little ol' baby sure had a great pair of lungs on him—and then the phone did go dead.

A quick call to Lenny Archer cemented the deal. He said "yes," and I said "yahoo." Under my breath, of course.

After that good news, I was more than ready for a burger and a little word play with Andy Ballou. Humming "When The Sun Goes Down" off-key, I showered, and wrapped in a towel, stood in front of my closet trying to figure out what to wear. That was always a problem. I tended to either tart things up or dowdy them down. Tonight I didn't want to look like a pole dancer—or a nun, either.

Snug jeans with my suede, high-heeled boots and a pretty black top—something low key but not low cut—would be perfect for the Toole Shed. Decision made, I put on my make-up, a little heavy on the eye shadow, and screwed on silver earrings. One armful (not two) of silver bangles, and I was good to go.

Already seated at a table in the corner, Andy leaped up when I strolled in and helped me off with my down jacket. "You're lovely tonight. As always."

"And you're a wizard with the words, as always."

His smile faded a bit and no wonder. I had taken his compliment and turned it against him, as much as said he didn't mean those pretty words he was forever spouting. My daddy also had a habit of feeding a smooth line to the ladies. And that sure hadn't made my momma's life happy. A fact that popped up in my mind whenever Andy's voice dripped oil. Even so, I smiled as I took my seat, figuring I was here for Joanne's sake not my own. Besides, I'd better accept his words in a kindly spirit or Grandma Ingersoll would be paying me a visit.

He shrugged. "I'm a lawyer. I earn my living with words. You could say they're my pick and shovel."

"See! That's what I mean. Nobody else I know says such things."

He laughed. "Is that good or bad?"

A shadow fell across our table. "Hope you're not talking about the Shed."

I glanced up, fast. It was Tim O'Toole, treating us to a toothy grin. "What do you want to drink, Counselor?"

"Table service tonight?" Andy asked. "That's a surprise."

"Yeah, thought I'd save you two love birds a trip."

Why couldn't I warm up to Tim? He had a big, ready smile. Too ready maybe, his teeth out for everybody who came through the door. And he had big meaty hands, always eager to clap somebody on the back. Neither tendency was enough to make me feel cold toward him, but somehow, I did.

"Where's your bargirl tonight?" I asked, glancing around the room.

"She's out back, doing a little office work. She's a college girl, good with the books."

"Hey, Tim, you're needed over here," yelled a pot-bellied guy perched on a barstool.

"Hold your horses," Tim hollered back. "The beer won't dry up." He raised his chin at Andy. "So, what'll it be?"

"Take care of your pal over there. We'd like another minute."

When Tim hustled back to the bar, Andy said, "Want to leave, go some place quiet where there's no TV blaring?"

I shook my head. "No, this is just fine." A shout roared up from the bar. "Besides, I love basketball. Wow, look at him go. Did you see that shot? Missed the rim by a hair."

"I had no idea you were a Razorbacks fan."

"Love the game, Andy. Love it. And my daddy before me."

"Before we get into the fine points of the game, would you like something to drink?"

"A Bud Light would be mighty welcome."

"Not something more interesting? Tim keeps a few top shelf brands."

"Thank you kindly, a Bud will do."

"You're the boss. Be back in a minute with your beer. I'm sure it'll be wonderful—like drinking silk."

"See. There you go again, sounding so elegant. How do you do that?"

He laughed and rose from a scarred wooden chair that looked like it had seen better days.

I was searching in my purse for lip gloss when a soft voice said, "Hi, Honey. I've been hoping you'd get here early." Joanne glanced over at the bar where Tim was busy filling Andy's order. "I found something. Will you show this to Mr. Ballou?" Keeping her back to the room, she reached into her jeans pocket, removed a folded slip of yellowed paper and handed it to me.

The paper was blank. "Is this what I think it is? Same stock as the suicide note?"

She nodded. "There's half a box of it in the office."

I slipped the paper into my purse. "Can you help me get something out of here without it being seen?"

"I don't know. What?"

"A beer bottle. I need to put it in a paper bag so I won't smudge the prints."

"Sure, I can do that. I'll leave one in the ladies' room under the towels. See you later."

She turned away and hurried over to the bar. In big, black letters the back of her shirt said, "Shed Your Worries."

"Good idea," I muttered as Tim came hot-footing across the floor toting a tray loaded with two bottled Buds, chilled mugs, a bowl of pretzels and another of nacho chips.

"The counselor will be right over," he said. "He's having a few words with Joanne." Tim's eyes narrowed into slits as he set the drinks and snacks on the table. "Saw her talking to you, too. Didn't know you were acquainted."

"That so?" Cool as glass, I plucked a pretzel out of the bowl.

He tucked the beer tray under one arm. "How did y'all come to meet?"

I riveted him with a single, cold stare. "I found her mother's dead body up at the Moose. You make friends real fast that way."

"Yeah, I guess so."

"Enemies, too."

"No doubt. So you're trying to sell the Moose, huh?" He glanced over a shoulder and cocked his head at the bar. "In case anyone asks, I've got your business card by the cash register. Good luck. You'll need it. Ol' man Huggins let the place go to hell."

I put down the pretzel I was about to bite into. "You've been in the Moose?"

"Sure." He shifted the tray from one armpit to the other. "After the business closed, of course."

"Of course."

"Before he passed, ol' man Huggins practically wrote his name on that last bar stool over there. Nights when he had too much, I'd drive him up the street so he could sleep it off at the Moose."

"Interesting." I bit off a hunk of pretzel and glanced over at the bar stool. The big-bellied man sitting there tonight looked familiar. Apple cheeks and a tiny button nose on a man that size weren't something a body was likely to forget.

Still gripping the tray, Tim stood there like he wanted to say more but couldn't figure out what it should be. I didn't help him out, either, just ate another pretzel. Finally, taking the hint, he sauntered off.

While he was busy trading quips with one of the stool sitters, I slung my purse over a shoulder and carefully picked up one of the Bud Lights by the very bottom. Acting like I was afraid if left the bottle on the table something might get dropped into it, I sashayed over to the ladies' room. Luckily, it was empty. Folded under the towels piled next to the sink, just as Joanne promised, I found a paper bag. I poured out the beer, slipped the empty bottle in the bag, and put the bag in my purse.

As if I had taken the advice printed on Joanne's T-shirt to heart, I strolled back to the table without showing a worry in the world.

A few moments later Andy rejoined me. "Tim only brought over one beer?"

"No, the other one's in my purse."

*"What?"*

"I figured the bottle would have more of his prints on it than the mug. Was I right?"

He shook his head, like he couldn't believe what I was spouting. "It might be a toss up."

"Good. I didn't steal the wrong thing then."

# SEVENTEEN

"You want to get me disbarred?" Andy asked.

"Over a beer bottle? Don't be silly."

"It isn't the value, it's the intent."

"Right. And I intend to prove Tim's fingerprints are all over Juanita's suicide note and all over the hate note too."

"Then what?"

"You said prints would prove something."

"Yes, *something*. If Tim's prints are on the skeleton note, you've likely found a prankster. On the letter, a person of interest in a suicide."

"*A possible* suicide."

"I'll concede that. In neither case would you have proven he's the culprit. And suppose there are no prints?"

"Tim's hands were all over that beer bottle. Of course, there'll be prints."

"But if not on the letters, you're back to square one."

"Not the point—"

"All right then prove your point. Get the bottle to the sheriff and ask him to test it for prints."

"So it's okay that I swiped it?"

Andy heaved a sigh. "Sometimes, despite the wisdom of the ages, the end does justify the means."

"There you go again." I shrugged into the down coat and picked up my purse.

"No burger?"

"Not here. Let's go to Josie's Diner. That fat guy on the last bar stool is creeping me out. I've seen him someplace but I disremember where. He knows me too. He keeps sneaking peeks over here."

IN THE FRIGID parking lot, the Shed's red neon sign cast an eerie glow against the night sky. As we strolled toward our cars, our breath visible in the cold air, something suddenly whizzed past my head and crashed into the car up ahead of us.

"Get down!" Andy grabbed my hand and pulled me to the ground beside him. We crouched behind a Ford pickup, silent, listening. Footsteps crunched on the gravel, a spurt of light, then the lot went neon eerie again.

"What was that?" I asked.

"Not sure. A rock. A pot shot. Whatever it was, I think I've been hit."

I glanced over at him. "Omigod. There's blood all over your face."

He fingered his temple. "Thought so. It must have ricocheted." He reached into a pocket for a handkerchief and pressed it to his cheek. "Whoever it was took off. I didn't hear a car start up, so he may have gone into the Shed."

"You mean one of those good ol' boys in there meant to harm us?"

"Could be."

"But *why*?"

"Doesn't like the questions you've been asking around town. Doesn't like my being counsel for Joanne Petty. Or Darlene before her. Or it could have been a random attack. A prankster acting out."

"You don't believe that, do you?"

"No." He stood and held out his free hand. "Come on. We need to call 911 and report this."

"Not 911. The sheriff. I have his number."

Ten minutes later, Matt screeched up to the Shed's front door and hurried inside. By this time, the bar flies had gone out to inspect the old Caddy with the spider-webbed windshield, and Andy was seated on a chair, holding ice wrapped in a bar towel to his face.

When Matt strode in, Andy lowered the towel. The bleeding had about stopped. Using some peroxide from Tim's first-aid kit, I dabbed at the cuts then covered them with Band-Aids.

Andy didn't wince a bit, either, not until Matt said, "Now that Florence Nightingale is through, why don't you tell me what happened?"

"Matt Rameros, that's so, so—"

"Never mind, Honey," Andy said. "I'm fine. Just a couple of scratches. Sheriff, the rock that hit that vintage Caddy was aimed at us. It missed Honey by inches. As for me, I'm glad I've got such a hard head."

"What the hell's going on around here anyway?" Tim asked. "I'm running a clean operation and all of a sudden I got criminal activity."

"Yeah." The apple-cheeked man lurched off his stool. "The windshield on my prize Caddy's all busted up. My daddy outran the revenuers in that baby, and now I can't even see to get home. Oughta be a law."

"There is," Andy said.

"When Honey and Andy left, you see anybody follow them outside?" Matt asked Tim.

"And leave the game? Not a chance. The Razorbacks were ahead fifteen to fourteen, and MacLeary was about to—"

Matt cut him off. "Wouldn't know. I'm a Houston fan myself. Anything happens in your lot again, let me know. You might have to have it patrolled for a while." He tipped his hat at me as if I was a strange woman he had never, ever, been to bed with and turned to Andy. "In the meantime, I'll report this as a random act of mischief. Without a witness, anything else will be hard to prove, unless you saw someone throw the rock."

"We saw no one," Andy said. "But somebody saw us leave. I'd wager it was somebody here in the Shed."

The apple-cheeked guy staggered across the barroom floor, lurched to a stop in front of me and stuck out what would most likely be a sweaty hand. I didn't take it, but that didn't stop him from going squinty eyed and looking me over real good. "I'm Kenny Knight. Pleased to meet you. I finally figured out where I saw y'all before."

"Oh?"

"Up at the Moose. I dropped in to see the ol' place last Saturday. Don't want the little woman to find out though. She always says you can't trust nobody around here, and she oughta know."

Like a tree caught in a wind storm, Kenny began to sway, back and forth, left and right, first one leg and then the other.

"He's goin' down!" one of his stool buddies hollered.

Sure enough, Kenny slumped to the floor, closed his eyes and commenced snoring.

Matt toed him gently enough with the tip of his boot, but Kenny wasn't about to rise and shine.

Hands on hips, Matt shot Andy a look loaded with a poisoned-dart tip. "Great place to bring a date."

# EIGHTEEN

"WHY ARE YOU seeing Ballou?" Matt slammed the door to his office. "He's a shady mouthpiece, and you know it. Case in point, taking you to that dump last night and—"

"It was my idea."

"Why?"

"None of your business. You're not my keeper."

"I'm not your brother either. I'm a guy who's crazy about you. I sat back while you got it on with Saxby Winthrop, and I watched you carry a torch for Sam Ridley. But I'll be damned if I'll sit back and let you throw yourself away on a smooth-talking phony like Andy Ballou. Not without a fight."

"I appreciate having you worry about me, Sheriff," I said in what I hoped was a cool, big city voice. "But there's no need to upset yourself. From what I've seen of marriage, it isn't worth the aggravation."

Half way to his desk, he spun around on his heel. "*Marriage?* Who said anything about marriage?"

"You have. You've been hinting about it for months. And to tell you the truth, it makes me downright nervous. I'm not in a marrying mood, Matt Rameros. Not with Andy Ballou, not with anybody, and that's the God's honest truth."

"So the prisoner gets a reprieve."

"What?"

"Never mind. A figure of speech is all." He sank onto the chair behind his desk. "What brings you here today? *Me?*"

"Absolutely, darlin'. You're my go-to person with stolen goods."

He thumped his elbows on the desktop. "Meaning?"

I took the paper bag holding the bottle out of my tote and carefully placed it on his desk.

"What's this? My lunch?"

"Have a look."

He peered into the bag and glanced up fast, an eyebrow cocked. "Isn't it a little early in the day?"

"It's from the Shed. I want you to have it dusted for Tim O'Toole's prints."

"Just like that? Mind if I ask why?"

"Because of this." I held out the slip of notepaper Joanne had found in the Shed's office and gave it to him.

He glanced at it and turned it over. Another eyebrow went up. "Your answer's a blank piece of paper?"

"It's from Tim's office. I swear it's the same stock as the suicide letter and that hate note."

He surprised me by not arguing a single bit. He removed the manila envelope marked PETTY from his file cabinet, pulled on his cotton gloves and laid the papers on his desk side-by-side. "They do look the same."

"They *are* the same."

He nodded. "Could be. I'll have Tim come in and see me ASAP."

"Won't that tip him off?"

"Not if I ask him to write a report about last night's

incident. And get his prints on something. Unofficially, of course. At least for now. The problem is prints are hard to lift off paper unless the hands that touched it were oily or sweaty or the person used some kind of hand lotion. Though that said, in recent years the technology has improved. The newer rubber gelatin lifters can be effective. So we'll see. As for the bottle, looks like you handled it with care, and the bottle's the decider. If there's a match to the letters, we're onto something." He shrugged, put the notepaper in the manila envelope and pulled off the gloves. "If there's no match—"

"There will be."

He sighed. "Right. While you're here, I want to get a set of your prints so they can be eliminated. I'll need Joanne's too. Every attorney in the state has prints on file, so we have Ballou's, and we took Darlene's after the murder. None, of course, for the deceased Miss Nevins."

Deep in my tote, the cell chirped. "Mind if I get this? I have a client interested in a townhouse on Main… oh, it's Joanne."

"Honey, are you busy?"

"Sort of. What's up?"

"I just got a call from Mr. Ballou. He wants to see me as soon as possible. He sounded real serious. Something's wrong. I don't know what, but I'm scared. Could you possibly go with me?"

"Yes, I could. When?"

"Meet me at his office in thirty minutes."

Before I left the station, Matt took my prints, just for the record or so he said, and I hurried off. Joanne was waiting for me, shivering on the sidewalk outside Andy's building. When we walked into his office together, his face lit up at the sight of me. I was a bit surprised, since our Saturday night burger date hadn't ended well. After the rock tossing, Matt insisted on following me home in the cruiser and Andy, with blood seeping out from under the Band-Aids, had headed for home, too. Today, with nothing covering the cuts, his cheek looked raw and achy.

"Joanne asked me to ride shotgun today," I said.

"Delighted to see you. As always," he added, a smile lifting the wounded cheek in a way that looked painful.

Not waiting to be asked, like it was sit or fall, Joanne slumped into one of the chairs facing Andy's desk. I sat, too, my pulse pumping a little fast. What was the news that had brought us racing over here?

Wearing a funeral director face, he sat across from us and cleared his throat, not a good sign. "You were right, Joanne, your birth certificate was in with your mother's other legal documents. I found it this morning."

"Thank goodness." She moved closer to the edge of her chair. "I've been so worried. I can't get a passport without it."

"You going on a trip?" I asked. What I didn't say was "at a time like this," but I sure did think it.

She nodded, uncertain. "Next semester. There's a dig in southern Peru at the Wari Temple site. I don't want to go, not with Momma…and all, but it's a degree requirement and, more than anything, she wanted me to graduate. I'll be the first college graduate in my family. Knowing that made Momma proud. So I'm real glad you found the certificate, Mr. Ballou."

Andy opened his desk's center drawer and removed

a folded document. "Here it is. And isn't. So let's not rejoice too soon."

"What do you mean?" I asked.

"The document's not authentic."

"A *fake*?"

"Afraid so."

"Are you sure?"

"I handle documents at the county courthouse nearly every day. Several years before this certificate was issued, the county updated its record keeping to a computer system. Take a look at this."

He turned the birth certificate around so we could read it and pointed to one letter after another. "Look at the b, the a, the t. If this document wasn't typed on a Remington Electric, one of those old timers with a daisy ball, I'll eat my shirt."

"But the county clerk signed it," I said. "See, her signature's right here—Reba Knight."

"That signature can be verified. Or not, as the case may be."

"Why would my momma want me to have a fake birth certificate?" Joanne asked. "It doesn't make sense."

"Or maybe it does," Andy said. "Maybe it does."

I was almost too shocked to pay heed to what they were saying: The certificate listed Darlene Petty as Joanne's momma, but the slot for her daddy's name said, "Unknown."

# NINETEEN

Joanne shrugged on her backpack. "I don't have to be at work until three. That gives me plenty of time to get to the courthouse and see what's what."

"Kind of thought you'd say that." Andy reached into his desk drawer and handed her a copy of the birth certificate. "Take this with you. I'll keep the original in my safe."

"Why, if it's a fake?" Joanne sounded as bitter as a person could possibly be, and who could blame her?

"It's evidence of fraud." He glanced at his watch. "I'm due in court in an hour, or I'd go with you. Can I persuade you to wait until tomorrow?"

"No, sirree. I'm heading over there right now." She turned to me. "Honey, you want to come along?"

Try to sell a townhouse or try to solve a mystery? That was easy. The townhouse wouldn't walk away.

Reba Knight, a short, middle-aged woman with a Dolly Parton chest, approached the documents counter as slow as syrup oozing uphill.

"Yes?" she said, none too friendly.

Joanne slid the copy across the countertop. "This your signature?"

A quick glance, just one, and Reba's eyes darted up

to Joanne's face then to mine. Her mouth settling into a tight line, she picked up the document and squinted at it.

"Looks like my writing. Who's asking?"

"My name's Joanne Petty. I'm here to see the official record of my birth."

"That so? You're a stranger to me, gal. Nothing's getting opened up without proof of who you are."

Joanne lifted the pack off her shoulders. "Here's my driver's license."

Reba gave it a fast once over. "Don't mean a thing. It was issued in Fayetteville. Sorry, I can't help you." She turned away from us, ready to stomp off.

"Reba Knight," I said, "get your ass back here."

A quick gasp and she whirled around. "Why you've got—"

I held up a hand, one finger pointed at her nose. "Don't even go there. This girl's asking for a public record, and she's going to see that damned record—fast—or all hell will break loose."

"Why, I've got a good mind to—"

"You want to call the cops, go right ahead. It's illegal to deny access to public records, and you know it. So let's get the sheriff here. He'll be happy to thrash this out."

"I've never—"

"There's always a first time. So hustle over to wherever the records are kept, find the book with Joanne's date of birth in it and bring it right the hell back here for us to take a look at."

"Honey?" Joanne had a shocked, I-can't-believe-you-said-that look in her eyes.

I tossed her a wink. "A person can't be professional twenty-four seven."

Whether Joanne knew it or not, I was just warming up. The gloves were off, and I was smoking hot, ready to deck Reba if need be. Good thing I didn't have to. Matt would have had trouble understanding that. No need for such extremes, anyway, thank the Lord. After a few "Humphs," and "Who do they think they ares?" she turned on her heel and, meek as a sullen lamb, disappeared behind the stacks of county records.

A few minutes later, she came back toting a thick, dusty black book and dropped it on the counter. She flipped through a number of pages until she came to the proper date. Giving the book a shove, she swiveled it around toward us. "Have a look."

Whispering "thank you" to me, Joanne drew her index finger down the list of babies born on her birth date. The list was short: seven baby boys and three girls.

But no Joanne Petty.

The color draining out of her cheeks, Joanne flipped back several pages and then forward a few more without finding what she wanted. "I was hoping to see my daddy's name on the record. Momma never would tell me who he was. Always said, 'some day when the time is right,' but she never got around to it. And now he's not in the record book and neither am I. Guess I was never born," she said, turning back to her birth date page.

"Let me take a picture of that," I said. Using my smart phone, I snapped the page once then again for safe keeping.

I swiveled the book back to Reba. "How do you explain that Joanne's birth isn't listed?"

She shrugged and, with a *whoosh*, snapped the record book closed. "Human error. Somebody forgot to make the entry. It happens." She picked up the book and hugged it to her chest. "The birth certificate's what matters. I looked it over good. It's got a seal. That makes it official. You can use it anywhere, for anything—to get a driver's license, get married, get a passport. This here record's just a history book, so to speak. It doesn't prove a thing one way or the other."

That Reba would lie about the county record was bad enough, but that she would think Joanne and me…I… were stupid enough to believe her was freaking infuriating. Maybe I'd deck her after all. Of course, I'd have to leap over the counter to get at her.

Well, there was more than one way to pluck a chicken, to use one of those figures of speech Andy's always spouting. Come to think of it, Matt spouts them too.

I made my voice honey smooth. "Reba, your husband named Kenny, by any chance?"

"Yeah," she said, slowly kind of like she wished she could deny it. "Why?"

"Oh, just wondering. Kenny and me…I had us a nice long chat the other evening. Over at the Toole Shed, don't you know?"

"That right?" Her tone might have been cool, but her face looked hot.

I'm not proud to admit it, but sheer devilment made me press on. "He had a lot to tell me about a lot of things, including the Chocolate Moose. Before he passed out, that is. Guess he knew the Moose real well."

"I'm busy." She turned away, the record book still clutched to her chest.

"And you're a liar."

Joanne gasped, grabbing my wrist so I'd shut up. But no way would I let Reba walk off like she had a perfect right to be pissed. "Miss Petty's birth certificate's a fake and you know it. What are you covering up?"

Joanne's grip on my arm tightened.

"Let go of me, girl," I whispered in her ear. "At times, a body can't be professional. It just don't...doesn't... work."

Reba whirled around. "That certificate's got the state seal on it. So I don't know what all you're talking about."

"But I do, Reba, I do."

Who was lying now? The truth was I didn't know a darned thing about this whole mess, but I was determined to find out. Though she stood quietly by my side, Joanne's jaw had taken on a firm look. At the sight of that, I guessed she was not only determined to get to the bottom of all this too, but she was mad into the bargain.

Figuring it was better for her to be ripping mad than teary-eyed, I didn't mention that I'd just made an enemy out of the county clerk, the person who, among other things, issued legal documents for real estate transactions—property lines, acreage, liens, title deeds, tax records.

Without half trying, she could screw up my business real bad. But to save myself, I couldn't have played nice just now. Joanne and her mother before her, and likely her Aunt Juanita, had all been used and abused by folks who meant them no good. I knew that feeling only too well, still, I shouldn't have...

*Buck up, Honey.* Grandma Ingersoll again. *You got nothing to fear. You were right to give this Knight woman hell. You're gettin' at the truth. She's the one who should be shakin' in her boots.*

To that, I said "Amen" right out loud in the middle of the records office. It kind of sounded like a prayer.

# TWENTY

AFTER DROPPING OFF Joanne in town, I raced to my one o'clock appointment with high hopes for a sale. An urban renewal project was gentrifying an old mattress factory on Main Street into three-level, walk-up townhouses, and I'd been named sales agent for the first one to go on the market. Its sleek, modern design featured a garage on the ground floor, a wall of reused bricks, the kind of bricks people in the business call "restored" in the second floor living room and granite countertops in the kitchen. With only one bedroom on the top floor, though, even if the bath included a Jacuzzi built for two, the townhouse wouldn't appeal to everyone. A buyer would likely be young—all those stairs—and unmarried or newlywed—that single bedroom.

A thirty something professional with enough income to meet the mortgage payments would be ideal. But how many of those lived in a small town like Eureka Falls?

Kelsey Davis's insurance company had replaced the fancy camera he'd had stolen at the Moose's open house. He was still disgusted the mugger hadn't been caught, but pleased about the new camera. So I had him take some shots of the interior for the *Star's Sunday Supplement*. The ad worked, too. Mindy had a number of calls asking for particulars about the property. Better still, a half hour ago she'd made an appointment for me with a Mr. Jeffrey Bruce.

Luckily, I got back from my encounter with Reba Knight in time to open the townhouse, turn the lights on high and the stereo system on low. I even had a few moments to spritz the rooms with air freshener and run a comb through my hair.

Ingersoll Realty needed this sale, and I was ready for Mr. Bruce with a history of the building, an estimated cost breakdown of principal and interest rates, utilities and even a sales agreement—just in case.

What I didn't have to show was a list of comparable houses in the area and the prices they had sold for. There weren't any. So far, the townhouse was one-of-a-kind, but that was about to change. Under the elevator music, the faint sound of a hammer echoed through the building. As a reward for being first, a pioneer in a way, the buyer of this unit would get a big price break. That was my selling ace in the hole, and I'd save it for last, after hearing whatever Mr. Bruce's opinion about the place might be.

Pulse humming, I paced the living room. Right on the nose, the door chimes rang. Before I got half-way down the stairs, the door opened and a tall, thin, fifty-something man in a gray business suit, starched white shirt and silk tie stepped in on shoes as polished as mirrors.

*Really? He wanted a trendy townhouse? A middle-aged man with a comb-over?*

The fit didn't seem right to me, but in sales you never knew. That's what gave the game its excitement.

Anyway, hand outstretched, smile in place, I hurried

down to greet Mr. Bruce, aware of his lemony after-shave and glad, for some reason, that I'd switched out of my boots into stilettos and had on my good black pants suit. He took my hand with fingers that were icy cold. I let go real quick.

He followed me up the stairs, pausing at the top to glance around the living room. "I like the brick wall."

"I do, too. Feel free to explore the other rooms. The contractor staged them with enough furniture to give you an idea of how the spaces work. So go ahead and poke around. "

He hesitated, almost as if he wanted to say "no," but instead murmured, "Might as well, now I'm here."

*How strange.*

"Take your time. I'll be in the kitchen when you're through."

He nodded in an odd, uncertain way. Polite as he was, something about the man made me uneasy. He was dressed for success but acting like he didn't know what to do next. The mix made the hairs on the back of my neck rise. I took the cell phone out of my purse. "I have another client coming over in a few minutes. While you're having a look, I'll let him know I'm here."

I was lying through my teeth. But with all that had been happening lately, I'd lost a good deal of trust in my fellow man, and this particular man didn't add up to a solid prospect for a sexy, three story townhouse.

"I'll hurry then." Almost at a run, he headed for the stairs.

"No need to rush," I called. No answer. A few minutes later, his footsteps sounded overhead. I wondered what he thought about the Jacuzzi built for two.

I pressed in my office number. Mindy picked up

right away. "I'm at that townhouse on Main Street," I said. "Call me back in ten minutes. If you don't get a good answer, or any at all, contact Sheriff Rameros."

"Wait, don't hang up. I want to ax you—"

I hung up with a sigh as Mr. Bruce hurried back into the kitchen.

"That was quick," I said. "What do you think?"

"Very nice. Very clean, I must say."

I set the phone on the granite countertop within grabbing distance. "I have a list of the contractor's upgrades. They're included in the asking price which makes this a very good buy. A steal really. Also, the furnishings are negotiable, so—"

"Miss Ingersoll. Stop."

I picked up the phone, thumbs at the ready.

He watched me, frowned, and said, "My name isn't Jeffrey Bruce."

I stiffened. "Oh? Then who are you?"

"Roger Ledbetter. My father was the Reverend Ledbetter. You may have heard of him."

"You're Verna's son?"

"Yes, indeed, I'm her son, that fact is very clear." He smiled a bit for some reason I couldn't fathom.

"Are you interested in buying this house?"

He shook his head.

"Then why are you here?" I nodded at the phone in my hands. "Make it good or I'm calling 911."

"No need for that. I'm not here to cause trouble. I've already caused enough of that."

"You haven't answered me."

"I'm here because I need your help."

Suddenly weak-kneed, I sank onto a stool by the counter. From the pale look of him, Roger Ledbetter was in the same state. "Why don't you take a seat, Mr. Ledbetter?"

"Do call me Roger."

He took a nearby stool, perching on the edge like it was a seat of needles. A lot of throat clearing and then he dropped the hammer.

"I…uh…I'm Joanne Petty's father."

*Oh, my.*

His eyes filled with tears. "I couldn't hold it in any longer."

"If this is true—"

"It is." He glanced around the room, his gaze jumping from wall to wall, everywhere but where I sat.

"Why tell me?"

He snapped his wet eyes back to my face. "Darlene was asking questions before she was murdered. Joanne's doing the same. It has to stop. You know Joanne. You've been seen together. You were out at the courthouse with her, making inquiries."

"Ah, Reba Knight. She called you?"

He nodded. "An hour ago. She's worried. So am I."

"What about?"

"It concerns Joanne's birth certificate. You were correct. It's invalid."

"Well, for openers, it doesn't name her daddy."

"I know. We kept that a secret. It would have killed my mother to know what I…what I did."

"You say 'we' kept it a secret. Who do you mean? You and Darlene?"

"No, my father. He took charge. Covered up everything. We knew Darlene would care for the child. Love her." His tears spilled over. "And she did. I'll always be grateful for that."

"Why aren't you telling this to Joanne?"

"I can't bear to face her. Don't you understand?" His voice shrill, he paced the floor. "I've let her down. I've never been a father to her, never acknowledged her. For my mother's sake, I couldn't. But I fear the truth is about to come out." He stood still long enough to reach into a breast pocket and remove a carefully folded linen handkerchief. He mopped his eyes and the beads of sweat popping out on his forehead. "Joanne obviously trusts you. Will you tell her what I've just confessed?"

A snowman in the sun, he was melting in front of my eyes, but I couldn't seem to find it in my heart to feel sympathy for his past, only pity for his weakness. "Well, I don't know. It's your place, not mine, to—"

"I can't. I simply can't, Miss Ingersoll. You see, there's something more to the story. I *am* Joanne's father. But Darlene Petty was not her mother."

# TWENTY-ONE

WHEN A MAN you just met tells you he fathered an out-of-wedlock baby with a mysterious woman that sure puts you on a first name basis fast.

"Roger, if Darlene wasn't Joanne's mother, who is?"

"I can't say. I vowed I never would."

"Sometimes promises have to be broken. Besides, the secret's about to be busted wide apart. Joanne's hell-bent to learn the truth. She's probably at the sheriff's office even as we speak."

If pale before, Roger turned bed sheet white. "Word gets out that I talked, I might be killed."

I didn't bother to point out that by telling me he had already let the word out. Though he was making me very nervous, I had to keep him talking and asked, "Who would do the dirty, Mr....ah...Roger?"

"The same person who killed Darlene."

"Darlene wasn't asking questions about you. She was looking into her sister Juanita's suicide." I sucked in a breath. *Ooooh.* "Are you saying Darlene's death had something to do with the Moose? With what happened there years ago?"

He nodded without speaking.

"So, they *are* connected?"

I was talking to myself as much as to him, but he answered, "Yes, they are."

"How?"

No response.

On a hunch, I asked, "Was Juanita the mother of your baby?"

He looked up quick, his blue eyes, so like Joanne's, opening wide. "No, no, not her."

"Who, then?"

No answer.

"Was it one of the other girls who worked at the Moose?"

He hung his head, studying the pattern on the granite counter. Finally, softly, "Yes."

"Does this woman want to kill you?"

"God, no." He lifted his gaze to meet mine. "We loved each other."

*Phew.* "I'm mighty happy to hear that, but telling me isn't enough. You have to tell your daughter and the police."

He shook his head so hard, part of his comb-over loosened up and slid onto his forehead. "You don't understand. I'll lose my job. The whole town will hate me. My mother most of all. Can't you see that? All I want is for my daughter to stop asking questions. She's putting her life in danger and mine, too."

"How can you expect her to do that? If what you're telling me is true, she's found her daddy at last, but the woman she called momma was a stranger."

"Maybe this will convince you."

He reached into his breast pocket and took out a wad of bills held together with a rubber band. He laid the wad on the countertop. "This is ten thousand dollars. It's for you and Joanne. But you both have to let the past go."

"You're *bribing* me?"

"Think of it as a gift."

"You're asking me to help you cover up a felony. I can't do that. This is a police matter. Either you call them or I will."

As soon as the words were out of my mouth, I knew they were the stupidest thing I'd ever said. Roger's lower lip was quivering, his fists were opening and closing. No telling what he might do next. I needed help fast. I grabbed the cell off the countertop ready to punch in 911. Before I could, it went off in my hand. Startled, nerves on edge, I nearly dropped it.

"You all right?" Mindy asked.

"No," I said, feeling like a rat. "I'm not."

DURING A SHOWING, I always leave the front door of a property unlocked. Habit, I guess. Anyway, during the longest ten minutes of my life, I soothed Roger with stories about Joanne, how sweet she was, how good a student, how loving she'd been to Darlene's memory. He was listening to me as if I was spouting the greatest story ever told when Matt came busting in without knocking, raced up the stairs and rocked to a halt in the kitchen's open doorway.

Though he worked out every other day and was in great shape, he was gasping and could barely choke out, "What's going on here?"

Roger slid off his stool and took a step or two toward the stairs. "Nothing much, officer, I was about to leave. I understand you're interested in this property. You'll like the Jacuzzi."

"Miss Ingersoll?" Matt asked.

I shook my head, mouthing, "I'm scared."

Legs apart, hands on hips—the right one cradling his gun—Matt blocked Roger's way out. "I need to see some ID."

"That's not necessary, officer. I don't want to bother you."

"No bother. Let me see your driver's license."

"What's the problem? Am I under arrest?"

"ID, please."

Like birds longing to take flight, Roger's eyes darted around, from Matt to me, then back again, frantic to escape. "You have to have a reason to detain me. It's the law."

"I'm responding to an emergency call. The law dictates that I get the facts. So I'll ask one more time. Let me see some ID."

Sweat beads popping out on his forehead, Roger backed up a step at a time, moving away from Matt inch by inch. "No. Nobody must know. Nobody."

"Know what, sir?"

"Who I am. What I've done."

"It's too late for that, Roger," I said, throwing caution and whatever common sense I was born with to the four winds. "I already know."

He blinked, again and then again, as if the light was suddenly too strong for his eyes. "You're the only one. So far, you're the only one."

"You can't hide the facts forever. Tell the sheriff the truth. He'll help you."

"No. He'll tell. You'll tell too. Unless I stop you." Eyes wild, hands quick as a snake's strike, he reached out and grabbed me. His arm went around my neck in a stranglehold. I couldn't move, I couldn't breathe, I couldn't do anything except stare at Matt.

Behind me, his aftershave in my lungs, his breath in my ear, Roger panted like an uphill runner. When I tried to wrench out of his grasp, his arm tightened around my throat cutting off what little air I had. Afraid he was going to kill me, I wanted to scream, but couldn't.

*The stilettos.* I raised a foot. I'd kick him in the shins and break his grip.

"Don't fight him, Honey," Matt said, his voice as smooth as a well-oiled machine. "No need. You're free to leave, sir."

*What?*

"You're lying."

Matt stepped to one side of the kitchen doorway and swept an arm wide. "Feel free to go."

Still clutching me like a shield in front of him, Roger force-walked me one baby step after another toward the stairs. Like a statue in a park, Matt didn't move. He wouldn't really let Roger leave with me, would he? A moment of panic caused me to claw at Roger's arm. A wasted effort. His arm didn't ease up a single bit. Together we kept on taking baby steps, getting closer and closer to the stairs.

From the corner of my eye, I saw Matt's right hand, the one cradling his holster, move. Not much, just a tad. I should have known he had no intention of letting Roger force me down the stairs. He'd blow Roger's head off first—all over the brand-new paint job.

That's when I lost the fear and found some smarts. If dead weight, I'd be hard for Roger to lock step out of the kitchen.

Pretending to faint, I closed my eyes and slumped in his grip, letting my knees go limp and the stiletto heels drag along the hardwood floor.

"She's fainted," Matt said, real panic in his voice. "Let her go. *Now.*"

*Uh-oh.* My eyes snapped open. Just as I thought, the Glock was out of the holster and pointing straight at Roger's head. Which was only inches from mine.

I screamed. How dumb can a body get? I could have caused Matt's trigger finger to twitch. But calm and in control, he didn't react. Roger did. Startled by my outburst, he let go, dumping me like a sack of meal onto the kitchen floor.

"Don't move," Matt said, and he sure wasn't talking to me.

Paying no heed to the warning, Roger lunged for the stairs. As he jumped over me, I reached up, grabbed his pants leg and yanked on it with all my strength. Down he came, headfirst onto the floor.

Matt leaped on him, pinning him in place. He holstered the Glock then cuffed Roger's hands behind his back. Still straddling him, he asked, "You okay, Honey?"

"I think so," I rasped. "But he isn't." I pointed to Roger. He was moaning and blood was pouring from his nose.

Without getting up, Matt hauled out his cell phone and punched in 911. "This is Sheriff Matt Rameros. Send an ambulance to 558 Main Street. I have an assault perpetrator here who needs medical help."

# TWENTY-TWO

"WHAT DO WE tell Joanne?" I asked Matt as the ambulance drove away with Roger strapped inside along with a police order that he be hospitalized forty-eight hours for psychiatric evaluation.

"The truth."

"Oh, God. How can we say your daddy's a mental case, and no one knows who your momma is?"

"Roger knows."

"She can't ask him that. Not now that he's had some kind of breakdown."

"He's not the only one who can be questioned. He had help in concealing Joanne's birth. His father for one."

"The reverend's dead," I pointed out.

"True, but Reba Knight's still alive. She was probably paid handsomely for that false document."

"You think she knows the truth?"

"I'd put money on it. But you can bet she was sworn to secrecy."

"Maybe it's high time she came clean."

Matt nodded. "By the time we can get out there, the county offices will be closed, but we can make a house call."

"I'm for that! Let's go. When Joanne gets off work tonight, we might have something more to tell her."

We turned off the lights, hurried down the stairs and locked up the townhouse.

Matt followed me to my apartment so I could drop off the Lincoln. When I joined him in the cruiser, he said, "Before we drive out to the Knight farm, I'd like to change out of this uniform. It's got Roger's blood all over it. Do you mind stopping at my place?"

"Course not." Actually, I was curious as all get out to see where he lived. Though I'd known Matt for several years now, and we had dated a few times, I'd never been to his place. Either I had met him somewhere or he had picked me up at my apartment. So this was kind of an exciting first.

He headed for the south side of town and, after a ten-minute drive, he parked in front of a small, square-framed house painted a happy green with bright yellow trim. The house sported a little scrap of frozen front yard and a shiny metal mailbox out by the road. Like kissing cousins, all the other houses on the block looked much the same, so it fit right in.

"Welcome to Barista Street," Matt said.

He didn't need to tell me Barista Street was home to a number of migrant families who had come to Arkansas years ago from places like Louisiana and Arizona and Texas. Finding work in the fields and farms surrounding town, many of them had stayed on in Eureka Falls. I guess they felt safe here, something I could understand, for I felt the same way, at least I did until lately.

"You live here alone?" I asked.

"Yeah, it belonged to my folks." His face got quiet and serious. "They left it to me, and I haven't been able to bring myself to sell it. But if I do," he said, sending me a flash of white teeth, "nobody except Ingersoll Realty gets the sale." He unlocked the cruiser and swung open his door. "Come on in. Okay if I grab a quick shower? I promise I won't be long."

"You're the boss." He laughed and led me up the narrow concrete walk into the house. "Oh wow," popped out of my mouth the minute I stepped inside.

"You hate it, huh?"

"Well, I wouldn't say that, but to be truthful, the colors aren't quite pleasing to me." I glanced around the small front room. "There's a lot of red and all."

"My mother loved color. Lots of it. Picked out every can of paint and painted every inch of the place herself. That's why I haven't been able to part with it. It reminds me of her…of them."

"That's sweet, Matt, it really is. I understand, honest I do. It's just that the—"

"I know. The red living room, the yellow dining room, the green kitchen. When I come in off a shift, I feel like I'm still on traffic duty."

"Did your mother crochet all these doilies?"

"Yeah. Every night while she watched TV."

I ran a hand over the back of a dark, polished chair that gave off the faint aroma of lemon oil. "The furniture's nice and solid." It was also heavy and big and *everywhere*, like a fat lady in a too small dress.

"My folks didn't understand the concept of less is more."

Not quite sure of what that meant, I just nodded.

"Have a seat. Help yourself to anything in the fridge. I won't be long."

I slipped off my coat, and when the shower went on,

I had a sudden notion to sneak a peek at Matt's bedroom. After all, a bedroom tells a lot about a person, and the more you know about your local police the better, right? Anyway, moving fast, I tiptoed out of the living room into the dining room…phew, all those chairs… and into a kitchen that was dated but tidy enough. A short hallway off the kitchen led to a bathroom where the water was running full blast, sending steam billowing out from under the closed door.

Separated by the bath were two bedrooms. The one on the right couldn't be Matt's—those rose-colored walls and the double bed with its pink coverlet and pile of crocheted pillows. The next one then. Like a critter on a hunt, I snuck past the steamy bathroom.

The door to the second bedroom stood wide open, and in I went. This was more like it—blue walls and a king-sized bed, a big HDTV at the foot. A couple of Razorback posters over the headboard that I hadn't seen before. Who was that leaping at the—

"Aha!" Barefoot, wearing nothing but a big grin and a towel around his hips, Matt strode in, giving me a full view of his nice, hairy chest. "Had to see where I sleep, huh?"

"Well, no, I was—"

"Well yes, you were—"

"—taking a look at your posters."

"At my what?" A grin threatening to crack his cheeks wide open, he came over to me, towel and all, and drew me close. His dark eyes swept my face. A single finger stroked my cheek. "I have a confession to make."

*Two in one day.* "You're the daddy of a secret baby?"

He laughed. "Not yet. You'd know about it, Honey, you'd know about it."

Fearing he was working up to the M word again, I tensed in his arms. "So, what's your confession?"

"This is a set-up. A sting operation."

"A *what*?"

"A trap to see if the suspect bites. I'm not saying that's nice. I'm saying it's effective. Usually."

"Matt Rameros, what all are you jawing about?" I go country real fast when I'm aggravated, and this was one of those times. My question didn't seem to bother Matt a single bit, though. A tiny smile lifted the corners of his mouth.

"I lured you here. I staged the shower, hoping you'd do what you did. Get curious…come looking to see for yourself. Also, as part of the plot, I changed the sheets."

I reared back a little. "*Why?* For me?"

He nodded, abashed as a school boy.

"But you didn't know I'd be here today."

"Last week. I changed them last week. I've been sleeping in my folks' old room, keeping things neat in here in case, just in case…"

He kissed me, and I didn't pull away, didn't say "no," didn't say "stop." All I said was, "Are you getting cold in that skimpy little towel?"

HE WASN'T COLD at all as it turned out. And he warmed me up real fine too.

A good man, Matt Rameros, solid and capable and loyal to a fault. Though my knees didn't exactly go weak each time I saw him, I have to admit I enjoyed making love with him. But the big question I couldn't answer just then is did I *love* him?

Cozy and warm in his blue-walled bedroom, in the center of his king-sized bed, I tried to make those thoughts go away. They were bringing me back from bliss to the real world when I longed to have the world and all its problems disappear and leave me in this wonderful peace.

Then another thought hit me. *Was this love?*

As if ready to answer the question, leaning on one elbow, Matt gazed down into my eyes. "Thank you."

"You don't need to thank me."

"I want to. I also want to stay here all night. Order in Chinese. Watch some old reruns." He arched an eyebrow. "Muss up the sheets some more. But duty calls. We're on our way to see Reba Knight, remember?"

I did and, hauling myself out of my comfy nest, I got dressed for the second time that day.

# TWENTY-THREE

REBA KNIGHT LIVED outside of town in a clearing her daddy, and his granddaddy before him, had carved out of the woods. Back in the day, it had been a working farm. Her folks, the Floodys, had mainly grown rye and corn Matt told me, adding with a smile, "I heard they kept the revenuers busy chasing them up and down the hills."

"Shine?"

"So the story goes. The best in Yarborough County. No more though. The old Floodys died off, and Kenny Knight apparently didn't have the stomach for running his in-laws' still." Matt shrugged. "But who knows? There are lots of glens and hollows hereabouts, and nowadays there's money in cooking meth." He took his gaze off the road for a second to send a frown across the front seat. "That stuff's so bad it makes you long for the good old rum-running days. A jug of corn likker didn't rot your brain, at least not right away."

"You saying Reba's family's been on the fringes of the law for years?"

"That's my understanding. Personally, I haven't had any problems with them, except for Kenny's occasional toot. I've driven him home in the wee hours a few times, but that's all."

As we wound our way through the hills, we passed thick stands of evergreen trees. The cold had persisted all week, keeping the air crisp and clean and smelling of pine. In the fading light, any scars or ugliness the ground might have suffered were covered with white. The whole scene was so sinless and pure a body could be fooled into believing that was the way of things out here. But it wasn't. Even I knew that.

"Matt, if Reba's family had this history of thumbing their noses at the law, how did she get a job in the county records office, handling everybody's legal papers and such?"

"Good question. Reba was already ensconced in the courthouse when I came on board. Connections, I suppose."

Daylight had nearly fled behind the hills when Matt pulled the Ram off the highway and up a steep rise. The rutted road led to an oddly shaped farmhouse on the top of the ridge. Though sizable, the house appeared to have been added onto willy-nilly over the years, a room here, a room there, with no mind given to the final outcome. In the half light of dusk, lamps in the downstairs windows sent yellow beams onto the front porch and down to the yard where a couple of pickups stood in snow up to their hubcaps.

"Guess Kenny doesn't believe in shoveling," Matt said as we climbed out of the Ram's cab and tramped over the lumpy yard to the porch. No sooner had his boots hit the first step when a howling straight out of hell rose up. I froze in my tracks. "Attack dogs."

"No, Kenny's coon hounds," Matt said. "They're harmless. As long as he's home."

While I waited in the snow, ready to sprint back to

the truck, Matt strode onto the porch and banged on the front door.

Those dogs, I have to admit, were better than any alarm system ever invented. They kept on howling then suddenly got quiet as death. The front door opened a crack, and Kenny Knight peered out into the gloom.

"Sheriff, that you? God almighty, what brings you way out here?" His voice tightened. "Don't tell me you got bad news."

"No, no, nothing like that."

*Ha.*

Kenny leaned to one side and peered around Matt. "Who's out there with you?"

"Honey Ingersoll, the Realtor."

"Well, she's mighty welcome, but I'll tell you right off this place ain't for sale." Beckoning to me, Kenny yelled, "Come right on in, Miss Honey."

"Is it okay with your hounds?" I yelled back.

"Don't you worry about them none. They're just like me, all bark and no bite." As I climbed the porch steps, he added, "All of us guys like pretty girls. Don't we, Jake?" A skinny hound, gray as a wolf, had followed him out the door. Kenny stuck out a foot and kicked it, yelping down the steps. "A sullen one, that Jake. Never did take to him much. Have to show him who's boss once in a while." Kenny snapped his suspenders then held open the door to a pine-paneled front room furnished with big, well-used easy chairs. "What can I do for you, Sheriff? A drink maybe?" His voice was hopeful.

"No, thanks. We're here to see Reba."

"Too bad, you missed her. She came home from work, got some kind of a call and headed right back out again. Said it was a job emergency." Kenny switched his attention to me. "How about you, Miss Honey? Can I interest you in a little refreshment? A shame to come all this way for nothing."

I shook my head. "No thanks."

He waved an arm at the chairs. "Well, at least go sit by the fireplace and warm yourself. It's a cold one tonight."

Kenny was acting friendly as could be. So I guess he wasn't holding a grudge over our Saturday night set-to at the Shed. Either that or he'd forgotten all about it.

"How's the Caddy?" Matt asked, making no attempt to sit down. "Get the windshield fixed?"

"Yup. Set me back a few bills, but she's good as new." Kenny scratched at his scalp with one of his long fingernails. Itch relieved, he said, "Don't know why anybody would throw rocks at a pretty girl like you, Miss Honey. I was telling Reba all about it, and she said she could guess why somebody might." He roared like he'd just said something rib-slapping funny. "That's womenfolk for you, always in the know."

Well, well. Maybe Kenny hadn't forgotten a thing. That little speech sounded mighty like a threat. I shot a glance Matt's way. His brown eyes met mine, held steady, and then he winked. So, he'd caught Kenny's drift too.

"We'll be heading along." Matt moved toward the front door where the hounds stood guard, ready for a signal to pounce. "Tell Reba we were sorry to miss her."

"Sure will. You want to leave her a message or anything?"

"No, I don't think so. I'll catch up with her tomorrow. She'll know what it's about. You know, womenfolk and the way they have of figuring things out."

Going squinty-eyed, like he wasn't sure if Matt was joshing him or not, Kenny walked us to the door and swung it wide, letting in a blast of cold air. "Sorry to see you go so soon but you know best."

As we headed over the snowy ruts to the Ram, Jake came sniffing after us, his tail all droopy.

"Poor dog," I said, "what with Kenny kicking him around and all, he's feeling too blue to lift his tail out of the snow." The sight of that low-down tail caused my fear of him to flee. I waggled a finger. "You're not an attack dog. You're an ol' coon dog and a sweetheart. That's what you are, aren't you, boy?" I kept my voice soft so as not to scare him. "Don't be shy, come on over and say hello."

Tail twitching a little, not sure what to expect, Jake sidled up to me slow and easy. When I went to pat his head, he sprang back and growled. I crouched on the snow and held out a hand. "I won't hurt you, boy, come on, say hello."

It took a few minutes of coaxing, but finally Jake inched over and let me stroke his head. In another minute or so, he was stretching his neck, reaching out for more. "I wish I had a treat for you, but I don't."

"Looks like you made a friend," Matt said.

"Wonder if Kenny would let me adopt him?"

"That's a surprise. I didn't know you wanted a dog."

"I don't. But I don't want Kenny kicking him around either." I glanced up at Matt. "You think Kenny would let him go?"

"You're serious?"

"Yes, look at him. His coat's all matted, and I can feel his ribs through it. He needs love, Matt."

Matt heaved a sigh. I figured I knew what his sigh

meant, but I didn't feel up to tackling it right now. I had Jake on my mind.

"He's a coon hound," Matt said. "They like to roam. He's used to a lot of freedom."

"A lot of abuse, you mean. He's not a pup. Maybe his roaming days are behind him."

"You can't save the world, Honey."

"No, I can't. But maybe I can save one mangy ol' dog."

The front door burst open suddenly, outlining Kenny against the lamp light. "Y'all still out there?" he hollered. "What's the matter? Car won't start?"

"No, that's not it. We got a proposition for you," Matt called. "Want Honey here to take Jake off your hands?"

"Am I hearing you aright? That pretty girl wants a scruffy mutt like Jake? Why, his better days are long gone."

"Yes or no, Kenny. It's cold out here."

"Darned right." In the lamp light, his shrug was clear to be seen. "Sure. It's okay by me, and I can tell you for a fact Reba hates the mutt. So take him and good riddance."

He half-turned to go inside, but did a Uee instead. "You take him off the place, no changing your mind. He goes, he goes for good. Got it?"

"Of course. Thank you," I called.

"Don't mention it. You made my day."

"Jake's too," Matt said under his breath. He sent me one of his fast, white smiles. "And mine, of course."

Kenny slammed the front door shut.

"You think he has fleas?" I asked.

"Who? Kenny or Jake?"

"Very funny."

"You better hope not. It's too cold to have him ride into town in the truck bed, so he's riding in style. On your lap."

Oh my. And me in my best black pants suit.

Matt opened the Ram's passenger door and whistled. "Come on, boy, hop in."

While Jake decided what to do, I stood, a little stiff in the knees and shivering in the night air. That's when the car's overheads caught the glint of something shiny. I bent down, peered closer, and after a split second of fighting my conscience, I picked it up and slipped it in my coat pocket without saying a word.

# TWENTY-FOUR

ALL THE WAY HOME, I had Jake on my lap and guilt on my conscience. Swiping a beer bottle was one thing but pocketing a smart phone was out and out theft.

I kept sneaking glances at Matt, wondering if I should tell him what I'd done. He wouldn't approve, of that I was sure, so maybe it was best I not say a word, at least until I found out who owned the phone. Maybe it wasn't Reba's at all. And even if it was, what would it prove? That along with forging Joanne's birth certificate, she was involved in other dirty doings? A long shot is what my daddy would call it. Either I had a pocketful of gold or a pocketful of nothing. I blew out an exasperated breath that rose like a puff of fog in the cold cab.

"Regrets?" Matt asked, glancing across the front seat.

"About Jake? No. He needs me. Don't you, boy?" He licked my cheek. "See, that's a yes. Tomorrow I'll have the town vet look him over, and after that he's going to a groomer. Then he's coming to work with me. Every day. Okay, boy?"

*Woof!*

I laughed. "See! He likes the plan."

"As long as you're sure."

"I am." I hugged Jake to prove it to him. Why not?

I was so covered in doggy hair a few more wouldn't matter a bit.

"He'll make a great watchdog. That makes me feel better though my conscience is bothering me right now."

*His too?* "Whatever for?"

"If I hadn't lured you to Barista Street, we might have caught Reba at home."

"You regret our detour?"

He reached across the seat to squeeze my hand. "Never. I could never regret being with you, Honey. But I forgot for a while something I shouldn't have forgotten. Not only has a document been forged, a woman's been killed. It's not impossible the two are connected." He sent me a lopsided smile. "Bottom line, I shouldn't have forgotten."

"Isn't solving the murder in Detective Bradshaw's hands?"

"Technically yes, but—"

"And if the truth about Joanne's birth waited twenty years, will one more day matter?"

"It might. Tonight I would have taken Reba by surprise. Now that element's been lost. Given a chance to think things over, she may refuse to talk."

I patted my coat pocket. *Or she may spill her guts.*

I wanted to tell Matt about the phone, I really did, but he'd probably get all official on me and start in on the owner's right to privacy or some such police folderol. Anyway, while I was fretting over the situation instead of trusting Matt the way I should have, his cell phone rang. He listened a moment, said, "I'll be there ASAP" and hung up. "Highway patrol's short-handed. They need backup tonight. I have to go home and get suited up."

After Matt dropped me at my apartment and hurried off, I brought Jake inside, shrugged out of my hair-covered coat and gave him a bowl of water. He needed something to eat too. I yanked open the pantry door. A box of spaghetti, a jar of tomato sauce, some Oreos… he might like those…ah, in back of a box of grits, a can of tuna fish.

"You're not a cat," I told him, just in case he didn't know, "but this might hold you till we can get to a grocery."

Sure enough, he loved it. While he wolfed down his food, I took the phone out of my coat pocket, collected a note pad and pen and carried everything out to the kitchen table.

The phone was a dated flip top with no entry code. That was a lucky break, and heart thumping, I pressed the phone icon and scrolled down the list of names and numbers.

Judging from what I read, the phone was Reba's, all right. It included the courthouse, Yarborough County Hospital's records division, even the Toole Shed—most likely for the nights she was looking for Kenny. Others were of people I didn't know. That made no difference. I wrote down every name and every number. Then my fingers and my heart nearly stopped at the last number on the list: Andy Ballou's.

*Oh, my.* Before I could dwell on what that might mean, I got another shock. Gretchen Wilson came on shouting out *"Redneck Woman."* I nearly dropped the phone on the kitchen floor. Pulse going like a trip hammer, I let Gretchen go on until the call went into voice mail. A woman came quavering onto the line, sobbing so hard I could hardly make out her words.

"Reba, something terrible's happened. Worse thing in the world. I have to talk to you. Call me soon as you can, no matter how late. I'll be up all night anyway."

Crying into my ear was the reason why I shouldn't have swiped the phone. I was interfering in someone's life—Verna Ledbetter's. She had a problem and was looking for help she wouldn't get any time soon. I thought I knew what her problem might be. It no longer seemed important to wait until Joanne's shift was over to tell her about Roger's bombshell.

I changed into jeans, pulled my hair into a pony tail and shrugged into my hairy black coat. "Come on, Jake. That tuna fish wasn't much for a big boy like you. How would you like a hamburger? Medium rare on a toasted bun?"

His tail wagged.

*Yes!*

"We'll get you a burger for sure. But we're going on an errand of mercy too. At least, I hope it will be. Joanne needs to hear some heavy news and, all of a sudden, I don't think it can wait another minute."

# TWENTY-FIVE

THE TV OVER the bar was blasting out an NBA game and, as usual, the Shed's steamy air smelled of fries and beer. Joanne topped off a tall lager, closed the tap and sent me a big, welcoming smile.

I looked around. The stools and tables were studded with customers, but I didn't see any other help. "You on alone tonight?"

"Tim's out back. His cook up and quit on him, so he's running the Fryolator." Joanne's smile got wider.

"I need to talk to you, but first, can he fix me two burgers? One rare, one well done?"

"It'll be a challenge for him, but I'll see." She settled the lager in front of a round-shouldered guy whose red face said he'd been enjoying a mighty long happy hour. "Be right back."

He glanced over a hunched shoulder. "You better be, or I'll help myself."

"That's your last one, Willy," Joanne told him as she hurried off.

"Who says?"

"The State of Arkansas."

"What's the state got to do with it?"

She didn't bother to answer as she pushed open the swinging door into the kitchen.

While waiting for the burgers, I went out to the Lincoln to check on Jake. He wasn't allowed in the Shed, and I was afraid he'd be cold sitting out in that freezing car.

Sure enough, when I opened the car door and called to him, he came out shivering. I patted him, and he rubbed against my leg, looking for warmth, I guess. Poor thing.

"Come on, boy. To heck with the rules. Let's go see Joanne."

Tomorrow, along with dog food, I'd buy a leash, but for tonight I hoped he'd be a good boy and listen to me.

The Lakers-Cavaliers game was neck and neck when I strolled back inside, Jake at my knee. With everybody focused on the TV, nobody paid any attention to him as he snuggled under a table by my feet until Tim came out of the kitchen looking like a thunder cloud and took over at the bar.

"Hey, what's that dog doing in here?" he yelled. "It's against the law."

"He's waiting for his burger."

"The kitchen's closed."

"He'll eat one raw."

"No, he won't. Get him out of here."

"It's ten degrees outside. You force him to go, I'll slap an animal cruelty suit on you. Sue the pants off the place."

"Oh, jeez." Tim leaned his elbows on the bar top and held his head in his hands. "First the cook and now this."

"A raw hamburger, Tim, how hard is that? No need to heat the bun. He could use a little water, too. And while you're at it, would you tell Joanne I want to talk to her?" I was pushing the envelope and that wasn't mannerly, but something about Tim made doing so feel downright joyful.

"Not a chance. She's busy."

"Never mind." I reached for my purse. "I'll go tell her."

Tim put aside the glass he'd been rinsing. "No, you won't. No customers allowed in the kitchen."

"Think of it this way—I'm not only a customer, I'm a Realtor. You should let me look around. Some day you'll want to retire, and you'll need help selling the place."

"I ain't retiring any time soon, and when I do, I'll sell the Shed myself."

"You want top dollar, you need a professional—"

A sneer twisted the corners of his mouth. "That what you are? A professional? I heard stories about you and your—"

A roar rose out of the TV.

"Pipe down, Tim," a Lakers fan shouted. "We got a game goin' over here."

I leaped up and snapped my fingers. Jake growled to his feet. I had to grab his collar to keep him from lunging at the bar.

Tim took a swipe at the bar top with a towel that looked as old as he was and upped his chin at me. "Go on then. Keep that mutt under control."

THE GREASE IN the Fryolator had already stopped bubbling and the chopping block in the middle of the kitchen had been wiped clean. Busy stowing hamburger patties and uncooked fries back in the fridge, Joanne looked up and grinned. "Hey, nice dog you have there, Honey, but Tim's closed the kitchen. Sorry about the burgers."

"So he told me. I was hoping you'd have a raw patty for my pal here."

"Better than that. Here's one that's cooked. Medium rare. Someone must have canceled an order."

She stroked Jake's coat then set a plate with a burger and a bun on the floor and a bowl of water next to it. He was on the burger in no time, gobbling it down like the tuna had never happened. A few slurps of water and he returned to his station by my knee.

"Can you stop working a minute?" I asked as she was about to hose down the sink. I nodded at two metal stools beside the chopping block. "Come sit for a spell. There's something important you need to know."

"Is it about my momma? Did Detective Bradshaw contact you?"

"No, it's—"

"The birth certificate? You found out something."

"Well, you could say that, but—"

She sank onto a stool and sat twisting the hem of her black bar apron between her fingers. "Honey, whatever it is, tell me straight out. I can take it. Momma raised me to carry a weight."

I inhaled a lungful of smoky, oily air. How often did Tim change that Fryolator grease, anyway?

Across from me, her face pinched and strained, Joanne waited, hardly taking a breath as if whatever I was going to tell her wouldn't be, couldn't be, good.

"I found someone. Someone who belongs to you."

She stiffened like she was about to be slapped or something. That, more than the strain on her face, reminded me of how much she'd been through in the past few days.

"No one belongs to me." Her voice trailed off, kind of wistful like. "Now that Momma's gone, I'm alone."

"Not quite." I held her hand and squeezed it tight. "You have a daddy."

It took a second or two for the words to hit home, but as soon as they did, a shock rocketed through her body. She tensed, gripping my fingers so hard I winced. Her eyes, bluer than ever in her pinched face, rounded in amazement. "Who?"

"His name is Roger Ledbetter."

Her hand let go of mine and flew up to her mouth. "Ledbetter? That's Verna's name."

I nodded. "He's her son."

"Omigod. Is this true? How did you find out?"

"He told me."

While she slumped on the stool, her arms wrapped around her body as if cradling herself against another shock, I told her about Roger's visit to the townhouse and how it ended.

"So I have a daddy in the Yarborough Hospital, but I'm not supposed to know he *is* my daddy. Is that what you're telling me?"

"I can't be sure, but I think he wants you to know. I think he loves you and is sad about many things. Especially—"

The kitchen door swung open and Tim came busting in. "That dog still here? The board of health sees him, they'll shut me down for sure."

"Not if they see the Fryolator first."

"What's that supposed to mean?"

"We need a few more minutes." Joanne looked

him straight in the eye. "I just found out I've got me
a daddy."

Now it was my turn to be shocked. She didn't trust
Tim, so why let him in on her news? To judge his re-
action maybe? Later, when I had a chance to dwell on
things a bit, I remembered the Ledbetters had once
lived in the church manse right across the street from
the Shed, and the owner of a pub knew all the local
gossip, didn't he? Anyway, whatever her reason, when
she spoke up like that my jaw fell open. As for Tim,
well, his jaw damn near hit the floor. But like any wily
dude, he recovered fast. "Of course you got a daddy.
Everybody does. That's no surprise."

"It sure is to me," Joanne snapped back.

"And who would your daddy be?"

"You mean you don't know?"

"Of course not. Why should I?"

"Why do I think you do?"

*God Almighty, she was riding him hard.*

At the sharpness in Joanne's tone, Jake rose from
the floor, bared his teeth at Tim and snarled. I reached
for his collar. "Sit, boy, sit."

Tim pointed a finger at me. "Five more minutes, you
and that mutt better be out of here." To Joanne, "Like I
said, I know nothing about your daddy. Now get back
to the bar. I got a business to run."

He left, sending the kitchen door swinging behind
him.

"He *knew*," Joanne said, leaping to her feet, color
flooding her cheeks. "I bet he's known right along."

"Could be." I checked my watch. "If Tim comes
back, I'll have to leave before Jake goes for his throat."
I patted the empty stool. "So please sit down. I have

more to tell you." I knew the words I was about to speak would be hurtful, but holding them from her any longer didn't strike me as right.

When she had settled down, I said, "Roger…your daddy…talked about Darlene too."

"He mentioned Momma? Did he say why he never lived with us? Never took care of her?"

"Well, here's the thing." I took in another deep breath before letting Roger's long-held secret escape into the greasy air. "He said she…ah…wasn't really your birth momma. She adopted you when you were born."

"That's a lie!" Joanne burst into tears, her whole body trembling so bad I was afraid she'd fall off the stool.

Somehow, I didn't think Roger had lied. He'd been very…well, fevered up in telling me about his past. But the last thing Joanne needed now was an argument. "There's one way to find out. It's foolproof, folks say."

"DNA?" Sobbing, she could barely spit out the letters.

"Yes."

She whipped her head back and forth so hard the tears jumped off her cheeks. "No matter what any test says, Darlene was my momma. She loved me. She sacrificed everything she had for me. Even worked a second job so I could get through college. She was my momma in every possible way."

I blew out a breath. "Right."

Joanne's feelings were so powerful, how could they not be true? At least to her. But if Roger hadn't lied, another woman was Joanne's birth momma, and I knew that given time, Joanne would discover the truth. After all, a person who would travel to Peru to study long gone strangers would move heaven and earth to learn everything she could about her very own folks.

I stood, ripped a piece of paper toweling off a roll near the grill and pressed it into her hands. "For your tears. I want to show you something." I reached into my purse for Reba's smartphone. "I found this on the snow."

"Oh?" She wiped her eyes and sniffled up her nose, but the tears kept on flowing, her nose kept on leaking. Clearly, right now, she didn't give a hoot or a holler for somebody's lost phone, only for the earth-shattering news I'd just dumped on her. And who could blame her?

In too far to back off, I said, "It's Reba Knight's. Listen." I clicked on voice mail, and Verna's message came quavering through the line.

"She sounds familiar," Joan began. "Is that—"

"Verna Ledbetter. According to Roger, she's your grandmother."

"Play it again, Honey." I did and Joanne listened to every word, her teary eyes hardly blinking. "She's upset about something."

I nodded. "I suspect it has to do with Roger's past coming to light."

"But you can't be sure. Reba never got this message." She heaved a sigh. "You shouldn't have kept the phone, Honey."

At Joanne's scolding tone, my glance darted across the room at the dingy back wall, the Fryolator, the fridge, the sink, everywhere but at the frown on her face. "Lord knows, it was wrong of me, but I thought it might shed some light on your birth certificate. Tell who Reba phones and texts. Lead us to some people who might help."

"All it led to was my…my grandmother." Joanne stood and tossed the damp paper towel in a trash bin. "She might be in trouble."

I couldn't deny what Joanne was saying. She'd found some kin folks at last and was standing by them. I loved her for that and hated myself for borrowing… swiping Reba's phone. "I'll return it first thing in the morning. Promise."

"Okay, but Verna might need help now. I'm going up the street to check on her."

"Is it all right if Jake and I come along?" I had to ask. Her stern face put me in mind of Grandma Ingersoll when something vexed her, and there was no messing with a strong woman like that.

She hesitated—which hurt me a bit but was no more than I deserved—then nodded.

"Let's not wait till my shift ends." She untied her apron and flung it on the chopping block. "The cook's not the only one who's quitting tonight."

# TWENTY-SIX

WITH JAKE PEERING over our shoulders from the Lincoln's backseat, we drove up Sugar Street, our breath like little puffs of smoke in the cold night air. Along the road, house lights gleamed here and there, but at the top of the street, in the cul-de-sac, the Moose stood tall and dark.

Across the way, lamp light filtered through the curtains on Verna's front windows. "Oh good, she's awake." Joanne seemed hell-bent to call on this cold, floor-scrubbing woman who had no smiles for anyone and no joy in her heart.

Of course she was eager, I told myself, she had questions for Verna. Verna was kin. For the first time in her life, Joanne was about to learn who her family was, what manner of people she had sprung from.

We hurried up the front walk, and I rang the bell. Again. Then again. The chimes played their tune loud and clear, but no one answered.

"Something's the matter." Joanne turned away from the door, panic in her voice. "On the phone, she said she'd be up all night."

"It's late. Maybe she fell asleep."

"I can't leave not knowing."

"We could try calling her."

"Yes!" Joanne pulled her cell phone out of her parka. "You have the number?"

"No, not with me."

"We better call 911 then."

"Let's look in the windows first. She might be dozing in a chair. It'll only take a minute to find out."

"Okay." Not wasting any time about it, Joanne crept behind the evergreen shrubs outside the parlor windows and peered inside, straining to see something through the sheer curtains. After a minute or so, she crept back, shaking her head. "Nothing's moving in there, but I couldn't see real good."

"Let's check the back windows," I said.

We tiptoed through the snowy yard leaving footprints—human and doggy—all around the house. In the morning light, anyone with half an eye would know what we'd been up to. Not that it did us a speck of good. Verna had pulled her blinds and shades all the way to the window sills. I should have known. She was too neat to leave anything half done.

"Something's wrong," Joanne said. "I can feel it."

"Don't give up. We're not through yet."

The sensible thing would have been to call for help. Instead, I opened my purse, unzipped a side pocket and removed a steel pick. As I held it up, it gleamed in the lamplight. "Meet Plan B."

"What *is* that?"

"Something Saxby Winthrop, my former…ah…boss gave me. He said every Realtor needed one in case of emergency. Better still, he showed me how to use it. Come on, the back door would be safer."

"Is that what I think it is?" Joanne whispered as she followed me through the snow.

"Yes. Now pray Verna doesn't have a dead bolt on the door or we're sunk."

As it turned out, she didn't.

My lock-picking was a little rusty, but on the third try, the tumblers clicked, the door handle turned and we were in. Like two burglars up to no good, we huddled in the darkened kitchen.

"You think she has a gun?" Something I should have thought of before I picked the lock.

"One way to find out. Verna," she called. "It's me, Joanne."

I poked her arm. "Louder. She's a little deaf."

"Verna!"

No answer.

I switched on the kitchen overheads. The room was empty except for a cup of tea and a piece of pie on the kitchen table.

"Look at that." I pointed to the pie. "It's not like her to leave food sitting out."

"She's in trouble. I knew it."

Without waiting another second, Joanne ran out of the kitchen into the front parlor, glanced around it for an instant then darted down the hall to the bedrooms. I stood rooted to the kitchen floor, waiting, until a scream sent Jake and me racing toward the bedrooms.

In the back room, where the week before I'd found Juanita's suicide note tucked into a letter holder, Verna was stretched out on her back in the middle of the rag rug.

Joanne knelt beside her, pressing a finger to her wrist, searching for a pulse. Finding none, she laid her head on Verna's chest and listened for a heartbeat. A few moments only and she looked up, her eyes filled with pain. "I think she's dead."

But that wasn't the case. Jake sashayed over to Verna and gave both her cheeks a long, slurpy lick. At that, Verna's lashes fluttered and a low moan escaped from between her dentures. The next thing I knew, she was staring up at us. So that's where Joanne had gotten her beautiful blue eyes. Funny how I hadn't noticed the likeness till now.

"Where am I?" Verna asked.

"At home," Joanne said, patting her cheek.

Verna brushed off Joanne's hand and pointed a finger at Jake. "What's an animal doing in my house? And what are you two doing here? How did you get in?"

Her voice was a little quavery but, otherwise, Verna was recovering fast.

"You left the door open," I said, adding a lie to my list of other sins.

"I never do that."

"You weren't feeling well. You must have forgotten."

"I never forget." Vera sat up and looked around.

"Do you want me to call 911?" Joanne asked.

"Whatever for?"

"Your doctor then?"

Verna shook her head. "A doctor can't help me with what's wrong. I got some upsetting news earlier and skipped supper. I suppose with my blood pressure like it is, I shouldn't have done that."

"What news?" I asked as soft and sweet as I could.

"My boy, my Roger's in the hospital." She shot me such a dirty look you could rightly say she evil-eyed me. "Don't pretend, missy. You know all about it. I heard tell he was looking at one of your new-fangled townhouses when he had his seizure."

She struggled to sit up and fell back onto the carpet.

"Let us help you," Joanne said.

We each took Verna under an arm and lifted her onto a chair. She was hefty enough, but lighter than a body might suspect from listening to her.

"You need to eat something. I'll get that pie you left on the kitchen table. I'll make you some hot tea," Joanne said.

As if too wrung out to protest, Verna nodded. "That would be nice, but what I'm needing most of all is a ride to the hospital. I called a friend earlier, but she never answered."

The guilt nearly laid me out flat on the carpet we'd just lifted Verna off of.

"I'll take you," Joanne said, "but first your tea."

As she hurried out to the kitchen, Verna, wan but wary, stared at me without blinking. "Roger told you, didn't he? I've warned him over and over, never admit it to anyone, but he did, didn't he?"

"Did what?"

"Tell you what he's guilty of. He's been threatening to tell, said he couldn't keep it to himself any longer, it was eating at him." Tears slid out from under her lids. "Now everyone will know. A preacher's son...what a disgrace."

"She has your eyes," I said softly.

Verna pulled a handkerchief out of her apron pocket and wiped the tears off her cheeks. "I've noticed."

"You gave her a mighty fine gift. They're beautiful."

With a flap of her hand, she batted my words away like they were flies. "People talk. We'll be the laughing stock of the town." She was upset, all right, but her voice held its usual tart edge, a sign she was back to normal.

"How long have you known?"

I almost didn't think she'd answer, but she did.

"After my husband's death, I went through his papers and found a birth certificate. It lists Roger as the father. And a Gaylene Mills somebody as the mother. She was one of the...one of the—"

"Girls from the Moose?"

"So I was told."

"She died in childbirth."

"God's retribution, I say."

"God works in mysterious way." *Listen to me, spouting off like I really know.* "He's given you a beautiful grandchild."

"Humph."

At that, I snapped. In all my born days, she was the coldest grandma I'd ever met. "She needs you. Why don't you forget your almighty pride and be a loving grandma?"

Verna's jaw went stiff as a concrete block. "*Grandma?* She's no part of me and mine. She's trash."

"Trash, is that what I heard, *trash*?"

Hands on hips, I stomped over to her so mad I could spit. Whether she knew it or not, Verna had hit a nerve. I'd spent the last five years and then some struggling to overcome my own upbringing. God bless my momma and Grandma Ingersoll, they raised me best they could, but their good country manners and their country way of talking didn't help me sell houses to city folks, nor help me make my way in this hard-scrabble world of today. Still, they had loved me and given me everything they had, no matter how little it was. Just as Darlene had given her all to Joanne. Trash indeed.

Raising a hand off one hip, I pointed it in the direction of the kitchen. To my great vexation, my pointing finger shook. "That girl out there, your *granddaughter*, needs you, and that's what matters. As far as your almighty pride is concerned, suck it up and do the Lord's bidding. And while you're at it, show that girl her real birth certificate."

God in heaven, I sounded like a Sunday preacher, and I had no right to do so, no right at all. I lowered my shaky arm and sank onto the side of Verna's bed. My fanny told me the mattress was hard as a board. No surprise there.

A moment of heavy silence passed. "Miss Ingersoll?"

I glanced her way.

"My husband, the Reverend Ledbetter—"

"I know who your husband was," I said in a nasty tone.

"Well, here's something you don't know. If he was here, he'd tell me what you just said was the Lord's own truth."

*"Really?"* I almost fell back on the mattress.

"And he'd tell me he kept Roger's secret to spare me pain. But I know that without having him say the words. So I'll try to forgive my son and accept his love child—"

I leaped off the edge of the bed and went over to give her a hug. "Wonderful!"

"Even if it kills me."

# TWENTY-SEVEN

EARLY THE NEXT MORNING, the town vet checked out Jake and declared him to be in good shape—even his teeth—for an eight-year-old dog. Afterwards, I dropped him off at the groomers. She promised she'd make him beautiful, though from his awful howling when I left, he didn't give a rat's tail about how he looked.

Then I did the dirty and drove out to the courthouse to return Reba's phone. Trying to think up an excuse for having it kept me busy all the way out there. But as I pulled into a visitor's slot, I figured I'd told enough lies and broken enough rules in the last few days. So I just plunked the phone on her County Records countertop. "I think this is yours. You might want to take a look."

She snatched it up. "Well, I'll be darned. I tore the house apart last night looking for it." Her moment of gratitude over, she drew in a sudden breath as suspicion struck her in the chest. "Where did you find it?"

"Out in the snow. You must have dropped it."

I was sure she'd ask where in the snow, but she didn't. That would have been that if I hadn't added, "Me and Joanne...Joanne and I called on Verna Led-better last night."

"Oh?" The phone clutched in her hand, Reba stood there staring at me.

"Yeah, turns out she's Joanne's grandma."

"You don't say?"

"Yes, ma'am. And guess whose name is on her *real* birth certificate?"

She shook her head.

"Her daddy's."

I'm kind of ashamed to admit it, but Reba's shocked gasp gave me a certain amount of pleasure though I didn't turn the screws by telling her the sheriff would likely find Joanne's news mighty interesting. I didn't even ask why Roger's name had been left off the fake one her adoptive momma had. No need. I figured Reba already knew why. Now it would be up to Matt to find out the truth at last.

Besides, I had to buy dog food, a leash and get back to the groomers for my pooch. Sometimes it was easy to forget I was a real estate agent not a would-be crime buster with a few transgressions…I think that's the right Bible word…of my own.

When I stopped by the groomers to pick up Jake—all fluffy and smelling of pine soap—he was so happy to see me I knew then, if never before, why folks loved dogs so much. We were already best pals though we'd only met yesterday. Pals? Shucks, I was in love. And from the way his tail wagged, so was Jake.

"Come on, boy, we're going to work." I didn't add, "At last," but Jake understood.

As we walked into the office, Mindy leaped up to greet us. "Where have you…oh, a dog."

"Meet Jake. He's joining the firm."

"He's gorgeous, but I didn't know you had a dog."

"Yup."

"I've been so worried. The phone's been jumping off

the hook. The sheriff's looking for you. You got two inquiries about that new townhouse. And Carl Huggins called—three times."

"If you want to pet Jake for a bit, I'll call him back right now."

"No need. He's waiting in your office."

As I strolled in, Carl threw down a copy of *Home & Land*. "High time you got here, missy." Making a big point of eye-balling his watch, he said. "It's near ten o'clock. You sleepin' in or you runnin' a business?"

I took the swivel chair behind my desk—and the high road. "I've made three calls already this morning, Carl." Not that they had anything to do with real estate. And not that they were any of his business.

"Hmmph. We need to talk."

"About the Moose?"

He shifted in his seat. "That's the one. No action on it, right?"

"No. I warned you it would be a hard sell. Now with the murder and all—"

"No need to tell me what I already know." He leaned forward, took off his John Deere long enough to swipe an arm across his forehead and back on it went. "Here's the deal. One more open house and that's it. No bites, no offers, I'm razing the place and selling the land as a building lot."

"That would be a shame. Under the neglect…and, well, the history…the Moose is a fine piece of property."

"Lot of good that's doin' me. I been paying taxes on the place long enough and my daddy before me. So one more open house and no movement, in come the wreckers."

"You're the boss."

"Don't you forget it. Keep in touch."

"Of course, Mr. Huggins."

He stomped out and the front door slammed so soon afterwards, I figured he hadn't stopped to give Jake a friendly pat. I guess under the circumstances that would have been asking too much.

I hadn't heard from Joanne about the hospital visit with Roger, and she was heavy on my mind. I hoped the meeting had been a good one, that he'd been well enough to man up and acknowledge her face-to-face, even with his momma looking on. Especially with his momma looking on.

But I told myself Joanne was with kin now, and by keeping my mind on business, I cleared my desk, answered all my voice mail messages and set up an appointment to show the townhouse at five that afternoon. The prospect said he was a pharmacist recently hired by Walmart. He sounded young and let on that he was single. Perfect. He'd probably love the Jacuzzi—for more interesting reasons than getting squeaky clean.

Last, but far from least, I contacted Kelsey Davis at the *Star*. "Another open house for the Moose coming up, Kelsey. Saturday from one to five. This time make it a full-page ad and run it for three days."

A low whistle came through the line. "Sure thing, but it'll be pricy."

"I know, but I'd really like to see the place sold so it can shake off its past, become what it once was. The Moose didn't start out with a bad name. It used to be a home with big ol' rooms and plenty of space for a growing family. Besides, I owe you one. What with your camera being stolen there and all."

"Not to worry. Matt Rameros found it."

"He *did*?"

"Yup, in that Paradise Pawn Shop outside of town. He brought it in this morning. It's been wiped clear of prints, but they're looking at the shop's surveillance camera. Who knows, maybe the shop owner can ID the guy who pawned it."

I said goodbye with the feeling that things were heating up. For sure, the weather was. By noon, the last scraps of snow had melted away like the last few ice cubes in a glass, leaving the streets wet but not slick and the whole town washed clean.

By two, curious and curioser, I was about fit to bust when Joanne marched in, a great big grin splitting her face. I leaped up to give her a hug.

"I met him." Those were her first words. No need to ask who she meant.

"And?"

"He's nice. Real nice. The nurse only let Verna and me stay a few minutes, but I promised I'd go back later. They're keeping him for observation. I guess he has some problems." Her smile dimmed a bit. "But that's all right. Between us, Verna and I'll take care of him."

"Shouldn't Roger be caring for you?" was on the tip of my tongue, but she was so happy I couldn't spoil her joy with such a hurtful question. Instead, I asked, "Have you heard from Sheriff Matt?"

She nodded. "I called him this morning while Verna was getting dressed. She gave me my birth certificate, and I want him to see it. He said he'd meet me here at two-thirty. I hope that's all right."

"Of course it is."


AT TWO-THIRTY on the nose, Matt, along with Deputy Zach, arrived bringing with him a whiff of the lemony aftershave I remembered only too well from…yesterday.

"Ladies," he said, with a devilish wink tossed in for me. "You have something I should see?"

"Yes, sir." Joanne took the birth certificate out of her backpack and handed it to him with a little wave of her wrist.

A quick reading and he shot her one of his big, white smiles. "Looks like the real McCoy. The question is why the other fraudulent document? Zach and I need to pay a little call on our county clerk. I suspect she won't be happy to see us darken her door, but I also don't think she'll be surprised." He tapped a nail on the paper. "Before we leave, Honey, can you make a copy of this for me?"

"I already have, Sheriff." I plucked it off my desktop and held it out.

Matt reached over to take it, his fingers brushing mine. "Thank you." I had a notion he wasn't talking about a piece of Xerox copy paper. Though to be honest, I do suffer from a fanciful mind.

Anyway, he turned to Joanne. "You'll be informed of any decisions regarding your documents, Miss Petty."

Then he and Zach stomped out, leaving me and Joanne…Joanne and me alone with our half empty coffee mugs and our curiosity which, as it turned out, was eating holes in both of us.

"Why do I have to wait for the police to tell me what's what? I can do my own digging." Joanne plunked down her mug. "Before I go out to the hospital, I'm going to the courthouse."

"Right. And you know what? My next appointment isn't until five o'clock when my client gets out of work. Could you use a little company?"

"Yes!"

"Let's go. I'll follow you in the Lincoln."

MATT'S SHINY, BLUE cruiser sat right in front of the courthouse entrance. Joanne parked next to it, and I pulled up beside her. By the time I got the engine turned off, she had already jumped out of her Jeep and was hustling up the stone stairs, racing straight for Reba in County Records. How she could move so fast with that satchel strapped on her back, I didn't know, never having toted around a bag of books in my life. I followed after her, a little slow maybe, in my red stilettos. But those shoes did so much for my legs they speeded up my life in other ways. What was a wee bit of inconvenience compared to that?

With my heels making a racket on the green and tan tiles of the courthouse floor, I stomped along the main hall toward County Records in back. Halfway there, I spotted Matt and Zach standing outside the washrooms, legs wide apart, like they were guarding a bank or something. *What on earth?*

Usually Matt lit up the second he laid eyes on me. But not this time. As I approached, his eyes went dark like what he was looking at wasn't pleasing to him. *Hmmph.* I might as well have worn bedroom slippers.

"First Joanne comes barreling through. Now you, making enough noise to raise the dead. What are you doing here, anyway?"

"Don't you go all snarly on me, Matt Rameros. This is a public building." I flung my hands on my hips so fast the handbag slid off my shoulder and banged into my side. "But since you asked, I'm accompanying Miss Petty while she finds out all she can about her birth record."

Matt's face softened a tad. "She may have trouble finding what she wants." He upped his chin in the direction of County Records. "We were about to do that very thing when the clerk back there said Missus Knight was in the ladies' room."

"You standing guard to make sure she takes care of business?"

At least Zach lightened up enough to snort.

"We're waiting on her return." Matt glanced at his watch. "She's been in there quite a while. Want to do law enforcement a favor?"

"If I can."

"Go see if she's in there. Or not."

Did he actually think Reba's clerk would lie to the cops? From the firm set to his jaw, I guess he did, so to be obliging, I pushed open the door to the ladies' room and sashayed on in.

Reba was there all right. No question about it whatsoever. Spread-eagled on the floor, she lay flat on her back, her beehive hairdo off to one side, her mouth open as if she wanted to say something—but couldn't.

# TWENTY-EIGHT

THOUGH REBA SURE wasn't moving, was she breathing? I couldn't tell, not without touching her, and that was something I couldn't bring myself to do.

"Matt," I hollered. "Come here. Hurry up."

The door banged open, and Matt and Zach hustled in. One startled glance at Reba and Matt dropped down beside her to search for a pulse. A few moments only and he shook his head. "I'm not finding anything. Call 911, Zach."

To keep out of the way, I stood against the sinks by the wall. I'd never had warm feelings for Reba, but to see her like this…her beehive hairdo piled to one side of her head not up top where it should be and her hose bunched around her feet…well, it made my heart want to weep. "Do you think she's…do you think she's—"

"Dead?" Matt nodded. "The question is why?" His gaze roved over her still body. "No obvious signs of foul play, but that's for the coroner to decide."

"The ambulance will be here in three minutes," Zach said, just as one of the courthouse workers poked her head in, glanced around, and let out a little scream.

"Sorry, ma'am," Matt said, getting back on his feet. "Use the men's room. My deputy will stand outside for you." He turned to Zach. "Have somebody put up a sign. The ladies' room is out of order until further notice."

*Now what?*

Sad to say, I knew. First the medics. Then Detective Bradshaw. Then the coroner. And last, the ambulance that would bring Reba's remains to the morgue. For with a murderer still on the loose and questions about to be asked regarding suspicious county records, Reba's sudden death wouldn't be treated as an act of God. Not without first proving it wasn't an act of somebody more, well, *local*.

Anyway, all the commotion had workers and visitors alike clustering outside the ladies' room. It was all Matt and Zach could do to keep folks calm and clear the way for the medics.

As Joanne and I stood down the hall away from the excitement, she said, "I found my original birth certificate. It was there in the record book on my correct birthday, right where it belonged. Everything matches the copy Verna gave me last night. Names, dates, everything." Dropping her voice to a whisper, she lifted her book bag up off the floor. "I'm leaving. I want to see my…Roger. No doubt about it, Honey, he *is* my father."

"That's such good news." It was actually better than good, but why so much mystery around an innocent baby's birth? If Darlene had questions about Joanne's daddy's name being missing on her birth certificate, she hadn't questioned it over the years. Probably not until she found her sister Juanita's farewell letter to their aunt. That might have raised questions in her mind about the past and sent her searching for the truth. A search that cost her her life.

Of course, Reba had denied knowing anything about

anything. Not that I believed her. It may not be nice to talk mean about the dead, but if I was a gambling woman, I'd put my chips on the person who knew the most, Reba Knight, who for the last thirty years had been queen of Yarborough County Records.

Joanne took off for the hospital, all eager and happy. I hoped Roger would be strong enough to be a true father to her at last. As for Reba, why had she taken such a chance with an official document? Risked her livelihood and a possible jail sentence? Only two reasons came to me as I stood in the drafty hall, breathing in the stale odor of old cigarettes and old faded records: threats and money. One or the other, or both. Then another thought struck, pulling me away from the wall I'd been leaning on. Suppose Joanne wasn't the only one whose papers had been tampered with? Suppose Reba had doctored up others over the years? Had a cottage industry going in fake documents? That might include real estate transactions. *Omigod.* Any sale with a lien, a disputed deed, a land variance she had stamped as valid could be at risk. If that turned out to be the case, houses all over the county might be in legal jeopardy. A question for Andy Ballou, if ever there was one.

Though the thought of what might be wrong made me want to retch, I didn't have time to buckle. It was four thirty and even if I left right away, I'd be late for that five o'clock showing with the pharmacist. While I stood there trying to decide what to do, Doc Evers, the coroner, a tall man with a weary, overworked look about him, shuffled along the hall carrying his black medical bag. He and Matt went in to where Reba's body lay and closed the door, leaving Zach to stand guard outside.

I went up to him. "Zach, is it all right for me to leave?"

"Couldn't say." A man of few words, Zach wasn't about to change for my sake. I could bolt for town, but I found the body, so Matt or the coroner might have questions for me. I'd better wait around for a while, but I sure hated to miss that townhouse showing.

Then it occurred to me. *Ah! Why not? There has to be a first time.*

I whipped the cell pone out of my purse and called the office. Mindy picked up on the first ring. Good. That kind of proved she wasn't doing her nails in the front window. "How would you like to take over for me this afternoon?" I asked.

"Me? Really? How?"

"I want you to handle a showing. Close the office and get right over to that townhouse on Main Street. You have the address and there's a set of keys on the consol board. Light some of the aromatherapy candles and turn on the lamps, put the stereo music on low. Very low. Set the stage."

"What?"

"Pretend you're getting ready for a date."

"Oh, okay. I got it."

"Now write this down. It's the asking price. It's negotiable. Got that too?"

"Not to worry, Honey. I'll be just fine."

"I know you will. He's a pharmacist. Name is Thomas Wynell."

"Is he cute?"

*Oh God, what have I done?*

IN REBA'S LITTLE box of an office, Kenny Knight sat slumped at her desk, sweating big time. Beads of it had gathered at his hairline and darkened the underarms of his plaid shirt.

"I'm sorry for your loss, Kenny," Matt said, though he looked more troubled than sorrowful to be honest about it, "but I have to ask. Do we have your permission to perform an autopsy?"

"A *what*?" Kenny shot upright in his chair. "An autopsy? You want to slice her up?"

"The coroner can't establish a cause of death without one. Should foul play be involved…" Matt let his voice trail off.

The silence seemed to unsettle Kenny, for as the room went still, he glanced around the small space like he was dazed to find himself sitting there in Reba's seat.

"You have an answer for me, Kenny? About the autopsy?"

He shook his head. "I hate the thought of it."

"We wouldn't ask if it wasn't necessary. Suppose she was poisoned? Wouldn't you want us to nail the person who did it?"

Kenny paled like a body about to slide to the floor. "You think she *was*? Poisoned?"

"No, we don't know. The cause of death is unknown. An autopsy will help."

"All right, if you say so, but what a thing to do to my gal." Kenny wept then, hiding his face and his tears behind his thick, stubby fingers.

"Stay with him, will you, Honey?" Matt asked. "I'll be back in a few minutes."

I snatched a handful of tissues from the box on Reba's desk and pressed them into Kenny's fingers. Shoulders heaving, he took them without looking up.

As I watched him bend under the weight of his grief,

his shoulders shuddering, his eyes hidden from the light, I knew that if there was ever a chance he'd tell the truth it was now when sorrow made his life and his future seem unimportant.

I patted his heaving back, murmuring comforting things like a momma might to a hurting baby.

"Kenny," I whispered in his ear, "Reba was a good woman. One of the best." *Forgive me, Lord.*

His head nodded. *Yes.*

"So, who made her do it?"

"Do whaaat?"

"Doctor up those records. I know she wouldn't have done such a harmful thing on her own. Not our Reba."

"No." His voice a little uncertain.

"So, who forced her? Who was so cruel to such a God-fearing woman?"

Without warning, Kenny's tear-stained head popped up off the desk nearly banging into my chin.

"It was that snake-in-the-grass. Carl Huggins. That's who."

# TWENTY-NINE

MATT WASN'T BUYING IT. "Even if Kenny told you the truth, his story can't be verified. It's his word against Carl's. Furthermore, do you, in your heart of hearts, think Kenny Knight is a trustworthy person?"

"No, of course not. Except for this one time."

"What are you basing that on?"

"His tone of voice. The look in his eyes when he—"

"Give me a break, Honey. I can't accuse Carl Huggins of bribing a county official based on the look in a man's eyes. And you know it."

He spoke truly. I did know it and, like a pricked balloon, all the certainty whooshed out of me. "Kenny's confession is of no use?"

"Not without corroboration, and what that would be, I can't imagine. Carl sure isn't going to incriminate himself *if*—and this is a big if—he's guilty of wrongdoing in the first place."

"Okay. Sorry. I was just trying to help."

"Understood."

The walls of Reba's little office were closing in on me. The perfume she had favored, Flower Bomb from Walcott's Drugs, was getting stronger the longer I lingered there, making me faintly nauseous. I shrugged into my coat and slung my purse over a shoulder.

"Thanks, Honey." Matt was grinning.

"For what this time?" Too disappointed to ask nicely.

"For wearing those red high heels."

"Matt Rameros, that is the most sexist thing I've ever heard you spout."

"If those shoes aren't sexy, why wear them?" He grinned. "Since they kill your feet and all."

*Hmmph.*

THE NEXT MORNING, I left the red stilettos in the closet. I wasn't exactly mourning Reba's passing, but black fit my mood. So it was a black turtleneck, black pencil skirt and plain black pumps. I kind of looked like a widow, but it seemed appropriate...I think that's the word...somehow.

Jake and I got to the office early, only eight thirty by the clock outside the Savings & Loan. The lights were on, the heat turned up and the aroma of hazelnut coffee filled the air.

The front door had hardly closed when Mindy hurried out of the storeroom where she'd been brewing the coffee and rushed over to greet us.

"You're going to be happeeee..." She darted to her desk and held up what looked mighty like a check.

"Don't tell me—"

"Yes, yes, and yes!" She broke into a happy dance, whirling around the office waving the check in the air. "I sold the townhouse."

"On your first sales call? Why, that's *wonderful*. Beyond wonderful. I can't hardly believe it."

"Oh, you can believe. Tommy loved the place. Especially the Jacuzzi. He liked that best of all."

"Tommy?"

"Yes, the guy you wanted me to meet."

*"Guy?"*

"You *know.* Tommy Wynell."

I was afraid I did and sat down in a hurry.

"That Jacuzzi is so cool. On my way over there, I bought a bottle of champagne, you know, just in case. And like you said, I lit candles around the edge of the tub. We had to use plastic glasses for the champagne, but Tommy didn't mind. The Jacuzzi's *so* roomy—"

I held up a palm. "You didn't. Tell me you didn't."

*"What?"* She went all wide-eyed and innocent.

"Get in the Jacuzzi with him."

Her chin shot up. "I sold the townhouse, didn't I? On my very first try, didn't I?"

"Answer the question."

She shrugged. "What difference does it make? Results are what matter."

"You have any *idea* what you've done? If word gets out, every male client who comes through that door…" I pointed to it like it wasn't big enough to see "…will expect the same treatment."

"Oh." Her chin came down real fast.

"Then what do we become here at Ingersoll Realty?"

She thought a moment. "Movers and shakers?"

"I'll let that one go by. Here's another question. What if Mr. Wynell's check bounces?"

"It won't."

"Well, it's made out to the Eureka Falls Savings & Loan. So why don't you get your coat on and go see Mr. Cletus Dwyer, the bank president. Find out if there are sufficient funds to cover it. And here's something else to think on. Mr. Wynell has seventy-two hours to change his mind. What if he does?"

"We have to give the check back."

"Bingo. And that will mean you got squeaky clean for nothing."

"None of that's going to happen. I personally guarantee it."

"Is that right?" My voice dripped ice water.

"Absolutely. Tommy and I have a date tomorrow night, and if I know anything about men, he won't want me to cancel. Not for any reason under the sun. If you get my meaning."

"I get it loud and clear." I held out the check. "See what Cletus Dwyer has to say. Oh, one more thing. You're working this Saturday from one to five."

"*Noooo.* I don't work on Saturdays. Besides, I'm having a pedicure at two."

"Wrong on both counts."

Though I didn't like Mindy's sales method, didn't like it at all, to my own ears I sounded mighty like a boss from hell, and that wasn't mannerly. So I softened the blow. "When the townhouse sale is a done deal, you get a bonus."

The happy smile Mindy started out with had gradually slid off her face. Now it returned bright as a Fourth of July sparkler. "Oh thanks, Honey. That's terrific! I saw this darling little dress in Belinda's Boutique the other day. It has a…"

*Maybe I'd gone soft too fast.* "But if you ever use that same sales technique again, you'll be axed."

"Axed what?"

"Oh for heaven's sake."

# THIRTY

On Saturday, Jake and I got to the Moose a half hour early. I sat in the car, staring at the house for a while, trying to figure out what someone seeing it for the first time might think. A dump? A diamond in the rough? Like a show girl gone to seed, the house had good bones under its neglect and, though shabby and abandoned, to me at least, it didn't look like an ol' wreck waiting to be torn down.

I loved the way the winter sun caught the colors in the door's stained-glass panel and sparkled off the front windows. The broad verandah with its tall columns put me in mind of bye-gone days when the house had likely been home to a family with children. There was a big yard to play in, and a funky barn out back and that was just the outside. Inside, under all the screaming colors were high-ceilinged rooms and fireplaces that would make the holidays and all the cold, snowy days cozy and warm. Even the—

I heaved a sigh. *Get real, Honey. The place is a money pit. Maybe Carl's right. The wrecking ball is the way to go.* But my heart was heavy as Jake and I plodded up the weedy brick walk to the verandah. Sensitive to my moods, Jake let his tail go droopy as all get out. "You keep on like that, you're going to trip. You know that, boy?" I scratched him behind the ears, his favorite sweet spot, and when his tail took to swinging back and forth, I unlocked the front door and we strolled into the Moose together.

By one-thirty, the rooms hummed with a steady stream of folks coming and going. I guess there's nothing like a murder in a former bordello to ratchet up interest. Anyway, Mindy was stationed upstairs on bedroom patrol and Jake was hunkered down next to me by the front door when Matt Rameros in jeans and a cable knit sweater strolled in.

"I'm off duty today. Thought you could use a helping hand." He patted Jake for a bit then tilted his head at the kitchen. "Out there?"

I nodded. "Thanks, Matt, that would be perfect."

As he left to keep an eye on the back of the house, a middle-aged man in heavy-duty work clothes who'd been here since one sharp hustled on over to me. My pulse nudged up a notch. Maybe he was The One. The Buyer.

"Pardon me, young lady," he said. "What's the asking price again of this here property?"

When I told him, he whistled through his front teeth. "I been a contractor since knee-high to my daddy, and I'm saying straight out, you won't never get that money. Not for a place in this shape." He politely tipped a finger to his work cap and stomped on down the verandah stairs.

With my pulse sagging back to normal, I glanced quickly around, hoping no one had overheard him. It didn't look like anyone had, but I was afraid he was right.

By three, the hum of voices and the busy stir almost made me forget about the lack of heat. My feet weren't fooled, though. Even after piling on woolen socks, boots, two sweaters and a heavy scarf, I was chilled to the bone. Worse, I had to face facts. The Moose was an overpriced, rundown shell of a house with a bad name. I was spinning my wheels with this open house full of curiosity seekers. People had turned out in droves, no question about that—to see the bedrooms or to ask about the murder. But other than the contractor, no one else had asked me the golden question. By three-thirty I was sure no one would.

At four we hit a lull, and I called up to Mindy. She came shivering down the stairway, her arms wrapped around her body. "I'm frozen."

"Give me a few minutes to talk to the sheriff and then you can leave, okay?"

"Don't be long, *pulezz*." Hugging her elbows, she went over to stand by the front door with Jake.

I hurried out to the kitchen. Matt was alone, finishing a text message. "How's it going out front?" he asked, pocketing his phone.

"No bites yet. How about in here?"

"A lot of traffic through the mud room. Everybody wanted to know where Darlene's body was found." He shrugged. "Not so many inquiries about the house." He glanced around at the dingy, gray kitchen. "Too bad. It's a big, roomy place. Lots of potential."

"I think so too. A shame nobody else does. I've been wondering, Matt…" using my palms, I hoisted myself up and sat on a countertop "…any news about what happened to Reba?"

"Some. It looks like death by natural causes. Heart failure. But just for insurance, in view of Reba's messing with the Petty family documents, the coroner's ordered blood tests."

"Do you think all the poking about into Joanne's birth certificate pushed her over the edge?"

"Doubtful. From the condition of her organs, Doc said she'd been a ticking time bomb."

"So I shouldn't feel guilty for vexing her?"

"You did nothing wrong, Honey. You were helping out a poor kid who needed somebody in her corner, and there's something else you should know. It's not for publication but..." he shrugged "...since you brought it to our attention..."

My ears turned into radar. *"What?"*

"That beer bottle and the notepaper you asked me to have tested?"

I nodded. "Yeah?"

"The prints matched. Long story short, they're Tim's."

"I knew it! He's involved in Darlene's death then."

"Hey, lady, not so fast."

"Land's sake, you just said he's implicated."

Matt waggled a finger under my nose. "I said no such thing."

"But—"

One finger, up straight this time. "Okay, say he pulled that skeleton prank on Carl Huggins. He earns points for stupidity, but no real harm was done. The prints on Juanita's suicide letter are another story. They ID him as someone who was involved in her disappearance. To what degree remains to be seen."

Hands on hips, I asked, "So what's the next step?"

Matt sighed in that I-have-to-be-patient way he sometimes hauled out when he didn't much care for my questions. "I'll pay him a visit first thing Monday morning."

"Why not today?"

"Because the Shed is crazy busy on weekends. He won't have time to talk. And since I have no call to arrest him, I have no call to push. Not yet. But enough about that for now." He moved in between my dangling legs and pulled me close.

I might have resisted. I mean, only two days ago I'd read the riot act to Mindy for non-professional behavior and, besides, this was an open house. Somebody could pop around the corner at any moment. How would it look for the realty lady to be seen snuggling with the town sheriff? But I was so darn cold and Matt was so warm, I caved and cuddled right up to him.

He put his cheek against mine and inhaled. "Your hair smells of apples. So nice."

"Matt?"

"Um."

"I have to ask you something."

*"Now?"*

"Yes, it's been burning inside me for days. You think Reba falsified other documents over the years? Real estate documents, maybe?"

He loosened his hold to step back a bit and smile into my eyes. "You're proving what I've always known."

"Meaning?"

"You're beautiful *and* smart."

"That sounds nice, Matt, but I'm serious. I'm worried."

"Bradshaw and I discussed the possibility of further tampering, but as far as we can tell, no questions have ever been raised. The problem is the county doesn't have the money or the manpower to check all the thousands of transactions that passed through Reba's hands. If anything suspicious surfaces, her replacement has been told to notify us immediately. Other than that, there's little to be done. Ergo—"

"Ergo? Is that an American word?"

"There's nothing wrong with your vocabulary, Honey."

"My what?"

He laughed. "Cut it out. All we can do at the present time is assume Joanne's case was an anomaly."

"A what?"

"Okay, you win. The only one of its kind. Creating a false birth certificate is relatively easy. Especially when the birth mother dies and the father relinquishes his rights to the child. With real estate transactions, too many people are involved, too much money changes hands to easily falsify the legal documents. So we won't borrow trouble—not yet at least." He reached for me again. "When we're through here, what do you say we go out for dinner and maybe take in a movie later?" A brow arched up. "At my place."

"A movie? On the HDTV at the foot of your bed?"

He grinned. "If you insist."

I shook my head. "Sorry, Matt, I really am. But I'm busy tonight."

Though I hated turning him down like this, I had no choice. Or so I told myself. By staying tight—to some degree—with Andy Ballou, the man Darlene Petty had confided in and told all her secrets to, I might be of help to Joanne in finding her mother's killer. Anyway, that was the reason I was seeing Andy tonight, and when Matt learned the whole truth, and nothing but, he'd understand. At least I surely did hope he would.

# THIRTY-ONE

BY THE TIME I fed Jake, took him for a walk and then left him snoring on the sofa, it was nine or so before I got to the Toole Shed. Andy was already seated at a table in the corner, the one with the rickety chairs. He'd dressed up kind of fancy for a joint like the Shed, in a tweed jacket, tan pants and a soft, blue shirt. Looking at him decked out in his finery, I felt a little too country in jeans, cowboy boots from high school and a fuzzy purple sweater. But heck, this was a pub, and besides, I'd been so cold all afternoon I needed sturdy clothes to keep the chill from returning.

Anyway, when I slipped off my coat, he hugged me close, then bowing a little from the waist, he held out a single rose wrapped in a piece of green tissue paper.

"A rose for a rose."

"There you go again, sounding so pretty." I sniffed the flower. It had no perfume and was a pale pink, not the bright red I liked best, but that was okay, a rose was a rose. "Thank you, Andy. I'd wear it behind my ear but the stem is too long."

He laughed and helped me onto my wobbly seat. "It's great to see you." He spread his arms wide. "Even in a dump like this." He leaned over the scarred table-top. "Tell me something, Honey, why do you insist on

coming here? You know I'd take you to a decent restaurant. One with dim lights and table cloths. Maybe
even menus."

He laughed and so did I. But I had agreed to meet
him here with the rowdy bar flies telling their stale
jokes and the juke box spinning out old Kenny Rogers
hits, hoping such a smart guy who had been to Vanderbilt and all would get the message. I just wasn't into
him. He was the lawyer of a murder victim, and for that
reason only I wanted to stay friends—just friends...

"Honey," he was saying, "I asked Tim to open a bottle of what he calls his top shelf wine. A merlot. Hope
that's all right." He actually looked worried.

"Sounds wonderful." I wanted a beer, any kind.

"Whataya know, the love birds are back."

Startled, I looked up fast. Tim stood by our table, a
bottle of red wine in one hand, a corkscrew in the other.
"You like the place, huh?" He half-turned and cocked
his chin at the bar. "The Shed does that to a lot of folks.
Most of those guys over there never want to go home."
He winked at Andy. "That won't be your problem. Not
with a looker like Honey to go home with."

Darn that Tim and his big mouth, anyway. I felt like
stomping all over him.

Andy was none too pleased either. "Just leave the
bottle, Tim," he said, his lips going thin. "I'll open it."

"Sure thing. That'd be a help. My bar girl quit with
no notice. Heard tell she's staying up the top of the
street with Verna Ledbetter. After all I done for her,
you'd think she'd come on down and give me a hand.
She knows what Saturday nights are like around here."

"You have any wine glasses?" Andy said, his voice
kind of flat.

"Oh, yeah. Be right back."

Andy plunged the corkscrew into the bottle neck. "Honey, I have an announcement to make."

"Oh?"

"This is my last visit to the Toole Shed. From here on, you'll have to pick a different place. Capiche?"

"Does *capiche* mean understand?"

"It certainly does."

"Well, don't fret. I do."

He didn't answer and, for a silver-tongued attorney, that told you something. While he struggled with his bad mood and what looked like a dry cork, I excused myself for a few minutes. So far, we hadn't even touched on the murders, or the mysterious suicide of Darlene Petty's sister, or Joanne's faked birth certificate. If we didn't get to something useful soon, the evening would be a bust. To avoid that, I'd have to raise one of the issues, but how? To give myself a little thinking time, I picked up my purse and lit out for the ladies' room.

It was empty, so I took my time, mulling over the situation while I brushed my hair and reapplied some Passionate Pink lip gloss. I didn't need to pee or anything, but I washed my hands anyway. I was wiping down the sink with the damp towel when I heard angry male voices just outside the ladies' room. One voice I didn't recognize and one I did—Tim's.

I put an ear to the door. "Here, take it," the stranger's voice said, "but make no mistake, O'Toole, this is the last payment. Do whatever you want. Tell whatever you want. I don't give a damn any more. This has gone on long enough."

"You know what you're sayin'? After what I did for her, she owes me. You owe me."

*Who was Tim talking about? Joanne?*

"I don't owe you a dime. As of tonight, you're shut off."

"Cut the payments, she's heading for jail and your name's in the toilet. What happens to the both a you then?"

"What happens then?" A short bark of a laugh. "I'll kill you. That's what."

A hoarse shout from the bar. "Hey, O'Toole, where the hell are you?"

"I gotta go. The troops are callin'. Do anything drastic, you'll live to regret it." Tim chuckled. "Or maybe not. You got my drift?"

I waited by the door without moving as footfalls became faint and then got lost in the tinny juke box music and loud bar chatter. Taking a chance, I cracked open the door and peeked out into the back hall. *Uh-oh.*

A tall, balding man in a camel-colored topcoat over what looked like a gray business suit stood leaning against the wall, a hand up to his brow like he was rubbing life back into his head or something. I'd never laid eyes on him before so was pretty sure he hadn't been in the main bar area when I came in. Like Andy's clothes, his would have stood out in a roomful of jeans and nylon jackets sporting Go Razorbacks in big, white letters. That he'd been the man arguing with Tim, I had little doubt.

After staring down at his shoes for a while, he drew himself upright, squared his shoulders and headed for the kitchen. From the look of him, he was no short order cook, but the back door leading out to the rear lot happened to be located in the kitchen. Clearly, this wasn't his first visit to the Shed.

Over the bar noise, Kenny Rogers had given way to Waylon Jennings. The Saturday night crowd had the place jumping. By now Andy would be wondering where I'd gone to. If I hadn't had a fresh manicure, I'd have bitten my nails down to nubs. What to do? What to do? If I took time to tell Andy about the squabble I'd overheard, the man would be long gone. Maybe for good. I couldn't chance that, I simply couldn't. Whoever this well-dressed stranger was, he knew something about Tim's past and Tim, sure as shootin', knew something about the Moose's past.

Okay, that settled it. I had to follow the guy. That meant leaving Andy sitting alone at the rickety table. As soon as I could, I'd call him, ask him to forgive me and tell him not to worry. Not a good plan, but it was all I had. I grabbed my purse, rushed out of the ladies' and hurried into the kitchen.

"Hey, what's goin' on here?" the new cook hollered as I raced past the Fryolator. "This ain't no bowlin' alley."

I flung open the back door and, without a coat, shuddered in the frigid night air. No one in sight. Where had he disappeared to? I peered around the dumpster. Rear lights flared red across the tarmac. Someone was backing up what looked like a late model sedan, a Lexus maybe. But I couldn't get a clear look at the plate, or the driver, and I wasn't even sure the car was a Lexus. A glance around the lot showed nothing else moving. It had to be him. Forcing my cold fingers to search through my purse, I found my keys in record time and ran, shivering, over to the Lincoln.

Wheels squealing, I sped out of the parking lot. Luckily Main Street traffic wasn't heavy, and under the streetlights I spotted someone heading east, in what sure looked like a shiny new Lexus. Staying two cars behind like they do in spy movies, I turned on the heater and followed him out of town. Well, I was following somebody. I hoped it was him.

Gradually, with my fingers warmed up enough to work the phone, I called Andy.

"Honey? Is that you?" His voice aggravated as all get out. "Why are you calling me? Where are you?"

"In my car, heading down route eighty."

*"What!"* From his tone, I figured he had jumped to his feet. "What the hell are you doing that for? Your coat's here. I'm here."

"I'm following a Lexus. Sorry to leave you like that, but I had to. I'll explain later."

"You'll explain *now.*"

*Oh, ordering me around, are you?* I hung up, dropped the phone on the passenger seat and gripped the wheel. Route eighty leading out of town had grown scary dark. No more street lights, no more cars. Only two red blurs up ahead. Fearing he might notice me on his tail, I dropped back a bit. The road went on and on, curving around hills black as pitch. Where was he headed anyway? This was the way to Little Rock, a two-hour ride at least, and I hoped that wasn't where he was heading. But where else could we be going? Except for a house light peeking through the bare branches every now and then, there wasn't much to be seen, no traffic, no activity, just the steady red lights of Mr. Mysterious up ahead. If only I could make out the plate number, but the road was too curvy, too dark.

I eyeballed my gas gauge. Half full. Well, at least I had that and four good tires. I gripped the wheel like it was a lifeline, which in a way, it was. The last thing I wanted was to get stuck out here in the middle of nowhere on a freezing cold night, and me with no coat. No mace. No gun. No nothing. Good Lord. And all these years, I'd been thinking my momma had raised no stupid child.

I heaved a sigh that fogged up the windshield. This wasn't the time for regretting. I was doing what I needed to do, and I'd keep on doing it until I ran out of gas or out of nerve. Whichever gave way first. For now, I'd watch the road and hope the drumming of the tires didn't put me to sleep.

*Uh-oh.* Not a chance. Without warning, not even the flash of a directional signal, the Lexus pulled off the highway onto the driveway of Dicky Bob's Motor Inn.

*Darn it.* I shot past too fast to make the turn. Good grief, what kind of spy was I, anyway?

The road was all mine now and totally dark. I leaned over the wheel as if that would help me see better. What I needed was a driveway, a path, a side road. Anything I could use to turn around in. Nothing but trees and more trees on both sides of the highway. I slowed down and, after going for what seemed like miles, the branches thinned out, and off to the right I spotted a pebbly lane and a house light somewhere deep in the woods. I eased onto the lane, put her in reverse and once back on the main road, I shifted into drive and stomped on the gas.

I swear the Lincoln loved it. She purred like a tiger as we ate up the highway, my eyes watching left for that flare of blue motel lights.

*Ah, there it was.* I slowed down and eased onto Dicky Bob's bumpy tarmac. My front tire hit a rut. *Figures*. I parked under the flashing road sign and glanced around. A long, single story building, the motel was painted tan with blue trim. It looked like the usual motel setup with the office in the center and rooms fanning out on either side.

A few cars were parked in front of some of the rooms. But no black sedan that looked anything like what I'd been chasing. Had he left while I wasted time turning around?

Maybe. But Dicky Bob rented rooms by the hour as well as by the night, so I figured not everyone who stayed there wanted the world to know about it. The back lot then.

Pulse revving up a bit, I slowly cruised around the far side of the building and onto a rear lot that backed up to a stand of trees.

Light from a few windows filtered out onto the rutted blacktop. I slipped into an empty parking slot, turned off the engine and sat, letting my eyes adjust to the dark. That helped, and in the dim glow, I spied about a dozen cars parked in front of the rooms. Three or so looked to be black.

I was getting cold fast and couldn't sit there all night. So, what to do next? The answer seemed simple enough: Number one, get a license plate for a car I think—*think*—may have been parked at the Shed tonight. Number two, find out if the driver of this car was the same man Tim had threatened.

In the icy front seat, I warmed myself up with a pep talk: *Trust your instincts. As the man said, trust but verify. The question is: How?*

*The plate number.* I rummaged in my tote for a pen and ripped a deposit slip out of my check book. Slipping them both into my jeans pocket—the pen almost didn't make it—I really needed to lose five, I stepped outside, eased the door closed and, like a tom cat up to no good, pussy-footed along the line of cars.

This should be easy enough. I'd get the number of any black car parked in front of a lighted window. He wouldn't have the lights out and be in bed so soon, even if he had a lady friend waiting for him. And from the sound of his chat with Tim, I doubted he was in a romantic frame of mind.

Up close, the car in front of the first lit window was maroon, not black. I moved down four doors. This one was black but dusty. Not a Lexus, either, a worn-out flivver. One more lighted window. *Bingo*. Just to be sure, I pressed my hands on the hood. Still warm. This was the one. In back of the car, I knelt by the trunk and peered at the plate. If only I had a match or a flashlight. Well, I didn't, but I had fingers, didn't I? Blind people read that way, didn't they? One by one, with the tip of my finger, I traced the bumps, five numbers and then a single letter. I wrote them on the bank slip, tucked the slip in my jeans and, stiff as stone, heaved to my feet.

Fast as a rifle shot, a door suddenly opened and a flash of bright lamp light flooded the tarmac. As quick as my knees would allow, I sank down by the side of the Lexus and held my breath.

A few parking slots away, a car door opened and a man hollered, "Hey, Louise? You sure you left that bottle in the trunk? Oh, never mind, I see it."

The truck slammed shut then a second later so did the room door. In the dark, I clung to the side of the car and gradually stood.

Now for part two. In the room behind the Lexus, curtains were drawn across the window, but light filtered through the fabric and escaped from a narrow slit near the sill. He was still awake.

*Show time.* I fluffed my hair with my fingers, smoothed the purple sweater over my hips and pasting on a big fake smile, I knocked on the door.

No answer. Louder then.

*Bang, bang, bang.*

The door opened as far as the guard chain would let it, and Mr. Mysterious peered out. Even in his shirt sleeves, no top coat, no suit jacket, it definitely was him—the same tall skinny frame, the same balding hair line. "What is it?" he asked, none too happy about being disturbed.

"Oh, my goodness." Going all sweet and southern, I put both hands on my cheeks and let my mouth gape open in surprise. "I'm so sorry. I must have knocked on the wrong door. This isn't one-o-ten, is it?"

"That would be two doors down."

"Thank you *so* much. Sorry I bothered y'all."

Before the door clicked shut, a woman called, "Honey, who is it?"

She sure wasn't talking to me.

# THIRTY-TWO

I HUSTLED BACK to the car as fast as my frozen feet could carry me and turned on the heater full blast. When my fingers could wiggle again, I peeled out of Dicky Bob's lot and headed for town on a lonely stretch of road that was no place for a sensible gal on a Saturday night. Why was chasing down some stranger so important to me, anyway? What did he have to do with my life?

I chewed hard on that question most of the way home, finally deciding it made no damn sense whatever for me to be driving all over the place like this. Except in one particular way. Not so long ago, I'd been a lot like Joanne Petty, trying to straighten out my life and needing a helping hand to do it. Josie, who ran the town's diner, came to my rescue. She gave me a job even though I was new in town and had no restaurant experience. Now if I could help another girl sift through the mess that had turned her life upside down, I had a duty to do so, didn't I?

The question lay unanswered for quite a few miles before I womaned up enough to admit all that sounded mighty noble, but the simple truth was I loved the excitement of chasing clues and looking for bad guys. I was hooked on crime busting. I wasn't so much doing Joanne a service, as she was doing one for me.

That jolt of reality made me turn off Brad Paisley and drive home the rest of the way in silence. As soon as I got inside, I'd call Andy and apologize, explain why I ran out on him without any warning. Once he knew the details, he'd understand. I was sure of it. First, though, I'd call Matt and ask him to run that plate number. But my hand, as I reached across the front seat for the tote, froze in midair. And not from the cold. He'd be home, wouldn't he? No telling. It was a Saturday night. He could have a date.

Well, only one way to find out. As soon as I got inside, I'd give him a ring. I grabbed the tote and stepped out into the cold. A little way down the road, a car door opened then slammed shut and hurried footsteps came my way.

Not good. Not good at all. With my key at the ready, I jogged over to my front door. Too late. A hand reached out and grabbed my arm. I drew in a breath, ready to let it out in the mother of all screams.

"It's me, Andy."

Like a leaky tire, all that sucked-in air whooshed out and turned into a cloud in front of my face. "Good Lord, Andy, you scared me half to death."

"What do you think your phone call did?" In the light from the street lamp, he wasn't wearing a smile. You could even say he looked downright pissed. Which he had every right to be.

Before I could explain that I wasn't really bad-mannered but had been chasing a Lexus for a very good reason, he said, "I've been stood up before, but not like this. I hardly got the cork out of the bottle and you were already on the highway. What the hell was your rush? You couldn't get away from me fast enough?

That it? Well, I've got news for you, missy. This was the first and the last time. Here."

He jammed something into my hands—my coat—and stormed off. I stood there watching until his rear lights disappeared into the dark. Was what I found out worth making an enemy? No answer came to me, but at least I'd learned something else: Andy didn't always spout poetry.

Lower than a foreclosed outhouse, I let myself into the apartment. I dropped the coat on the sofa on top of Jake. He didn't even stir, didn't jump up to say hello. Nothing.

I fished the bank slip with the license plate number out of my jeans pocket, dug the cell out of my purse and called Matt. At least my efforts were about to result in something worthwhile, the name of a man Tim O'Toole had been blackmailing. Someone I had a hunch knew Darlene Petty and maybe what had happened to her long-dead sister, Juanita. If so, my wild goose chase hadn't been just a crazy stunt. Maybe not, my heart murmured, but you lost Andy's friendship over it. Probably for good.

With that silent message ringing in my head, I hardly noticed Matt's cell phone go into voice mail. When I realized it had, I held my phone at arm's length and stared at it. No need to leave a message. Matt had Caller ID. Besides, he never went anywhere without his phone, even slept with it next to his bed. And he always answered. Every time.

Except, like now, when he didn't want to.

# THIRTY-THREE

AFTER A RESTLESS NIGHT—even Jake slept on the sofa like he was mad at me—I couldn't stand the silence of my apartment.

At nine, wrapping up real warm in black wool pants, turtleneck, dressy black boots and my black wool coat, I tossed a bright red woolen shawl over the whole she-bang. Checking twice to make sure my cell was turned on, I tucked it in a pocket and sashayed on over to Josie's Diner where I walked into steamy warmth and the welcoming aroma of coffee and grits and bacon on the fry.

As usual, the place was jammed, but I lucked out. At the counter, a big guy in overalls and a plaid shirt was finishing up his last bite of lemon meringue pie. He drained his coffee mug, plunked it down and stood. "The stool's all yours, Miss," he said, peeling off a ten and leaving it next to his plate. He winked. "Warmed up for you too."

I thanked him kindly and took my seat. As soon as she spotted me, Josie came right on over. Without asking, she filled a mug from the carafe that never seemed to leave her hand and set the mug in front of me. I wrapped my hands around it, enjoying the heat on my fingertips.

"About time you dropped by," she said. "I was beginning to think you'd left town."

Figuring I was already carrying a full load of guilt, I decided to beat her to the questions. "How's married life?"

A bride of six months, her face pinked up at that. "Still going strong." She gave the already clean counter a swipe with the towel she wore tucked in her apron waistband. "You oughta try it."

"Haven't met the right man yet."

She leaned over the counter so we'd be eyeball to eyeball. "Yes, you have, but you're too darn stubborn to admit it."

I sipped my coffee without answering.

"You feeling good?" she asked. "You look a little peaked to me. Have a late night?"

"You could say that."

"Thought so."

While I was loosening the shawl and unbuttoning the coat—or as my momma used to say, they'd be of no earthly good to me when I went out in the cold—Josie reached across the counter to finger the shawl's fabric. "This is mighty fetching on you, Honey. Puts me in mind of one I saw some time back. I remember those bright, embroidered flowers right well."

"That so?"

"Yeah, but that was years ago. Where'd you find this one?"

"At a church sale last fall. They practically gave it to me. Said a lady had come by with a box full of donations. This was in it."

"Interesting. The one I 'member belonged to a gal

named Juanita Petty. She passed, poor thing. Took her own life they say."

*Omigod.* "Who had that sale again?"

"Grace Church over at the corner of Sugar and Main."

"Well, maybe I'll go to the next one. This sure was a lucky find."

With no more interest in the shawl than that, Josie took my order—grits, two fried eggs, three sausages and one slice of raisin toast. I had the toast dry to make up for the other fatty stuff. Then full as a tick, I left the diner with a promise not to be such a stranger and hurried home to get Jake before driving over to the Moose.

Though my hopes weren't high, I'd hold the open house anyway, as promised. Matt still hadn't contacted me, a real bad sign that on top of the grits and all had my stomach tied in a knot. I needed to tell him what I learned last night. I needed to have him check that license plate. I needed…heaving a sigh, I tried his number again. *Voice mail.* How did he know I wasn't in trouble? In the hands of some bad guy? Fighting for my life?

He didn't, and yet he was ignoring my calls. This was a first, and I didn't like it. I didn't like it a single bit.

Andy was another story. Mad enough to spit, he'd shoved my coat at me and taken off without giving me a chance to explain. Running out on him wasn't nice, I admit, but it was necessary. At least I thought so at the time, but sitting in my car with a silent phone in my hand, I wasn't so sure about anything any more.

A knock on the passenger side window startled me into the moment. "Joanne!" I released the lock and let her in.

"I was over at Verna's and saw you drive up. I came to say goodbye. I'm heading back to school this afternoon. Spring semester starts tomorrow."

"Your last semester?" *At least I know that much about higher education.*

"Yup."

"Your momma would be so proud."

Her eyes welling up, she nodded.

"Verna…your grandmother…must be too."

After a moment's thought, she said, "It's hard to tell. She doesn't let on much about anything. I guess grandmas come in all sizes. They don't all like to crochet, if you know what I mean."

*Uh-oh.* "How's Roger doing?" I was snooping, but Joanne answered me willingly enough.

"Not well. He'll be in the Yarborough Mental Health Hospital for some time to come." The tears hiding under her lids seeped out and ran down her cheeks. "I always wanted a family. Guess I didn't know what I was asking for." She snuffled a bit before adding, "I'll be back in two weeks for my momma's funeral. Verna's not too pleased that I'm having the service in Grace Church. She's worried it will turn into a media circus, but Momma would have wanted it there. I won't be back before then unless I'm needed. In case something comes up, I called Sheriff Rameros to let him know."

"He take your call?"

"Yes."

"When?"

"Just now."

"Oh." I blew out a cold, foggy breath.

"Something the matter?"

I shook my head. "No, I've been trying to reach him

is all. Well, seeing as we're having an open house again today, I'd better get in and set up."

She nodded and leaned across the front seat to give me a brief, tight hug. A final pat for Jake and she was off.

Downhearted and downright discouraged, I stuck the open house sign on the front lawn and went into the cold, silent Moose with Jake.

At least for so late in January, the day was sunny as a body could hope for at this time of year. Maybe the sunshine would bring folks out to take a look, even if just out of curiosity, for I'd about given up on making a sale. Or a happy life. The self-pity bug had bitten me, and its fangs wouldn't let go.

Shortly after one, folks started trooping through—not as many as yesterday—but enough to engage me in polite chitchat and take my mind off what was troubling me. Nobody asked any serious questions about the house, though, which I didn't find disappointing since I hadn't expected any. I was just going through the motions. Tomorrow, I'd contact Carl Huggins to set his Plan B into action.

Still, what a shame. If someone could peel away the layers of neglect—and nasty history, well, that last might be hard—the house would shine like a gem.

I left my post at the front door and toured around the downstairs rooms. No getting away from it, one fireplace mantel was a hideous gold and the other one vomit pink, but the carvings on them were wonderful. Animal heads and flutes and twists. And those oak floors set in that French style…what's the word?…parquet. Yes, parquet. Without those ripped shades in the way, the big-ass windows overlooked a large grassy lawn with a scruffy patch that might once have been a flower garden.

In its current state, the kitchen was pretty hopeless, but it was big and high-ceilinged and had a walk-in pantry perfect for storing food and crockery and those turkey platters a body only used but a few times a year. I wonder if—

Heavy-booted footsteps echoed on the bare floors. I needed to get back out front.

"Honey? Where are you?"

*Omigod.* "Out here. In the kitchen."

Matt strode in wearing his full uniform, hat, boots, gun, the works.

"Oh, I'm so glad you're here. There's something I've been dying to tell you."

His face wasn't sporting its usual smile. "This isn't a social call, Honey. I've been asked to bring you in."

My jaw fell open. I know it did. I could feel the droop. "Bring me in. Where to?"

He eyed me under his hat brim without speaking.

"You mean…you mean?"

"Afraid so. Detective Bradshaw's waiting to question you."

"*Why?* About what?"

Hesitation sprang into Matt's eyes, and his face flushed under its year-round tan. "About Reba Knight's death. Turns out her heart wasn't the problem after all."

# THIRTY-FOUR

THOUGH IT WASN'T five o'clock yet, I asked the few curiosity seekers to leave, locked up the Moose and yanked
the sign out of the front lawn. Then Jake and me…I…
followed Matt's cruiser to the Eureka Falls Police Station.

My hands weren't exactly shaking, and my heart
wasn't exactly sprinting around in my chest, but I sure
wasn't calm and relaxed either. Worse, the grits and
sausage from this morning were still sitting mighty
heavy on my insides.

What could have happened to Reba? From Matt's
grim face and the fact that he wouldn't straight out tell
me likely meant she'd come to an evil end. And I'd
been alone with her in the court house ladies' room.
For that reason, maybe Detective Bradshaw considered me a person of interest in her death. And maybe
that's why Matt wasn't smiling or saying much. He
was worried too.

At the station, I pulled into a visitor's parking slot.
Matt, his jaw set stiff as a piece of concrete, came over
to me.

"I can't leave Jake in the car," I said. "It's too cold."

"Bring him on in. He can stay with Ellie at the front
desk." He bent down and gave Jake a long scratch on

that sweet spot behind his ears. Well, at least that was one show of affection.

"Are we still friends?" I asked, hoping to squeeze a smile out of his crabby face.

After giving Jake a final scratch, he stood and shook his head. "I don't want to be friends. I thought I made myself clear that afternoon…" His voice trailed off.

No need to ask which afternoon.

He took my arm; not like we were on a date or anything. More like he was bringing a criminal to justice.

I yanked free. "Wait up a minute, Matt. Before we go inside, I have something to tell you."

"I doubt I'll want to hear it."

"It isn't about you and me. It's about what I learned last night."

"Oh?"

"You can wipe that look right off your face, Sheriff. You're acting like a jealous lover."

One corner of his mouth curled up. "It shows, huh?"

"I never made any promises to you, Matt," I said quietly. "I'm too afraid to. Every man I've known, including my own daddy, has let me down. Everybody that is except you, and I'm having a real hard time telling myself you won't end up being the same as all the others. So right now, I don't have the trust a body needs to be more than friends. And that's a downright fact."

My little speech finished, I realized what I'd just spouted was the truest thing I'd ever said. And though I didn't mention his name, my list of disappointments included Andy Ballou.

Matt's face, so hard a moment earlier, softened up. "Honey, trust is something that builds slowly. It takes time." He smiled into my eyes.

"Okay." I nodded. "I'm all right with that as long as you are."

"It's not a perfect solution, but I'm a patient man."

This time when he held my arm, we went up the stairs together side by side. At the top step, I said, "Hey, I haven't told you what I found out last night."

"It'll keep. We'd best go in. Bradshaw's waiting."

IN MATT'S CRAMPED little office, Detective Bradshaw sat behind the desk looking for all the world like one of those TV judges. He frowned when we walked in and didn't get up or offer to shake hands or anything.

*This wasn't going to be good.*

He pointed to the molded plastic chair facing Matt's desk. "Have a seat, Miss Ingersoll."

What else could I do? I sat, didn't cross my legs and rested my hands on my lap like I was in a witness box or something.

Bradshaw cleared his throat. "I understand you were with Ms. Reba Knight at the time of her death."

"Not exactly."

Bradshaw shot a dark look at Matt then shuffled through some papers until he found my witness statement. He held it up, waving it like a flag. "According to this, at the time of Ms. Knight's death you stated—"

"She was already dead when I found her."

"Are you a physician?"

"You know I'm not, but it was plain as—"

He held up a palm for silence. "The day before Ms. Knight's death, you were overheard having an argument with her." He gave me the steely-eyed stare. He had that down real good. "*Did* you argue with the victim shortly before her death?"

"No, sir, I did not…" my heavy winter clothes were making me hot, so before going on, I took a moment to toss off the red shawl and unbutton my coat "…I told Reba that Joanne Petty's birth certificate was a matter of public record and all hell would break loose if she didn't get her ass in gear and let Joanne have a look at it. That's all I said," I finished primly, my two feet still planted side by side on the office floor.

"Miss Ingersoll simply used a figure of speech," Matt said.

"Were you there, Sheriff?" Bradshaw's voice was testy.

"No, but I believe her story."

I raised my hand like kids do in third grade. "Can I say something?"

Bradshaw gave me a short, irritated nod. "Go ahead."

"When I went in the courthouse ladies' room…" I paused so my next words would sink in deep "…at the request of Sheriff Rameros…I found Reba Knight stretched out on the floor. Dead. That's God's honest truth. Also, Detective, if you recollect, I helped the police solve the famous Senator Lott case a year or so back and again last summer I helped you nail Connie DeLuca's killer."

I drew in a deep breath and, lifting a hand off my lap, aimed a finger at Bradshaw's nose. "You might want to take another look at that statement of mine. On the day of her death, the husband of the deceased…" a polite way of saying corpse "…told me a certain Carl Huggins paid Reba Knight to fake Joanne Petty's birth certificate. Joanne Petty being the adopted daughter of Darlene Petty who was murdered outside the back door of the Chocolate Moose. So why are you jabbering at me today as if, as if…"

"Enough, enough." Bradshaw waved a hand in front of his face like a plague of gnats was tormenting him. "You're correct to remind me of the past. As you point out, Miss Ingersoll, you have been of considerable value to the department. For the present, I'll discount your argument with Reba Knight…" another quick glance at Matt "…though from all reports, that is what it was. Also let me assure you, Mr. Huggins's role in the case is on our radar screen." Then he surprised the starch right out of me. He leaned forward, looked me straight in the eye and gave me a for real, from the heart, smile.

"Please forgive my harshness, Miss Ingersoll, but a woman suddenly dropped dead and you were the first person to find her." Before I could jump in, he added, "strictly by accident, of course. Nevertheless, I had to question you. The fact is we have recently learned Ms. Knight was poisoned. We almost missed it, but due to the coroner's diligence that didn't happen." He paused for an eyeball-to-eyeball stare. "This is not for publication, of course."

"Of course. Understood."

*Phew. Poor Reba, poisoned.* Bradshaw was trusting me with some heavy stuff. I leaned against the stiff plastic chair back and slid the coat and the shawl all the way off my shoulders. Things had heated way up in here. Not only that, the deposit slip I'd written the license plate number on was burning a hole in my pocket.

I pulled it out and held it up. "Can I ask another question?"

DETECTIVE BRADSHAW LISTENED to my story as polite as can be and didn't interrupt even once. Then, after in-

structing Matt to let him know what the plate turned
up, he left the station and Matt ran the number. The
Lexus belonged to a Dr. Austin Hightower, 1500 Presidential Drive, Little Rock, Arkansas.

"You doing anything the next few hours?" Matt
asked.

"Yes, after we drop Jake off at my apartment, I'm
going to Little Rock with you."

Presidential Drive turned out to be a street not so
different from Sugar. Like Sugar it was lined with big
ol' Victorians and granddaddy elms that would shade
all the verandahs come spring.

Matt stopped at 1500 and parked in front of a property with a lot of curb appeal. Square-framed and well
kept, the house was painted light beige with white trim
and a black door as glossy as that Lexus I'd followed.
Lights gleamed from the downstairs windows, the verandah ceiling and from little side lanterns running
along a stone walk to the entrance.

"Nice," I said, thinking the Moose would look a lot
like this if brought back to its former glory.

Matt surveyed the house for a few moments before switching off the radio. Praise the Lord. He'd had
music playing all the way to Little Rock. I guess to
overcome the silence surrounding the subject of our
future together—or the lack of one. Anyway, I was
about Willy Nelson'd out when, still peering at the
house, Matt said, "I don't think the Hightowers pose
any kind of threat. There's nothing on the docket about
either of them. Not even a traffic violation. So you'll
be fine, and it will look more like a social call if we
both go to the front door together. You okay with that?"

*A social call, and him in a police uniform, driving
a cruiser. Men.* Anyhow, by way of answer I hopped

out of the car, and we walked up to the front door of 1500. Guitar and drum music came pounding out onto the verandah. I couldn't make out the tune…well, there was no tune.

"They'll never hear us over this," Matt said, ringing the bell a second time. The aroma of pizza wafted on the evening air.

Matt inhaled. "Pepperoni. My favorite."

I laughed and, as soon as the music paused for a split second, Matt leaned on the bell. This time the chimes rang out loud and clear.

"Someone's at the door!"

"Answer it, Tommy."

"I'm on it, Mom."

A heartbeat later, the door was yanked open. At the sight of Matt, a teenage boy of about fourteen or fifteen, brown hair hanging to his shoulders and an oversized T-shirt hanging to the ripped knees of his jeans, fell back a step. "Whoa. Officer, what's up?"

I had to smile. I could almost see the wheels of his mind racing while he flashed back over what had gone down in his life the last few days.

"Good evening, son," Matt said. "I'm Officer Rameros. This is Miss Ingersoll. I wonder if we could speak to Dr. Austin Hightower?"

"That's my dad. I'll find out. Just a minute." He half turned, then, "You want to come in while I get him for you?"

"That would be fine."

We stepped inside the lamp-lit foyer and, at first sight, I fell in love. With the polished dark floors, the deep moldings, the broad central staircase, the soft-colored walls, the oriental rugs, the—

"Officer, I'm Austin Hightower. What can I do for you?" And there he was, the same tense, worried man I'd spied on from the Shed's ladies' room. The same man who came to the door at Dicky Bob's Motor Inn. "I hope there's no trouble," he said, studying me as if trying to remember whether or not he recognized me.

Matt introduced us and glanced over at the boy who was staring like we came off a UFO. "Doctor, is there someplace where we could speak privately?"

"Of course, come into my study." We followed Dr. Hightower down the hall and into a wood-paneled room lined with books. He closed the door. "What's this about, Officer?"

"Miss Ingersoll here was at the Toole Shed in Eureka Falls last evening. She said you were there too."

The man shot a quick look my way that said: Have I seen her before? "There must be some mistake. I was with my wife last evening."

"At Dicky Bob's Motor Inn?" I asked.

"Ah." Hightower's jaw hardened as the pieces fell into place. "Is that against the law?"

"Not at all," Matt replied. "Blackmail, however, can be. *Have* you been blackmailed, Dr. Hightower?"

The man flushed. "Where I choose to spend my money is my own business."

Matt nodded, going still for a moment. "Allow me to rephrase the question. The layman's term is blackmail, the legal term is extortion. Are you a victim of extortion?"

Hightower fell silent.

"If so, we're here to help you," Matt said. "Law enforcement can put a stop to it."

No answer.

A bulldog on the scent, Matt had enough faith in me and what I'd told him about last night's happenings to drive all the way out here and challenge a man in his own home.

He wasn't about to give up now. I guess my word really mattered to him, and that mattered to me.

"You're no doubt a busy man, Doctor, so I'll cut to the chase," Matt said. "Last night, Miss Ingersoll overheard Timothy O'Toole threaten to harm you if your payments to him ceased. Payments for what? Protection? Old debts?" Like an actor on the stage, Matt paused. "Or for Tim's silence?"

Hightower turned his deep-set, troubled eyes my way. "Why should you involve yourself in my affairs, young woman? I don't know you, and you don't know me."

Matt stepped right up to the plate. "This is not about extortion alone. Recently, two murders have been committed in Eureka Falls. Both victims were well known to Mr. O'Toole."

That's when I jumped in. "And to people who lived—and worked—at a house at the end of Sugar Street. It used to be known as the Chocolate Moose."

Clutching the back of a leather wing chair with both hands as if without it he'd fall flat on his face, Hightower turned pale as a bleached sheet. "Please be seated," he said, sinking onto the chair and waving an arm at a tweedy couch.

Before we could, someone tapped on the study door. A woman peeked in. "Is everything all right, Austin? Tommy said a police—"

One glance at Matt's uniform and she stepped into the study, quickly closing the door behind her. Tall, and slim in all the right places, she had those high cheek-bones and the expensive blond looks you see in slick fashion magazines. Not young, not old, in tight green ankle pants and a well-filled pink sweater, she was the kind of woman a man would turn around to look at on the street. Even Matt who liked to think he gave nothing away—and seldom did—stared at her as if he couldn't get his fill.

"I don't understand," she said. "Is there a problem, honey?"

"You could say that," I blurted. "Oh, sorry. You weren't speaking to me."

Her eyes darted my way, a hand flying up to her mouth. "That shawl? Where did you find it?"

*Omigod. She recognizes it.*

I slipped the shawl off my shoulders and held it out. "Look at all the hand-embroidered flowers. This is one of a kind, I reckon."

She nodded, once. "Probably." She couldn't seem to pull her gaze away from the shawl, but she didn't reach out to touch it either.

"Can you believe I found it at a rummage sale," I said.

"Where?" In a whisper.

"Grace Church in Eureka Falls." Then acting on a hunch, I went all the way. "It's that church down the road apiece from the Chocolate Moose."

"Oh no." Like her bones had melted, she slid down the study wall and sat in a crumpled heap on the polished floor. Leaning her head back, she closed her eyes. "I gave it to my former cleaning lady. I should have burned it."

Her husband half rose out of his chair to go to her,

but Matt put a hand on his shoulder, easing him back into his seat. Matt didn't know a blessed thing about any shawl, but he knew more was at stake here than Mrs. Hightower's unexpected collapse. What came shining through to me was his trust in my judgment. He nodded, which I took as a sign to go ahead, pursue whatever the heck I was pursuing. So I did.

I bent over Mrs. Hightower where she sat with her eyes closed, maybe hoping the darkness would make her problems go away. "I heard tell this shawl belonged to a Juanita Petty." I waited a second or so to let the question sink in before asking, "Are you Juanita Petty?"

She nodded as if admitting it in words would take more strength than she could muster. Her eyes fluttered open. "Yes," she whispered. "Yes. Yes. Yes."

"Oh, honey," Hightower murmured.

"I'm too tired to pretend any longer." She managed to get to her feet, tossed back her blond hair—she wore it wavy on the ends like a forties movie star— and slumped on the sofa facing her husband.

He sat shaking his head, saying nothing, a defeated man whose barn had just burned to the ground.

Juanita looked over at Matt. "How did you find me?"

"Two weeks ago, a woman was killed outside the Chocolate Moose. Our search for the killer has led us here."

"For the *killer*? There's no killer here."

"Perhaps not," Matt said, "but I believe you know the victim."

I could see fear leap into her eyes. Afraid to ask, afraid of the answer, she finally mouthed one word. "Who?"

"Darlene Petty was her name."

Without a warning knock, the study door popped open. "Mom, I think the pizza's ready."

Startled, she stared at her son for an instant as if she couldn't fathom what he was saying.

"Pizza? Oh. Take it out of the oven, dear, and help yourself. We're busy, okay?"

"Sure." One glance at all our serious faces, and he shut the door fast.

"Well, Mrs. Hightower?" Matt said. "Did you know a Darlene Petty?"

"Petty's a common name in these parts. It could be a coincidence that a woman named Darlene—"

Matt didn't let her go on building her lie. "This particular Darlene Petty had a sister Juanita who left a suicide note, though her body was never found. That same suicide note bears Timothy O'Toole's fingerprints as well as those of an unknown person." He arched a brow. "Could that person be you?"

Without answering, she looked down at her trembling hands. Almost answer enough.

Matt swiveled his attention to her husband. "Those prints are from the same Tim O'Toole you met with Saturday evening."

"We've been—" Juanita began.

"Don't say another word," her husband ordered. "We need a lawyer."

Juanita was upset and trembling, but not ready to keep still. "We heard about Darlene's death on TV. It was all over the news. But that's all I know. What I don't know is why she was killed." She raised her big-eyed gaze to Matt. "Who would do such a thing? She was such a sweet girl…she was everything I was not."

"The police have no answer for you," Matt said,

"not yet, but there's a second letter bearing the name Juanita. Shortly before her death, Darlene apparently found it in her aunt's effects—"

"Her *effects*? Aunt Louise is dead too?"

"Of natural causes."

That's when Juanita lost it. Shoulders shaking, she sobbed into her hands. Her husband lumbered out of his chair and sat beside her. He pulled her to him and held her in his arms, cradling her from the harshness of the truth, as I suspected he had for years. "Shush, shush. It's all right, honey."

"No, it isn't. What have I done?"

"Shush. Shush."

When her sobs turned into quiet tears, and she was mopping her eyes with her husband's handkerchief, Matt said, "This second letter was postdated after your supposed suicide. It caused Darlene to ask questions about you around town. We think someone found out and wanted her hushed up. *Why* is what we need to find out."

Stricken, she raised her tear-wet eyes. "I have no idea. How did you come by the letter?"

"It was brought to our attention by Joanne Petty, Darlene's daughter."

Once more, Juanita's cheeks flooded with tears. "That would be my niece. The television coverage mentioned Darlene's daughter. We've never met," she added, not that she had to.

"Joanne's an adopted daughter."

"Adopted?" Juanita smiled. "Yes, the Darlene I remember *would* do something wonderful like that, but I left before…I never knew…"

Ignoring the sharp crease in his uniform pants, Matt

crouched down in front of Juanita. "Mrs. Hightower, I have only one reason for being here, and it's not to pass judgment on you. I'm looking for your sister's murderer. Will you help me?"

She swiped at her eyes one more time then rested the handkerchief on her lap. "How? I don't know who killed her. I'd tell you if I did."

"If you could tell me why you wrote the suicide note that would help. Who were you escaping from?"

Juanita gripped her husband's hand. "I hated the life. I had to get away. I was frightened, so frightened. Pretending to be dead seemed the only way out. You don't understand how it was…" she shivered, remembering "…he would never have let me go. I was his favorite." She sent a quick glance Hightower's way, but he didn't flinch. Maybe this was a tale he knew only too well. "It wasn't just the life I ran from. It was him. He knew I wanted to leave. Said if I did he'd follow me no matter where, no matter how far, and when he found me, he'd kill me. Pretending I was dead seemed like the only way out."

"Who were you afraid of?" Matt asked softly.

Juanita drew in a deep, shuddering breath. "Carl Huggins. His father owned the Moose."

# THIRTY-FIVE

EDGING THE HIGHWAY, ice-coated tree branches gleamed in the headlights as we flashed past. Snuggled in my coat and shawl and with Matt's heater purring away, I was cozy, a far cry from last night. Caught up in what the Hightowers had revealed, Matt didn't put Willy Nelson on the whole way, and that was more than fine with me.

"Going after that plate number was good police work, Honey," Matt said after a while. "Dangerous, though. No telling how it might have ended."

"Nothing happened."

"The point being it could have. Hightower seems a decent sort, but that's not always the case." He took a hand off the wheel to squeeze my knee. "I worry about you."

"That's mighty nice."

He laughed. "It *is*? Not for the worrier. Promise you won't take a chance like that again."

"Now that you know who the killer is, I won't have to."

"Who *is* the killer?" He actually tore his attention off the road to ask the question.

"Carl Huggins most likely. Juanita was so scared of him she faked her own death. Doesn't that say a lot?"

"A lot but not enough. All we have on Carl Huggins is Kenny Knight's accusation."

"And Juanita's fear of him."

"We'll bring him in for questioning, of course, but without substantive proof of wrong doing, it's a he-said-she-said."

"A dead end."

"Exactly."

"What about that blackmailing snake, Tim O'Toole?"

"Extortion is a miserable act but not necessarily a crime."

*"Really?"*

"Not unless the victim brings charges, and Hightower won't. He'll let the money go. What he wants is Tim's silence about Juanita's past. I can understand that. They have young Tommy to think about. Not to mention Hightower's medical career."

"Another dead end?"

"Not necessarily. We have O'Toole's prints on Juanita's farewell note to her aunt. The prints are a match to that prank note you found on the skeleton. Plus, you were witness to his blackmail threat. It's doubtful that's enough to establish a motive for murder, but collectively it does mean Tim's involved some way, some how."

Off in the distance, a faint glow lit the night sky. We were close to home if no closer to a solution.

"As long as we're in the mood—"

His head positively swiveled my way. *"What?"*

"For sleuthing."

He turned back to the road. "Be still my heart."

"Why wait for tomorrow? Why not tonight?"

He tore his attention off the road again. "Are we on the same page here?"

"No. But we can be."

He groaned. "You're playing me like a violin, Honey. Come right out with it. What are you getting at?"

"Let's stop by the Toole Shed and give Tim a little surprise visit."

"I plan to do that very thing."

"Good!"

"After I drop you off at home."

"No dice. I'm going with you."

"Let me remind you, Miss Ingersoll, that you're the Realtor, I'm the cop."

"Without my excellent sleuthing you wouldn't have found the Hightowers, so that—"

"Wrong. Sooner or later, we would have. It was only a question of time."

"Which I saved for you."

He stared straight ahead. And drove straight to my apartment, pulling up in front of my door. "You've taken enough chances already. This is a police problem, so let me do my job, an important part of which is keeping you safe."

From the set of his jaw, I could tell arguing wouldn't do a darn bit of good, so I thanked him kindly for the ride and said good night. As soon as the cruiser's rear lights disappeared around the corner, I went inside and woke up Jake.

"How'd you like to cruise for burgers?"

"Woof!"

"Thought so. Let's go."

We entered the Shed through the rear door off the kitchen. Judging from the eye-watering odor, the new cook was chopping onions on the butcher-block table. He glanced up as we came in. "You again? What the hell is this? A bowlin' alley?"

Cleaver in hand, he pointed at Jake. "Get him the hell out of here."

"He wants a couple of burgers."

"That so?"

"Come on. He's hungry."

"What am I, a vet?"

"He's got money, he'll pay. Raw is okay." I took a ten-dollar bill out of my pocket and laid it on the butcher block next to the onions.

Cookie eyed it, none too pleased. "That's ten each."

"No way. Jake's not getting buns, ketchup, mustard, lettuce, tomato or the two little bags of chips. Five each. Take it or leave it."

He snatched up the bill and pocketed it. From the fridge, he took out two raw patties and laid them on a paper towel.

"No dish?" I asked.

"He's a dog. I got health rules to follow."

"How about some water?"

"You're pushin' it, lady."

No doubt I was, so as soon as Jake licked the paper clean, we took off.

"Good thing you're leavin'. Another couple of minutes I'd call a cop."

"It's not too late. There's one out front talking to your boss. I'll tell him you're looking for him."

Though I was talking tough, my heart was racing as Jake and I strolled down the dingy hall out to the tap room. The bar was shuttered, the front door locked. In one of the windows, the neon CLOSED sign hummed its purple warning to the parking lot.

Huddled at a corner table, the one with the rickety chairs, Tim and Matt were so deep into their talk they didn't see me come in. Uncertain, I waited in the doorway, but not Jake. One look at the buddy who had scratched his sweet spot earlier and he bounded across the floor and flung his front paws up on Matt's lap.

"Whoa, boy. How did you—"

A quick glance around the bar room, and I was outed. "You shouldn't be here."

"Yeah, you come in the back way?" Tim looked none too pleased either. "That entry's only for deliveries."

"I'm making one, Tim." Pretending Matt was okay with having me there, I pulled up a chair and sat. "Unless, of course, the sheriff already delivered the package."

"I could order you to leave," Matt said.

"Nah, why bother?" Tim shrugged. "You said she knows what went down anyway. What's the dif?"

Matt stared at me under half-raised lids. Not happy that I defied him. Not happy at all. Without another word to me, he turned to Tim. "As I was saying, O'Toole, the Hightower spigot is turned off. Permanently. I doubt he'll prosecute, so until he does, you're off the hook. But let me repeat, so you understand real good. You stay buttoned up on the subject. One word gets out about Juanita's past, your ass is mine."

"Hey, I'm cooperatin'."

Tim sounded aggrieved. I think that's the word, like he was the hurt party. The nerve of him nearly lifted me off my chair.

"Why'd you do it?" I asked. "Why'd you help Juanita write those notes?"

Not bothering to deny the part he'd played, Tim waved off my question with a flick of his hand. "I dunno. She was pretty, she was scared. She wanted to get away from the Moose. I did her a favor is all."

Something about the way he spoke, a creepy little smile lifting the corners of his mouth, made me want to slap myself upside the head. Along with my temper, a light bulb exploded in my mind. Of course. Why hadn't I thought of it sooner?

"You were a nice guy and did *her* a favor? After that, how many favors did she have to do for you?"

That snapped the smile off his face. "What're you getting at?"

"As a payback, she have to have sex with you?"

"Naw, nothin' like that."

"Then when Hightower cut you off, you took his money instead."

Tim's behind came off the chair. "You're spoutin crazy stuff, why for—"

"Sit down, O'Toole." Matt was ordering not asking.

"Yeah, you're a—"

"Honey," Matt warned, "that's enough."

"Not hardly. Why—"

"Quiet. You're out of line."

No arguing with Matt when he hauled out his cop voice, so I shut up, though it wasn't easy. Especially with Tim wearing a smirk like he'd just bested me at arm wrestling or something. But he didn't wear it for long.

"Now that Juanita Petty is known to be alive, the county may sue for damages," Matt told him.

"*Damages?* What damages? Nobody got hurt. Nothin' was stolen."

"I'll ignore that appraisal." Clearly disgusted, Matt got up and shoved his chair out of the way. "At the time of her supposed suicide, taxpayers' money was spent searching for her body. Should the county try to reclaim that expense, you would be well advised to pick up the tab. I'm not a lawyer, but from the way things are shaping up, looks like you're going to need one." Matt got up and shoved his chair out of the way. "Before you start shooting off your mouth and throwing Juanita to the wolves, let me remind you that we're actively looking for the murderer of two women."

Tim reared back in his seat. "What's that got to do with me?"

Matt waved a finger in front of Tim's face. "No. I ask the questions. You give the answers. A few thousand in damages are nothing compared to a murder rap."

# THIRTY-SIX

"YOU SURE GAVE him what for, Matt. Good for you."

"He victimized the Hightowers. I don't like bullies."

Neither did I. "I'm proud of you," I said, meaning every word.

We were in the Shed's parking lot, our cold breaths making little clouds in front of our faces. He spread his legs apart in that super cop stance he got into when he had something on his mind. Like now.

"Thanks for the vote of confidence, but from now on in, put it in action or forget it."

At Matt's tone, Jake came to attention and stood guard by my leg. I patted him so he'd know everything was okay, though I wasn't sure it was. "I don't get your meaning."

"You had no business being here tonight. That's why I took you home earlier. These situations can escalate. Tim could have gone on the attack, thrown a punch, pulled a weapon."

"But—"

"But me no buts."

"I'm confused. You wanted me there when you called on the Hightowers."

"That was different. I needed you to ID Hightower, and there was another woman present. A bar at midnight—"

"Actually, it's ten thirty."

"—is different. If you pull a stunt like that again, I'll arrest you for interference."

"You wouldn't."

He arched a brow.

All right, he would. "I'm only trying to help."

He pointed at the Shed's front door. "You think you were a help in there?"

I hadn't been, and now I didn't have an answer either.

He sighed. "Are you watching my lips move?"

"Sort of. It isn't easy in this light."

"Meaning well doesn't cut it, Honey, so here's the deal. You work your real estate business and trust the cops to work the crimes."

"Some deal. I haven't agreed."

"Too late. It's non-negotiable. Now if you'll get in the Lincoln, I'll follow you home to make sure no one else does."

He was looking out for me, and how sweet is that? "When we get there, you want to come in?"

THE NEXT MORNING, Matt gave himself a so-so shave with my pink Lady Astra, drank a quick cup of coffee and left for work. He had looked happy enough standing in my kitchen wearing yesterday's uniform and a smile, but I knew he wasn't, not really, not after he said, "We need to talk. Soon."

He didn't mean about real estate, or the murders, he meant about the M word. He was old fashioned enough to think sleeping together without a commitment was wrong. Well, either old fashioned or right. I could hear

Grandma Ingersoll now, "Let the boy make an honest woman out of you, girl. Or else behave yourself before it's too late."

I sure did understand what "too late" meant, though having a family to call my own would be a blessing. Except for my late, loving momma, it was something I never had and always wanted. Matt did, too. He'd said so often enough. He still mourned the passing of his parents, and they'd been gone a good number of years now. Children, a home, a house, a husband…I liked the sound of it all.

Anyway, Station WXYN promised a break in the cold weather, so after walking Jake, I stripped off the sweats and dressed for work in black boots and pants and my bright purple, fuzzy wool sweater. Some chunky silver bracelets, my big-enough-to-travel-around-the-world tote, and I was good to go.

I felt mellow this morning, easy in my skin and happy with my world. Ditching the heavy coat helped. So did the sunshine. And so did the memory of last night with Matt. He was right. We did need to talk, but for now, I needed to keep my mind on business.

Except for Mindy's Jacuzzi surprise last week, sales were flat. Added to that, the fruitless open house had chewed up the weekend, so I'd better get busy making sales calls and following up on telephone leads. One hot spot was the strip of gentrified townhouses on Main Street. They'd created a buzz around town that warranted spending some money on a few ads. With no fuss, no muss, in move-in-condition, the townhouses appealed to millennials like me. Unpack and hop in the Jacuzzi with your girl friend. Or whomever. First thing, I'd work up a quarter page ad slanted to the young and single and contact Kelsey Davis at the *Star*.

Maybe I should buy one of the units. I'd been thrifty, country style, for the past few years and could swing a down payment. Well, it was a thought. One that flew out of my head the minute I opened the office door.

Mindy jumped up from behind her desk by the front window. "Honey, I thought you'd never get here."

"It's only eight o'clock, I'm early."

"Look, look, look!" She held out her left hand, but it wasn't the Passionate Pink polish that seized my attention, it was the ring in yellow gold with a diamond chip in the center.

"Nooo. Tell me it isn't."

"It is! I'm engaged."

"To?"

"Tommy, of course."

"Omigod, the guy in the Jacuzzi? The guy you only met last week?"

She pumped her head up and down. "Ten days ago, actually."

"Well, my goodness. You took my breath away. The ring's lovely," I fibbed, "but isn't this kind of fast?"

"Yes, that's what's so exciting. We can't wait to tie the knot. We're crazy about each other. Will you help me break the lease on my apartment? As soon as Tommy's mortgage goes through, he wants me to move into the townhouse with him."

Whether she knew it or not, Mindy had just said she and I had hatched from different nests. She had no trouble making up her mind about *everything*. Good for her. She'd soon have a husband and a home of her own, and if they kept enjoying the Jacuzzi the way they had been, maybe a family too. Suddenly my little rental seemed small and dry, and so did my life. Lately, I couldn't seem to pick out cookies in the Piggley-Wiggley, never mind dealing with the important stuff.

Anyway, I gave Mindy a big hug and wished her every happiness before going into my office and closing the door. As soon as I did, Grandma Ingersoll started in. "You pull yourself offa that slump, gal. Making decisions ain't the only thing that matters. Making the right ones is what counts in the end. So behave yourself then you won't have to go and do anything hasty and foolish."

"Of course not," I said out loud and, wondering if her advice might be a little late, I turned on the laptop and hauled out the smart phone.

By ten, I had returned all calls and lined up three prospects. One party was interested in that townhouse development. No surprise there. Two couples wanted to take a look at a fifties style ranch that needed some cosmetic fix-ups, but its ace-in-the-hole was an attached mother-in-law suite. As I mentioned to them, the suite would make a good rental property. No doubt they had figured that out for themselves, which was probably the reason for their interest.

Feeling a tad better, I was about to go to Josie's Diner for lunch when my office phone, line one, lit up.

"Yes, Mindy."

"A Mr. Carl Huggins to see you."

*Good Lord, so soon?* "Send him in."

He came stomping on in wearing work boots. But no John Deere covered his bald scalp today.

"Getting warmer out?" I asked.

"Yeah. High time too, missy." He lowered himself into the wing chair across from my desk and got right to it. "Any offers?"

I shook my head. "Not a one."

"Told you the open house was a bum idea."

"Well, you don't know until you try."

"Yeah? How come I did?"

I felt like swatting him, but the situation needed a little sugar. "Carl, you have your finger on the pulse of this town like nobody else."

He eyed me suspicious like, but I kept a poker face.

"I've come to a decision," he announced.

"Which is?"

"The Moose is comin' down. Right to the ground. No more paying taxes on the ol' place. And no more spent on upkeep."

*Upkeep?*

"First of next week, the bulldozers'll be there."

"What about the land?"

"I'm sellin' it as a house lot." He flung his right foot over his left knee and leaned back as easy as if he planned on staying a while. "You didn't do such a hot job for me, but I know you tried. And tryin's big in my book. So I got enough faith in Ingersoll Realty to let you represent the land."

"Thank you very kindly, Carl. The location is so desirable, there should be no problem selling it, providing the lot is priced right."

He slapped a hand on his knee. "There you go again, talkin' price. First, let's see some comparables or whatever you call them and go from there. I want to start high and move down slow. If we have to."

I picked up a pencil and resisted the urge to nibble on it. Instead, as I mulled over his plan for the Moose, I swiveled slowly, thoughtfully, and then surprised the daylights out of both Carl and myself.

"I have a proposal for you, Carl." I brought the

swivel to a halt and leaned in across the desk. "What do you say to this: I pay you the price of the land—a fair market price, mind—minus whatever the demolition company wants for the teardown. In return, you sell me the Moose."

His raised boot slipped off his knee and hit the floor with a clunk. "Well, I'll be damned. What all do you want with that ol' white elephant?"

"Why, I want it to live in, of course."

"Good God, missy, gettin' it up to snuff will cost a fortune."

An honest statement if ever there was one. "I know. That's why you can't pork me on the land."

He scratched the top of his head. "I dunno. It's an unusual kind of an offer."

"But not illegal."

He glanced over fast at that one. "No, I suppose not. But a pretty gal like you livin' alone in an ol' house of ill repute. Won't you be scared, you know, what with one thing and other that's happened there?"

"I will be, some. But when did being scared ever stop you?"

"Ha! I like that. You're all right, missy. You're all right." He stood and went to give his cap a tug, remembered he was topless and patted his scalp instead. "Tell you what. Get back to me with some numbers and, if I like them, I'll show you the demolition estimate. We'll take it from there."

With that, he gave me a wink and stomped on out the way he'd stomped on in.

I sat alone for a while. Even Grandma Ingersoll didn't surface.

Good heavens. What on earth had I done?

# THIRTY-SEVEN

"ARE YOU PLUMB CRAZY? The place is a money pit. You'll be taking on a boatload of debt and all for a property with a tainted history." Cletus Dwyer leaned back in his leather banker's chair and shook his head. "I cannot believe it. Of all the houses in town, you want to live in the Chocolate Moose."

"I'm painting it white."

"Paint is the least of its problems."

"I'm well aware of that, Cletus. But the house has wonderful potential."

"It's not worth the aggravation."

"Is that a no? You won't give me a mortgage?"

The richest man in town, Cletus owned the Eureka Falls Savings & Loan. His daddy and granddaddy before him were also the town's high rollers—an expression my own daddy favored. In other words, Cletus was a man to be taken seriously, though his elastic armbands and lavender shirts with the white collars made that a mite difficult at times.

Today, he looked so upset by my question, I had to smile. A good man, Cletus was married to my friend Amelia, and he'd made her very happy. From his expression, I could tell he wanted me to be happy too—by agreeing to give me a mortgage. But he didn't want to loan money for investment in the town's former bordello, and the struggle showed in his eyes.

*This called for salesmanship.*

"Cletus, in a sense we're in the same business. I sell properties, you make sales possible. We've worked together long enough by now for you to know I wouldn't take on a white elephant—"

"*See*, you agree."

"—without understanding what I was getting into. It's true, the Moose needs to be gutted. It needs a new roof, new wiring, new plumbing, new furnace and a complete face lift inside and out."

"That's what I mean, it's fool—"

"Once that's done, the property will shine like one of those diamonds folks are always finding down there in Murfreesboro."

"The cost, Honey, the cost."

"This would be out of the question if Carl Huggins hadn't agreed to my terms." Tense as a fiddle string, I paced Cletus's office. "For the price of the land alone, minus a demolition estimate, I'll own one of the town's historic properties. It's a steal, and you know it."

"A steal, huh?" He shook his head. "Well, if there's one dude in town I could be tempted to steal from, it's Carl Huggins." He pointed to his guest chair. "Make yourself comfortable, Honey. We need to talk some more."

LONG STORY SHORT, Cletus opened the bank's purse strings, and I strode out of the First National a proud woman. As soon as all the legal i's and t's were dotted and crossed, the Moose would be mine. What I didn't tell Cletus was my innermost reason for wanting the Moose. I was afraid it would sound silly to his ears.

For I didn't want the Moose for its fancy moldings, or the fireplaces or even the high ceilings, though I loved all of that. The Moose sang to me because like it, I too had a tarnished past. I too had needed a makeover and had a history to live down. Once I recognized that and worked to improve myself, a brand-new life opened up for me. Seven years ago, when I rode into town on the back of Billy Tubbs' Harley with only a ten-dollar bill lining my jeans pocket, I never dreamed some day I'd own a house of my own. And now here I was doing a happy dance. Proving good things can come of bad situations if a body sets her mind to it. Much like a person with a troubled past, a once beautiful house with an ugly history can be cleaned and polished and made whole again.

FOR THE LEGAL doings involved with the closing, I needed a lawyer. That meant paying a call on Andarius Ballou, Esquire.

My heartbeat, all on its own, kicked up a notch at the prospect of seeing him again. After leaving him stranded at the Toole Shed the other night, no telling what my reception would be, though the sensible part of my brain told me Andy was too professional to let a date gone sour mess with business. So why make an appointment? Why not surprise him?

Armed with that notion like it was a pair of pistols, I checked my lipstick in the Lincoln's rear view mirror, ran a brush through my hair and spritzed on some Yellow Diamond Cologne from a purse-sized bottle I kept handy for little emergencies like this.

A parking slot opened up on Main Street near Andy's office. A good omen. Telling myself my rapid heartbeat didn't show through my clothes, I climbed the wooden stairs to his second-floor office. Halfway up, I heard voices. No wonder. The door to Andy's office was open. Hmm. Though he had the only office on the second floor of the funky little building, his door was usually kept closed. So why not today? I stood on the top step and listened. Some fancy shoutin' was going on in there. Female shoutin'. Now and again, when he could get a word in edgeways, Andy struck a few pearly chords. His voice was easy to recognize even over the screeching.

"To think I trusted you with everything," she yelled loud enough for all Eureka Falls to tune in on. "My heart. My honor. My…my *body*."

Andy murmured something that set her off again. "Don't you dare say that. Don't you *dare*. I thought better of you. My momma thought better of you. And my daddy, why you've made a fool out of every fine thing he ever said about you."

A question from Andy that I couldn't quite catch. He was likely whispering to sound calm. If so, it sure wasn't working.

"No, I am *not*!" she shouted. "No thanks to you. At least I had enough sense to take care of that. Thank God I did. The thought of you as the father of my baby makes me ill."

*Wow.* I had to get a look at this gal. I tiptoed along the wooden landing, hoping the boards wouldn't creak. Though even if they had, Andy and, what could only be an ex-girlfriend, wouldn't have noticed.

I peeked into his reception area. He still didn't have

a full-time paralegal, so it was empty, as usual. The shouting was coming from the inner office overlooking Main Street. That door was open, too. I wondered if the female screecher had flung both doors against the walls when she stormed in.

Whatever. Done with tiptoeing, I strode toward the inner office and stood in the open doorway. Straight ahead, the girl had her back to me, giving me a great view of her expensive-looking fur coat and her crop of short, curly dark hair.

Trapped between his desk and the front window, Andy had the look of a hunted animal with no escape route in sight. What do you know? She had him scared.

"Furthermore, if you ever—"

I cleared my throat. The girl whirled around to face me then whirled right back to Andy. "Who's *she*? Another one of your bimbos?"

"Honey is not a bimbo."

"Oh, but I *am*? Is that what you're saying?" Without giving Andy a split second to answer, fast as a lightning strike, she grabbed the marble ashtray off his desk and flung it at him. He ducked in the nick of time and… *wheee*…instead of hitting his head, the ashtray crashed through the front window and, with a shattering of glass, plunged down onto Main Street.

A moment of silence. One only before Andy got his gumption back. "You could have killed me," he said.

"Keep that in mind."

"Or somebody on the street." He leaped up and poked his head out of the broken window that was letting in a blast of wintery air. He glanced up and down Main Street then turned back to face the music. "You're lucky, Rosemary. Nobody was passing by or you'd be up on charges."

*"Charges?* For *what*? Breaking up with a jerk?"

"You've said enough for one day. You're dismissed." To prove it, Andy sat down and began sorting through papers like he was really interested in them.

*"Oooooh!"* Words actually failed her, but her arm didn't. One long swipe across his desk sent everything on top—papers, pens, clock, folders, in-tray, out-tray—toppling to the floor.

Pink from effort and eye-spittin' anger, she turned her pretty face to me. "Watch yourself with him, honey. He's not worth a three-dollar bill."

With that she stomped off, her high-heeled boots banging every step on the way down to the street.

Andy rested his elbows on his desktop and leaned his head in his hands. The cold air from the broken window ruffled his hair. He sat up and smoothed it with a palm which didn't matter much. The air played with him again, but he didn't notice.

"You'll catch your death sitting in that draft," I said.

"Yeah, I better find a piece of cardboard and cover it up."

But he didn't move or say another thing. I shifted from one foot to the other and waited. Nothing. Finally, I said, "I bought a house and need to have you check the documents. And be at the closing."

He nodded, his mind elsewhere.

"Cletus Dwyer will call you when the papers are ready."

I had half turned to leave when he spoke. "Honey, I'm sorry you had to witness that little scene."

I shook my head. "I'm not."

# THIRTY-EIGHT

"I LIKE IT, HONEY," Matt said. "I like it a lot. The Moose has good bones, a good location. As for its history," he shrugged, "in time people forget."

"I'm hoping they will, but if they don't, I'll still have a beautiful house to call my own."

He grinned. "House being the operative word."

"Not funny."

"No, but good or bad, the Moose *is* a chapter in the town's history and you're giving it a happy ending. I like that best of all."

"You know something, Matt, you sound like a…a poet."

He tapped a finger on the tip of my nose. "Word of that gets out and I can kiss my crime busting career goodbye."

The last few days, heavy with damp and with the sweet promise of spring in the air, had melted the snow and turned the lawn into a soggy mass. For the sake of our shoes, we stood on the weedy brick walk, looking up at the Moose.

"Where do you plan to start?" Matt asked.

"For the neighbors' sake, on the outside. So the roof first. New black shingles."

"And after that?"

"Repair the damaged clapboards then paint the whole house white and put that elegant dark green, the one that's almost black, on the shutters. If possible, I'd like to keep the original windows." I pointed to the overgrown shrubbery bordering the verandah. "But all those big ol' boys need to come out." I tapped a toe on the bricks. "These weeds, too."

"Sounds like a plan, but that's only the tip of the iceberg. You still have the inside to deal with." He turned his attention from the house to me. "If you need extra cash to see you through, I'd be happy to chip in."

"Thanks ever so, Matt, but no thanks. I'm beholden to Cletus, and that's enough for now. I won't lie to you; I *am* mortgaged to the hilt. But once the house is improved, its value will increase, and Cletus will probably let me refinance."

"Probably?" A wavy line creased Matt's forehead.

"I'm sure he will. Not to worry. I know what I'm doing."

"Oh, is that so?" A frown replaced his worry line. "How many derelict, old houses have you renovated?"

"This is the first."

"Ergo—"

*"What?"*

"Therefore, when you start ripping out fixtures and old woodwork, you have no idea what you're going to find. Be prepared for some surprises."

# THIRTY-NINE

To MY GREAT RELIEF, on Friday I sold that fixer-upper with the mother-in-law suite. Turned out, it would be a father-in-law suite. The couple who bought it and the wife's daddy were so tickled at the prospect of moving in together it made my heart glad. It's good when a person can do something to make folks happy.

To celebrate, I took the afternoon off. Leaving Mindy to watch the phones, I went to Abe's Hardware for work gloves, scrapers, pails, a broom, a box of trash bags and a step-ladder. Then I lit out for the Moose. I'd hired contractors for the outside work, but to save money, I planned to tackle much of the lighter, inside chores myself and would begin by scraping off wallpaper.

The weather couldn't have been more beautiful, the sky blue, the air warm and smelling of thawing earth and greenery to come—or maybe the way I felt made everything brighter and sweeter. Whatever, I could hardly wait to turn my new-ol' home into the vision living in my head. It would take years, a mountain of hard work, and every dime I could lay hands on, but the project didn't scare me. It thrilled me so much that all the way across town, I sang along with Faith Hill, belting out "Take Me As I Am."

Earlier in the week, as soon as I took title, I'd had

the locks on both outer doors changed. Not that there was anything in the house worth stealing but, with a murderer on the loose, new locks made me feel safer. Though I wouldn't dwell on that today. Today I'd take the advice Matt was forever ladling out to me: Do your job, let the cops do theirs and, above all, be happy.

When I got to Sugar Street, I was happy to see my driveway clogged with cars and pickups. The contractors had wasted no time starting in on the redo. Good. A square stack of black shingles stood on the front lawn, and I glanced at the roof. Two men were tromping around up there as easy as if they were stomping on solid ground. The sight was enough to make a person dizzy. I parked out by the curb, took some of my do-it-yourself supplies out of the trunk and carried them around to the back door.

Near the spot where I'd found Darlene's body, a man with a weather-lined face and paint-splotched coveralls stopped working long enough to tap his cap with a finger. "I'm Dexter, ma'am, with Peerless Painters. Doing some preliminary chores before we start to apply the finish coat."

"Glad to make your acquaintance," I said, introducing myself before stashing the carry-in supplies in the mudroom then going back to the car for the ladder. I was thrilled work on the house had begun and would not, would *not*, let the general decrepitude of the rooms spoil my mood. I also had hope that even the memory of poor Darlene's death would, in time, fade. Else how could I live here and make it a happy home? A kind person like Darlene would want me to, wouldn't she?

Anyway, stifling a sigh, I lugged the six-foot step ladder into the living room, or the parlor as it was probably called back in the day, and scraper in hand, climbed halfway up the ladder then climbed right back down. The work would go smoother with fresh air to breathe. I opened the front door and wedged the extra scraper underneath to keep it against the wall. A clean, crisp breeze blew in. No doubt about it, spring was on the way.

Overhead, the workmen were walking around, tearing old shingles off the roof and calling to each other. I found the commotion comforting. I wasn't alone.

Without wasting any more time, I mounted the ladder and had at it. The hardware clerk said I'd need to sponge the walls and wait for the water to soak into the paper before scraping, but this paper was so old and dry, it peeled off in long, lovely strips. For an hour, I worked nonstop, moving the ladder from one spot to another and climbing up and down more times than I could count. A pile of gold-striped paper soon lay all over the floor, the exposed gray plaster, spider-webbed with cracks, proving it was the real deal, not dry wall. My arm had gotten heavy enough to need a rest, and my calf muscles were hollering when...

"Miss Ingersoll!"

The sudden outcry nearly sent me careening to the floor. Startled half out of my skin, I shot a glance over a shoulder and there, grinning up at me, stood none other than Roger Ledbetter.

"Fancy seeing you here," he said, staring like he was looking at a star in the sky or something.

I had grabbed one of the ladder steps for support and was clinging to it. "Wow, Roger. This is such a surprise." *To say the least.*

"For me, too. I'm staying with Mother now and was out for a walk. When I saw the front door wide open, I thought I'd take a peek." His face flushed pink to the hair-line. "For old time's sake, don't you know?" He barked out a little laugh. "Actually, you do." He peered around at the wallpaper littering the floor. "What's going on?"

I climbed down and, with our last meeting still a fresh and scary memory, I kept the ladder between us. "I've bought the house, and as soon as it's livable, I'll be moving in."

"Wonderful. You'll bring the old place back to life. So to speak," he added hastily, his cheeks pinking up again. "As long as I'm here, mind if I look around?"

"No, help yourself, but there's not much to see. All the rooms are empty."

A cloud settled over his face. "No matter. They'll always be furnished in my mind."

He strolled out to the hall, his soft-soled shoes hardly echoing on the bare floors. After a few minutes, I de-tected a creak or two over the roofers' noise. He had gone upstairs to tour the bedrooms.

Instead of getting back on the ladder, I'd give my aching legs a break and sweep up the mess I'd made. In minutes, a waist-high pile of scraps was ready to be packed into trash bags. For all my achy muscles, I'd only made a tiny dent in the redo, but it was a start. I'd just begun to…*what was that? A car starting up?*

Deep voices outside the front door, a laugh or two, and the sputter of engines revving to life. *Uh-oh.* The men were leaving for the day, and Roger was still upstairs.

I dropped the broom and ran to the front door. No one in the driveway. Now what? I was alone with a man who just a few days ago had gone plumb crazy. When I bought the Moose, I hadn't given a thought to the notion that Roger might be my neighbor. Well, too late to worry about that now. Now what I had to do was figure out how to pry him out of here.

I strode into the hall and yoohooed up the stairs. "Roger, time to leave. I have to lock up. Come down, please."

No answer.

"Roger! Come on, I have to leave."

Nothing.

Not a chance he didn't hear me in all this stillness.

"Roger!"

I sensed that I could call him till my lungs gave out and he wouldn't answer. I was too scaredy-cat, or maybe too sensible for once, to go up and get him. Well, instead of me, maybe Verna could flush him out. But what if she refused to step foot in what she considered the devil's workshop? Then I'd have to call Matt. Oh Lord, the first day I'd spent in my home and I needed the cops. Not good. Not good at all.

I leaned on the banister post and glanced up the stairwell, listening for footfalls but hearing none. There was an outside chance he'd snuck out without being seen, though I doubted it. No other way then, I'd have to get Verna.

I hurried out to the verandah, and relief like a warm shower washed all over me. The carpenter was standing by the curb, stashing his tools in the trunk of a beat-up Chevy. I ran across the weedy lawn to him.

"Dexter, will you help me?"

His hand on the open trunk lid, he looked up, surprised. "Yes, ma'am, if I can. What's the problem?"

"A man's hiding upstairs in the house, and he won't come down. I really need him out of there."

He narrow-eyed me, sort of skeptical at first, but not for long. "Okay, if you say so, a lady like you."

*A lady. Well, how about that?*

He reached into the trunk and pulled a hammer out of his tool box. "Let's see what the problem is."

I pointed to the hammer. "I don't think you'll need that."

"Then I won't use it. Let's go."

I hurried to keep up with his long-legged stride. "This man has been really sick. He, ah, just got out of the Yarborough County Psychiatric Hospital."

Dexter stopped walking for a second. "Oh, a nut case."

"Sort of. Do you have a cell phone?"

"Yeah. Back in the car."

"Hang on a sec. Before we go upstairs, let me get mine, just in case." I dashed into the kitchen where I'd left my purse, dumped everything in it on the countertop and grabbed my phone. *Why did I carry so much junk around anyway?* Dexter was already halfway up the stairs. Phone in hand, I hurried after him.

We looked into the bathroom and the two front bedrooms, even the small, narrow closets. No sign of Roger. Two rooms to go.

We found him in the back bedroom where the skeleton had been tricked out on the lumpy mattress. In the doorway, I put a hand on Dexter's arm. "Wait."

Huddled in a corner, head down, arms wrapped around his tented knees, Roger didn't look up when I walked into the room and called his name, soft and low so as not to spook him. "It's me, Honey Ingersoll. We have to go now, Roger. This here's Dexter. He'll help you get home."

"No, I can't leave. I love it here." He looked up, gazing full at me with those cornflower blue eyes that were so like the ones he had gifted to Joanne.

"There's nothing here to stay for, Roger. Not even a chair."

He sat up straight, leaning into the corner, stretching his legs out flat on the floor. "There's everything here. Everything." He glanced around the room from one wall to another, seeing things no one else could see, hearing voices no one else could hear.

"Oh brother," Dexter whispered.

"If only he hadn't helped," Roger said. "He was always *helping*. He ruined everything."

"Who?"

"My father, the Reverend Roger G. Ledbetter the third. He shouldn't have sent our baby away. I should have held her and loved her. I should have raised her. She was all I had left. He shouldn't have done that. Always helping...ask Juanita Petty, she knows...she knows he was a helping, god-fearing man if ever there was one." As tears sprang into his eyes and ran down his face, he burst into a laugh, a long, belly-bouncing laugh that went on and on.

"Back to the funny farm," Dexter said, none too softly.

"Shush," I said. "He can't help it. He's sick."

"Humph. If you say so."

We waited, Dexter with a hammer in his hand and me with a lump in my throat, for what would come next. Neither one of us moved, and after Roger's laughter faded into silence, he heaved a sigh and swiped a hand across his face. By now, I was edgy as a cat up a coconut tree. "Feel better?" I asked him.

"I guess so." Roger hauled himself to his feet. "The

memories kind of overtook me there for a spell." He nodded at Dexter, as if seeing him for the first time. "I'll go now. No need to come with me. I can find my way out." Halfway across the room, he paused. "I won't be back, Miss Ingersoll, so don't worry about that." He glanced around one last time. "There's nothing here for me anymore."

I RAN TO the front window. Looking neither left nor right, Roger stepped off the verandah and headed down Sugar Street. "He's taking a stroll," I said to Dexter. "I'm for locking up and leaving fast."

"Good idea. You going to be safe living here?" he asked as we went down the stairs.

"This is going to be my home. I better be."

"With that guy around, my advice is keep your doors locked from here on in."

"I'll do that, though it's not a friendly way to live. Besides, he said he wouldn't be back."

Dexter scoffed. "You believe him? Better safe than sorry."

He was right, and I knew it. "The next time I come back, I'll bring Jake along. He's a big, ol' softie of a hunting dog, but he's fierce when he needs to be."

"Good idea."

Dexter waited till I restuffed my purse and locked up. We walked out to our cars together and, after tapping his cap in farewell, he said, "Take care, miss," and drove off.

I was about to leave too when I glanced across the street. Verna's Ford, fifteen years old at least and shiny as a brand-new Lexus caught my eye. So she was likely home then. A quick glance up and down Sugar showed no sign of Roger.

*There might be enough time.*

On an impulse, I hurried across the street to Verna's back door. She answered on the second ring, wiping her fingers on the hem of her flowered apron. "Well, my goodness, look who's here. Come in."

She looked so pleased to see me I didn't want to spoil the moment by telling her she had a flour smudge on her cheek.

"What can I do for you, young lady?" she asked, beckoning me inside.

"Do you have a minute to spare?"

"Well, I'm in the middle of pie making, but I can always spare a minute or two." She glanced down at my shoes.

I rubbed them back and forth real good on the scatter rug by the door. "Can't forget your nice, clean floors," I said, following her into the kitchen.

"That's what I tell Roger all the time. But does he listen?"

"Well, speaking of Roger, that's really why I'm here, Mrs. Ledbetter."

"Oh?" She had had gone back to her pie and, with her thumb and forefinger, was crimping the edge of the crust.

"Apple?" I asked.

"Yes, apple's Roger's favorite."

"Nice of you to make it for him."

"That's what the Lord made mothers for. To keep their children happy."

I swallowed hard. "About Roger…"

"Yes?" She kept on crimping that crust, not looking up, more interested in her pie than in what I had to say.

"He just came over to call on me and I…ah…had trouble getting him to leave."

Crust crimped, she viewed her handiwork and smiled. "He shouldn't have done that. I've told him over and over again not to step foot in that godless place." She looked up suddenly and frowned. "I heard tell you went and bought it."

"Yes, but that's not—"

"Just a minute, I have to heat the oven."

As she turned toward the stove, I said, "I want to be neighborly and all, but he scared me walking in, *boom*, just like that."

She took a wet dishcloth out of the sink and mopped the tabletop, gathering the flour and pie crust scraps into a neat little mound.

"Are you listening, Verna?"

"Of course, I am. I've listened all my life. First to God and then to the reverend. And now I'm listening to you. I'm a born listener."

She wasn't making this easy. "What I'm trying to say is—"

"Just a minute." Using a palm, she swept the little mound off the table into her other hand and dropped the floury mess into a trash can by the sink. "I know what you're saying." She straightened up and turned to face me. "My son is insane and you don't want a crazy man in your *house*."

I bowed my head at the truth in that. "I'm afraid that's so."

"How did he get in?"

"I left the door open to air things out."

"Well, there's your answer. Roger's not to blame. Keep

your doors locked and you won't have a problem. Not with my Roger, anyway. At least not as long as I'm alive."

"Does that mean he'll be living here permanently?"

Using the dishcloth, she was polishing the kitchen table top. Pretty soon she'd be able to see her face in it.

"I don't rightly have to supply you with that information, but I will. Sorry if Roger makes you uneasy, but the answer is yes. Where else can he go? He's lost his accounting job. They don't trust him to handle their books any longer. He has no one but me."

"He has his daughter," I reminded her.

"A sweet girl, I must say. Too bad she's tainted."

*"Tainted?"*

"By her mother, by what she was."

"That's not fair of you, Verna."

"It's not me alone saying that. The Bible tells us sin is passed on down unto the third and fourth generation."

As I recollected from my long-ago Bible class, it was the sins of the fathers that were passed on to their offspring, but I wasn't about to hang that heavy burden around poor Roger's neck. So I kept my mouth closed and let Verna believe she'd bested me.

I'm glad I did. Whether I looked crestfallen or something, I don't know, but as I picked up my bag, ready to leave without having accomplished what I came for—a promise that she would help keep Roger away from my house—her next words just about blew me away.

I'd nearly reached the kitchen door when it happened. "Wait up a minute, girl," she said, leaving off wiping down the table to hurry over to me. "Just because I know my Bible better than you do, don't go away mad now, you hear? Peaceable neighbors need a meeting of the minds, don't you think?"

I nodded, wondering where she'd go with this.

"Truth is, girl, the Lord's given me some heavy burdens. I'm not complaining, understand, and I'm not saying I can't handle them, but He's trying me. He's trying me."

It might have been my imagination, but I'd swear tears hovered under her lids. If so, she ignored them, and they disappeared.

"First I lost the reverend," she went on. "That was a mighty blow. I admit it even to the Lord. And now Roger's in this helpless state, a baby all over again."

"I'm sor—"

She held up a hand, cutting me off. "No, no need to sympathize. I'm not looking for that. Long as you realize what I'm up against, we'll get along fine. I'll do my best to keep Roger out of your house, though if I had my druthers I'd tear it to the ground and good riddance. But keep your doors locked anyway. At least while he's still living here."

And then, no mistake about it, tears did glaze Verna's eyes, and the next thing I knew they were spilling down her cheeks.

All the ill feelings I'd ever held against the woman melted in that moment. She was worried for her son and for what the future held for them both, and as I watched, that fear was leaking out of her eyes. Touched to the heart, I opened my arms and reaching out, I pulled her to me and hugged her tight.

She didn't jerk back or push me away or anything but, still, she sure was a mighty stiff person to grab a hold of and try to love.

# THIRTY-NINE

On Saturday, Matt and I were working side by side scraping off wallpaper in the Moose's hallway. He was about to attack the cabbage roses when I brought up my visit with Verna.

"I never thought I'd say it, Matt, but underneath that hard shell, she's really a sweet ol' lady. She's worried sick and with good cause. Roger's off in a world of his own more often than not. Though the other day upstairs in the bedroom, I swear he was telling the truth. When he said Juanita knows more than she let on, he was too strung out to make up lies."

Matt sighed that cop sigh I'd heard plenty of times before, actually three times already today. "Everyone knows more than they let on. In psychology, it's termed preserving one's ego."

"There's something else," I said, ignoring his fancy talk. "Roger knows Juanita's alive. He spoke of her in the…in the…"

"Present tense?"

"Yes, that one."

"Could be a slip of the tongue."

"Uh-uh, it wasn't. While he was spouting out his feelings, in his…upset state he disremembered she had faked her own suicide. He knew she was alive, Matt, he *knew*. His father must have let him in on the secret and swore him to secrecy."

"While that is entirely possible, how do you suggest we question a mentally ill man for relevant information?"

That had me stumped. But not for long. "What about his mother? Verna might know something. If the reverend told his son what was going on, he might have told his wife."

"Or not."

"Well, either way, we need to find out."

He blew out a breath. "Who said anything about 'we?'"

No surprise there. I'd heard him say that before too. "Aren't you curious, Matt?"

"Yes. About many things. What, specifically, do you have in mind?" He gave me the wiggly eyebrows grin which I pretended not to see.

"I'd like to know whatever Verna and Juanita know."

"Let it go, Honey. The chance that Verna could shed new light on something that may—or may not—have happened over twenty years ago is slim at best. Furthermore, I have no justification for questioning her. As for Juanita, as long as the state is repaid for expenses incurred at the time of her disappearance, Bradshaw's willing to turn a blind eye on whatever ID she's been using these past years. At least while the murders are under investigation."

"By ID, you mean—"

"Her social security number mainly. How did she get a driver's license without one? Or get married? But let's leave the Hightowers in peace as long as possible. I feel strongly about that and so does Bradshaw." He waved his arms around the hallway. "Haven't you got enough to worry about right here?"

I had no comeback to that, so I shut up and went to work. The living room walls were stripped clean, but the hallway roses had to go.

While Matt climbed the scaffolding the painters had set up on the stairs, I grabbed a scraper and a lantern flashlight and ducked under the open area beneath the stairwell. Even in broad daylight, direct sun didn't penetrate this little, half-hidden space. To get a good look at what I was doing, I turned on the flash. In its beam, the cabbage roses practically leaped off the wall, but not the paper they were attached to. After a half hour of scraping, all I'd removed were pieces the size of my hand or smaller. No peeling off sheets in here. Maybe I'd have to take Abe Hardware's advice and sponge soak this area.

My scraping arm was already aching, so before starting the task, I flopped down on the floor for a little rest and stared up at the underside of the stairs. Like the wallpaper, the paint was as bright and garish as if it had been brushed on yesterday.

With a pillow and a blanket, I believe I could have fallen asleep for a bit. Between worrying about the size of my mortgage, keeping up Ingersoll's sales—more important now than ever—working on the house and fretting about a killer on the loose, no wonder I'd felt tired and nauseous lately.

I lay there for a few moments, enjoying the quiet, the only sound the scratch of Matt's scraper. But much as I wanted to, I couldn't laze there all day, staring at the underside of the staircase, getting nothing done. And then I saw it…a skinny, dull gray book tucked in a narrow crevice between one of the treads and the wall.

I reached up and tugged. In a shower of dust, the book fell into my lap. I sneezed then brushed it off and opened it. An old-fashioned ledger, it was the kind that back in the day a small business might have used to record transactions.

*Hmm, a funny place to hide a ledger.* In the flashlight's glare, I flipped the book open and stared at a page of neat, spidery handwriting. *Oh, my.* Slowly, as if my fingers couldn't believe what my eyes were seeing, I turned to the next page. To the next and the next.

My heart pounding out a crazy rhythm, I crawled out from under the stairwell and hollered at the top of my lungs, "Matt, look what I found!" I waved the book in the air. "You're not going to believe this. Come on down. I mean it!"

He leaned over the scaffolding. "What's all the shouting about? You find gold?"

"You'll never know if you don't come have a look."

"This better be good," he said as he climbed on down. "I was about to loosen up a whole strip."

Taking him by the hand, I drew him over to the bottom step. "You have to be sitting down for this."

Once he was, I opened the ledger, placed it on his lap and pointed. He bent over, peering at the fine, school marm handwriting. He read what it said, glanced up at me fast and looked down at the ledger again. Taking his time, carefully studying line after line, he went through the whole page.

Finally, "Hard to believe," he said when he came to the last entry. "But hard not to when it's in black and white. The Reverend Roger Ledbetter a Moose regular? What do you know about that?" He shrugged.

"There's still room for doubt, but who else could it be? Rev. RGL, that's pretty precise."

"I'm afraid so."

Though the ledger was filled with names and initials, except for one or two, most were of folks I had never met.

"Look how often he was with Juanita." I pointed to the dates that ran down the left-hand side of the page. "At least once, sometimes twice a week."

"Not Juanita alone," Matt said. "Did you get to page five?"

"I don't know. Why?"

"He started seeing another girl. A Gaylene. Look here." Matt pointed to one line after another. "Here. And here. This isn't good, not good at all. And look at these entries. In between visits with a Rev. RGL, Gaylene had other appointments. Some with an RL."

"Roger," we both said in the same breath.

"Oh God." I sank onto the step next to Matt. "If they were both sleeping with her, you know what that means?"

"I can guess at one possibility. Joanne's paternity is in question. She could be the Rev's daughter, not Roger's."

"Or somebody else's. And there's no way to prove it."

"Only with DNA. Even then, if she's a Ledbetter, I'm not sure a DNA test could determine which of the two men is her father."

*Phew.* I sank down on the step next to Matt. "Do you think Roger suspects the reverend was, you know—"

"Who knows? If Roger's thought of the possibility, he's probably buried it so deep he'll never uncover it."

"Could this be the reason for his mental state?"

"Could be. Sad either way." He glanced back at the

ledger, held it up closer to his eyes and broke into a laugh.

"What's so funny? I see nothing fun—"

He handed me the book. "We missed this." Here and there, on the right-hand side of the lines, were the letters IOU. "Can you beat that?"

*Would wonders never cease?* "I didn't know you could get credit at a cat house."

"Neither did I. Had I known that—"

"Oh, hush. Seriously, who do you think kept this ledger?"

"Carl Huggins' daddy most likely. He ran the place. No wonder he hid this so well. It's a vehicle for blackmail."

The instant the words left Matt's lips we looked at each other and mouthed the same name. "Tim O'Toole."

It made sense. If Tim would extort money from the Hightowers, why not the reverend? A man with a lot to lose in the community.

"Ledbetter went to his reward quite a few years ago." Matt snapped the ledger closed. "If what's in here is true, and if he had lived longer, his secret life might have been exposed." Matt shrugged. "But of course that never happened."

"What did he die of, I wonder?"

"Good question, Honey. It might be wise to find out."

Matt got on his phone to Ellie, the dispatcher at the station. "Check this out, will you, Ellie? The date and cause of death of a Reverend Roger G. Ledbetter."

He hung up, and we returned to our scraping but had hardly attacked a single rose when Ellie called back.

"According to the coroner's report, Ledbetter died on April 12, twenty years ago. Cause was cardiac arrest."

After Matt related her message to me, I stopped scraping for a moment as a notion flashed into my head. "You know, Matt, until the coroner tested her for poison, he thought cardiac arrest had killed Reba Knight."

# FORTY

"WE'LL HAVE TO dig him up," I said.

"There you go again with that 'we.' There's no 'we,' and there's no call to get out a shovel."

"That's extremely short-sighted of you, Matt. No telling what might have happened. A killer is still on the loose, and you're acting like—"

"An experienced sheriff should."

Due to the shouting, Jake had come over to sniff out the emotion.

"Bradshaw needs to see this ledger," Matt said. "He's the one who'll decide if there's sufficient reason to exhume the body of a man of the cloth…providing there is a body. The remains may have been cremated."

"Oh, true. I didn't think of that."

Jake snugged up against my leg. I leaned down to pat him. "Good boy."

"Who me?"

"Not hardly."

"Let me remind you, Reverend Ledbetter did a lot of good in his time."

"Any harm?"

"None I ever heard of, and this old tattered book isn't enough to hang a man over. So let's cut him some slack until we learn more." With that, he turned his back to me and went on with his scraping.

No wonder. I had been too quick to judge a man I never knew and that was wrong. Besides, Matt was giving up a whole day to work his heart out for free… for me…and I'd laid into him like a shrew.

I felt like a piece of dog poop. "Please forgive me, Matt. I'm sorry. I got carried away. A woman was murdered out by my back door and whoever did it is walking around free as air. I guess my nerves are on edge."

"That's understandable, but accusations have a way of boomeranging. You don't want to get hit in the rear by one you've thrown." He let the scraper dangle from his hand and peered down at me. "Is that really what's bothering you? Or are you discouraged in general? Sorry you bought the Moose?"

"No, I love it and know it'll be beautiful some day. If I keep at it." I scooted back under the stairwell, yanked the scraper out of my jeans pocket and went to work. So did Matt. And Jake? Well, Jake laid out flat on the floor between us ready to referee if he was needed.

But we were good. Until we weren't.

The loud banging on the front door was enough to make the dead sit up and take notice. Jake must have thought so too. He growled as if he could smell a ghost. As soon as the electricians rewired the place, I'd buy a set of front door chimes right off.

"Company," Matt called from his perch.

"I know." I crawled out from under the stairs, in my hurry banging my head and cussing. I wiped my hands on my thighs and yanked open the front door.

"Afternoon, missy."

"Well, my goodness, if it isn't Carl Huggins."

"Saw a couple of cars in the driveway so thought I'd stop by and see what all you're up to."

"Come in and take a look." I waved him on through. "Not much to see so far, but we've only begun to fight."

He peered into the living room. "You got the walls in here stripped clean."

"Yup, now we're working on the hallway."

"I can see that," he said, striding into the hall ahead of me as if he still owned the place. He peered up the scaffolding. "Afternoon, sheriff. Didn't expect to find you here."

"Carl." Matt kept on working, making no attempt to climb down and shake Carl's hand or exchange a little friendly banter. Hmm. Matt was usually very mannerly. Why not with Carl? And what had he done with the ledger?

Carl shuffled from one foot to the other but didn't ask to tour the empty rooms as Roger had. He fidgeted with his John Deere and hoisted up his jeans, looking like a man who wouldn't be at ease until he got something off his mind. And sure enough, my hunch was right. After a bit of hemming and hawing and jawing about the weather, he came out with it.

"Truth is, missy, I stopped by a few days ago to pick up something that got left in here…something you'd have no earthly use for. Problem is, you'd already gone ahead and changed the locks." He frowned, treating me to a stare from under half-raised lids. I figured the lock change didn't sit well with him.

"What is it you want, Carl?"

"Just an ol' book of my daddy's. I knew you wouldn't care if I took it. It wouldn't mean nothin' to you. Not worth a plug nickel, but since it belonged to Daddy, I'd like to have it, kind of as a keepsake, don't you know. I should have gotten it out of here before signing off on the place, but what with one thing and another, it slipped my mind."

"Of course, Carl. If you can find your keepsake, take it with my blessing."

Matt snorted but recovered fast and covered up with a cough.

"Thank you kindly, missy. If you don't mind, I'll get it right out of the hidey-hole Daddy kept it in."

Quick as a bunny, Carl dropped to his knees—faster than I would have thought possible for a man with a belly like his and—and slid under the stairwell.

A string of cuss words soon had Jake on his feet and ready to roll. I grabbed his collar. A moment later, all red-faced and dusty, Carl scurried out. "You sure you didn't find nothin' under them stairs?"

"Yeah, I did, lots of dust, a couple of spiders and some ratty wallpaper—"

"That ain't what I mean, and you know it."

Jake surged forward and bared his teeth, but he didn't need to. Matt hustled down the scaffolding and, by the time Carl got his cap on straight, Matt was ready for him.

"You're out of line, Carl. I suggest you back off. You know the rules. You sell a piece of property and what's in it belongs to the new owner."

"That right? Well, I should have torn the Moose down like I wanted to in the first place." With a yank on his cap brim, he stormed out, slamming the door so hard the walls shuddered.

I turned back to Matt. "Where did you put it?"

"In here." He reached under his sweatshirt and removed the ledger. "Glad it didn't drop on the floor while I was chewing him out."

"Glad you thought fast enough to hide it like that."

"A pissing contest would have been a waste of time, and I had no intention of letting Carl walk off with it before Bradshaw has a look."

"Meaning you think there's something to it?" My turn to do that Groucho thing with the eyebrows.

He laughed. "Yeah, exactly what, though, I'm not sure. The information in it is old, but it's potentially explosive. Carl knows that, too. Appears to me he has reason to be afraid."

"*Afraid?* Him?"

"Anger is the other face of fear, Honey. And that was a mighty angry dude who just slammed your door."

# FORTY-ONE

POOPED, AND WITH my right arm tired enough to fall off, I slumped on the living room floor and leaned against the wall. Matt was sweeping the fallen roses into a pile and stuffing them in trash bags. When I made a half-hearted attempt to help him, he insisted I stay sitting down or I'd fall down.

So I just watched, grateful and happy not to move. The queasiness that had been plaguing me on and off had disappeared, leaving me with the feeling that life was good and about to get better.

Matt had the wallpaper pile down to a few scattered scraps when someone knocked on the front door.

"I'll get it," he said, dropping the broom and going for the door. A moment later, I heard a pleased, "Hey there, lady! Come on in. Honey's in the other room."

A woman murmured something, and a moment later Joanne peeked around the corner, laughing at the sight of me propped up against the wall.

"Hi. What a nice surprise!" I went to scramble up.

"No, stay there. Don't get up. I'll join you."

In jeans, work boots, a padded vest over her T-shirt, she scrunched down beside me. "I'm glad I caught you home."

*Home. Yes, it soon would be.*

"I just stopped by to tell Verna and Roger that Momma's funeral is scheduled for Monday noon." She stared down at her boots. "I thought you might like to know."

I reached for her hand. "Of course, I do. I'll be there. Grace Church?"

She nodded. "My, ah…grandmother and my daddy are planning to go too."

*Her grandma and her daddy?* Oh boy. Were they? Maybe yes. Maybe no. But whatever the police discovered, one thing was certain: Darlene would always be Joanne's momma in spirit and in love—and in my book that was more important than DNA.

The morning of Darlene's funeral dawned sunny and warm, a February day that thought it was May. I had never been inside Grace Church and didn't quite know what to expect of the service. Would there be just a few sad souls weeping in the front pews, or would the church be packed with mourners?

*Packed, of course.*

The funeral of a murder victim whose killer was still on the loose, whose sister had been a hooker who supposedly had taken her own life and whose body had never been found? That was stuff movies were made out of. Then, too, some folks may have heard Darlene's daughter had been issued a false birth certificate. That she hadn't known who her real momma was until a few weeks ago. And that the jury was still out on exactly who her daddy might be. But not many folks, I hoped. Such information was Joanne's to share or not as she alone wished, but the problem was word got around fast in a small town.

Either way, big or small, funerals called for black. That meant my black skirt suit, even though it was a mite tight, black pumps, ivory silk blouse (well, rayon, actually), black and ivory striped Kate Spade bag (thank you, eBay) and pearl studs. Every slick fashion magazine would likely recommend the same thing, even for a burial in Manhattan. For Eureka Falls, Arkansas, I wouldn't have a single problem. Not, as it turned out, about my outfit, anyway.

I fed Jake, then drove to the church with plenty of time to spare, or so I thought, but the church parking lot was jammed. So was the Toole Shed lot and Main Street for five blocks on either side of the road. Parked cars even lined Sugar all the way up to the Moose.

I should have known. On top of everything else, Darlene had been the town's favorite librarian, checking out folks' books for years. Though I'll admit, not for me. I'm more of a magazine fan. In my opinion, nothing livens up a page like a few good pictures.

Anyway, between the murders, the Moose's history and the town's liking for Darlene, I figured the church would be as crowded as the Bijou on a Saturday night. For Joanne's sake I was pleased, but not for the sake of my feet. Spike heels set off a skirt suit better than anything, but these boots sure weren't made for hiking.

Oh, well, no help for it. I drove up Sugar Street, parked in my driveway and started trekking. I hadn't gotten but ten steps away when a long, black Caddy from Floyds' Funerals pulled up in front of Verna's house. Minutes later, the same car passed me heading down the slope to Main with Verna, Roger and Joanne in the back seats.

I waved as they drove on by and, a few hundred yards ahead, the car lurched to a stop. The driver stepped out from behind the wheel and waited by the curb till I got up close to him. "Morning," I said.

"Yes, ma'am. The family," he paused for a respectful moment, "would like you to join them."

"Oh, no, I'm not family. I couldn't. It wouldn't be—"

A tinted rear window rolled down, and Joanne poked her head out. "Please get in, Honey. In those heels, you'll never make it to the church in time, and I'd…I'd like to have you there."

Who could refuse an invitation, or was it a plea, like that? As the driver held a rear door open for me, I slid onto a leather-covered seat next to Joanne.

In her black dress and plain black coat, her dark hair flowing straight and smooth to her shoulders, she looked calm and ready for what was ahead. *Or maybe not.* She was gripping her handbag like it was the only raft in a sea of sharks. Her other hand held a tissue, and it sure wasn't for waving to a passing ship.

I took the tissue hand and squeezed. "You'll do fine."

She nodded. "For Momma. To make her proud."

A voice from up front said, "Miss Ingersoll?"

"Yes, Mrs. Ledbetter." I guess we were going to be formal today. Well, it was fitting, if strange.

Half turning in her seat to face me, Verna said, "Joanne asked us to sit in the front pew with her, right near the altar. That's where young Roger and I always sat when the reverend was alive so as not to miss a word of his sermons. He was a wonderful speaker, you know. Had a golden tongue, folks always said." Taking a crocheted hanky out of her purse, she wiped her nose on the lace. "Much as I want to be helpful, I just can't step foot in that pew. I'll look up at the pulpit ex-

pecting my Roger to come out from the sacristy but…
he won't. Not ever again."

I thought the day was warm, but judging from the
sudden chill in the air, I must have been wrong. As
Verna got through wiping her nose, I leaned forward
so she'd be sure to hear me. "That's so sad, Verna, but
why are you telling me this?"

"I thought it might be comforting for the girl to have
you sit beside her during the service."

"What about you, Roger?" I asked, baiting him.

"Oh, I have to escort Mother."

*Of course, you do.* I heaved a sigh and tried to put
myself in Verna's shoes. Finding out she had a full-
grown, ready-made granddaughter had to have been a
shock, and Verna *had* been kind to her—if not today.

Needing to lighten up, I sat back and turned to
Joanne with a smile. "I'd be mighty honored to share
the front pew with you."

"Oh, good." She clutched my hand so hard her
knuckles showed white through the skin.

"Now I can relax," Verna said, turning around and
leaning into her seat. "Don't you two worry about us,
we'll be just fine in the back row."

Okay, that killed my stab at lightening up. Vexed
by her coldness, I tried those deep breathing exercises
that are supposed to be calming. You suck in the air,
hold it for five then let it go like an escaped balloon.
It works too. By the time we approached the church I
was calm and had convinced myself that Verna was an
elderly woman carrying a heavy burden. I tried not to
give head room to what I really suspected: Verna didn't
want to share the front pew with Joanne because she

was afraid people had begun to suspect the girl was her son's love child.

*Or her husband's.*

Unlikely, but anyway, at Verna's request, the driver parked at the side of the church where there were almost no people, and at least he ran around the car to open the doors for us which was very elegant. While Verna and Roger held back, Joanne and I, like a small but united family, stepped around to the front entrance and climbed the stone steps.

In respect for Joanne's grief, both the mourners and the curiosity seekers stood aside and, like the parting of waves the Bible speaks about, they let us pass on by, down the center aisle, to the reserved front pew. Surrounded by organ music and the sweet-sick aroma of hothouse flowers, we took our seats. The organist, a frail-looking, gray-haired lady was pounding out "Rock of Ages." It sounded like thunder hitting the side of a mountain. No question, anyone playing arm wrestle with her would lose.

Straight ahead, a mound of floral arrangements filled the altar steps. In front of the flowers, on a small table covered with a long white cloth, stood a little metal urn surrounded by a ring of pink roses. *Darlene.* Oh my, so little, so reduced, so…nothing at all. I wanted to weep at the sight and sent a quick glance Joanne's way. Her chin wobbled, but no tears were falling. Relieved, I relaxed a little and looked around at the rest of the church.

Painted ivory with clear glass windows letting in the light, it was plain enough but not painfully so. A sky-blue drapery softened the wall behind the altar, and all the pews were padded in that same pretty blue. On either side of the altar and over the center aisle, rows of shiny brass fixtures were lit and blazing away like daytime stars. It was all so…

"Honey," Joanne whispered in my ear. "I have to use the bathroom."

*"Now?"*

"Yes. Right now."

"I don't know where it is."

"I do. Come with me, please."

She had entered the pew before me, so I stepped into the aisle to let her out, and wasting no time about it, she headed for a door in an alcove at the left of the altar.

Racing ahead of me, pulling off her coat, she ran down the stairs, dropping the coat and her handbag in her rush. I picked them up and followed her to the church basement, past a big assembly hall, a kitchen, a door marked storage and into the ladies' room. It was pitch black in there, but that didn't stop her. As if she had x-ray eyes, she ran into a stall—I could tell because a metal door slammed shut behind her. I fumbled for the switch, found it by the entrance and snapped on the overheads. Leaning back against the wall, I caught my breath while Joanne barfed up the contents of her stomach.

I draped her coat over one of the sinks and placed her handbag on top. After the retching stopped and the water flushed three or four times, I opened the stall door. Joanne was on her knees in front of the toilet, sobbing.

I yanked a handful of paper towels from the dispenser, ran them under a warm water tap and gave them to her. "Wipe your face and come on out. You can't hardly breathe in here now, and we need to clean you up. Listen!"

That little ol' lady was clobbering the organ. Her version of "Amazing Grace" had the ladies' room walls vibrating. A heavy shuffling of feet and, next thing you knew, the not-so muffled voices of the congregation were singing along loud as anything.

Holding my nose, fighting my own urge to barf, I said, "Come on out, Joanne, or you'll miss your momma's funeral."

That did it. Grasping the edge of the toilet, she hoisted herself up and stumbled over to the sink.

I ran the water and pumped some liquid soap into her hands. "Let's forget about makeup. You have beautiful skin anyway. It's the pukey odor we have to get rid of." While she stood, quiet as a tired child, I wiped a fresh, damp towel over her face.

"I don't know what happened to me, Honey," she said. "I've never done that before, not even at frat parties."

"It's the tension, is all," I said, sort of sounding like your average shrink.

When we had her scrubbed clean, Joanne rinsed her mouth and let me pop a peppermint between her lips. While she clung to the wash basin, I ran my brush through her hair and spritzed her with my purse-sized vial of Yellow Diamond cologne.

"We don't look a mite alike, but we sure do smell alike," I said. "Under the present circumstances, that's a good thing."

She gave me a wan smile, slipped on her coat and picked up her purse.

"Now let's go before the singing ends and the preaching begins."

We hustled up the stairs, our high heels clicking on the treads each step of the way. With everybody still upright for the singing, we were able to slip into the pew without creating too much of a fuss.

While I stood with the congregation and belted out the few last bars of the hymn, Joanne sat, listening and waiting. Finally, the music died and folks took their seats.

Pastor Ellis, a dignified, forty-something man in a black robe with purple trim strode across the altar to the pulpit and for a long moment stood there not saying a word. Except for a cough or two, silence fell over the packed church. When the coughing ceased and the only sound was the distant throb of traffic on Main Street, he began.

"We are gathered together this morning to honor a beautiful soul and the beauty of a life well lived." He raised his arms, and with the purple cuffs of his robe waving like flags, he gave the whole congregation a kind of big, loving bear hug. "Your presence here today, filling these pews to overflowing, is testimony to the woman who was Darlene Petty.

"Over the years, as our town librarian, she helped many of you, perhaps all of you, select that perfect book, whether it was the latest novel by your favorite author, a cookbook, information you needed for a school paper or for a job, or a piece of research you couldn't find on your own, but that she found for you because she knew it was important, not to herself, but to you.

"Always, and having been Darlene's pastor for going on twenty years now, I can state with conviction that

she reached out to help others in every way she could…
with her love of words, her love of learning, and certainly in her profession as our beloved librarian."

*Uh-oh.* I could feel my face flush. I didn't even own
a library card.

"In her short life on this earth, Darlene did much
good and one profoundly noble deed." He raised a purple cuff and pointed to our pew. "With love flowing
from her heart, Darlene brought her daughter to woman-
hood, alone, unaided, a single mother who sacrificed
herself…" his look grazed the congregation "…as so
many good women do, to give someone else a chance
at life.

"That's the kind of woman Darlene Petty was, generous of her earthly possessions, generous of herself.
Today," he paused and once more spread his arms wide,
"in this house of God, her generosity is being recognized one hundred-fold over. And since the Lord's love
never hurries us, we have ample time for remembrance.
So, I invite you, any of you who wish to, please come
forward and speak of the fellowship you shared with
our sister who has gone before us."

A shuffle of feet and a few fresh coughs, and even
a spate of whispers met the pastor's invitation. But no
one stirred for several seconds until, one by one, both
the shy and not so shy came up to the altar and told of
their deep affection for Darlene. Before long, all those
good words and those good feelings for her momma
reduced Joanne to a puddle of happy-sad tears. The
fellowship trail had about petered out when one more
witness to Darlene's character marched down the center aisle. Her pace slow but deliberate, her high heels
striking the stone floor with each step, she approached

the altar, nodded at Pastor Ellis and turned to face the congregation. She was in black with blond hair waving to her shoulders and the high cheek-boned face of a movie star.

I gasped. It was Juanita Hightower.

My outburst startled Joanne. She glanced over at me, alarmed. "What is it, Honey?"

"That woman," I whispered in her ear, "she's Darlene's sister. Your aunt." At least she was by adoption if not by blood.

"Omigod. Are you sure?"

I nodded. "In the flesh."

"And my momma never knew she was alive." From the corner of my eye, I could see Joanne's jaw harden and her eyes glitter with something more than tears.

Folks in the pews sat quiet and respectful, no doubt wondering who this stranger—for that's what she was—might be. And then she told them.

"My name, when I lived in Eureka Falls years ago, was Juanita Petty. Darlene Petty was my sister."

A buzz like wildfire flashed through the church. Those who remembered Juanita's career at the Moose and the suicide that followed passed the word on to their neighbors. Voices rose louder as folks stirred in their pews, their whispers turning into questions that echoed in the air. "Who? What? When did that happen?"

As the buzzing grew louder, Pastor Ellis leaned into his microphone. "Brethren, brothers, sisters, quiet, please. I'm asking for quiet. Remember where you are and allow this woman to speak for the departed soul who cannot speak for herself."

Pale under her makeup, her hands clenched in front of her—so the trembling wouldn't show?—Juanita nodded at him, closed her eyes for a moment and said, "All of my life, even in the years when life went badly for me, my big sister Darlene was my idol. To be like her, as warm, as gentle, as smart and funny the way only she could be was something I strived for. I never achieved her fineness and never will, but I'll always try to be what she was—a good woman. I'm here today, in this place of healing to tell her that and to ask for her forgiveness and that of my niece, Joanne Petty."

With that, Juanita stopped speaking and looked over at our pew, her hands trembling in the air like hummingbirds.

In that packed congregation, no one sighed, no one coughed, no one shuffled their feet. Breathless, everyone waited for Joanne's response.

"Miss Petty?" the pastor asked, a pleading note in his tone.

Well, poor Joanne, she never had a chance to give an answer for a voice rang out, shattering the silence. "No!"

Footsteps came hurrying along the center aisle.

"Easy now, easy now," Pastor Ellis said.

As if he hadn't spoken, the footsteps pounded on, coming closer and closer until Verna Ledbetter stood nose-to-nose with Juanita who now looked like she was about ready to pass out cold, right in front of the altar. And the whole town.

"You…you…" Verna's finger slashed the air, shaky but aimed at Juanita "…how dare you desecrate this church?"

"Mrs. Ledbetter," the pastor said, "that's enough."

Verna whipped around to face him. "*No, I say no!* My husband ministered here for over thirty years. He stood in your very place and now this…" she whipped back to Juanita "…this baggage returns to tear open old wounds."

"I came to heal, not to—"

"There is no healing for what you did to my husband."

What *Juanita* did? Even for Verna that was a stretch.

"Oh, my dear," Juanita, said softly, "if only you knew."

"I *do* know." *What was Verna getting at? Did she know everything? Had she read that ledger?* "You cost him his soul. I rejoiced when he told me you were dead."

"He told you that? But he knew I was alive."

"You *liar*."

Without warning, all her rigid, floor-washing, furniture-waxing control gone, Verna lashed out, slapping Juanita across the face, leaving a red imprint of her hand beneath those gorgeous cheekbones. Shocked, Juanita reeled back a few steps then quickly righting herself, she stood tall once again and gently fingered her cheek.

Like a hive full of bees, the church was buzzing. I turned in my seat and glanced around. Folks were talking out loud, not even pretending to whisper, and a few people in the back rows were standing to get a better look.

I shot a sideways glance at Joanne. She had turned the color of cold ashes.

Juanita looked up at Pastor Ellis and then down at her hands. "I'm so sorry. I didn't mean for this to happen. When I heard your call to the altar, I thought the time had come to make amends. I truly wish I could have."

Head held high, wearing the red welt on her cheek like a badge of honor, Juanita started up the aisle. I swiveled in my seat to watch her. Looking neither left nor right, her high heels tap-tapping on the stones, she passed along the rows of gaping, chattering people and strode out, the heavy church door, like the final note in a hymn, slamming shut behind her.

Pastor Ellis recovered fast. He stepped down from the altar and walked over to Verna who stood frozen in the aisle as if having said her all she didn't know what more to say or do or where to go.

"Mrs. Ledbetter," he said, soft and low like he was talking to a patient in a sick room. "May I help you to your pew?"

She stared at him blank-faced. "My pew?" Her eyes darted around. She didn't quite recognize where she was or that a hushed church was hanging on her every word. She pointed to where I sat with Joanne. "That's my pew over there. What are those interlopers doing in it?"

"Mrs.—"

"Don't Mrs. me. I'm nobody's missus. Not anymore."

"You're upset. Why don't you—"

As Pastor Ellis reached out to touch her arm, she snatched it away and, dashing past him, she ran across the front of the altar to the door in the alcove, the one leading to the church basement.

Nodding at the organist, the pastor mouthed something I couldn't quite catch and, before you knew it, the whole choir surged to its feet and launched into the opening bars of "How Great Thou Art."

Joanne half rose in her seat. "I'm going after her."

"No, don't leave." I tugged her back down.

"She's my grandmother."

"You need to be here." I squeezed her clenched hands. Locked between them was a sodden tissue. "It's your momma we're honoring, not somebody's hatred."

"Verna shouldn't be alone. She needs help"

"All right, you stay here. I'll go and see to her."

Before Joanne could stop me, I slipped off my trench coat, slung my purse over a shoulder and hurrying as fast as my heels would allow, I followed Verna through the alcove and down the stairs to the church basement. But where was she? A quick look around showed she wasn't in the big assembly hall or the room marked storage, or the ladies' room, either. I found her in the kitchen, a cloth in her hand, wiping down the stainless-steel fridge.

"Look at those fingerprints," she said when I walked in. "A disgrace, I call it, a downright disgrace. Why when I was the pastor's wife that wouldn't have been allowed."

"Of course not, Verna, but it sure is gleaming now."

She nodded and kept on buffing.

"What do you say I walk you home?" I said. "There must be a back entrance down here. We can slip out that way with no one the wiser."

Her hand stopped, mid-buff. "Why would I go out the back way? Roger and I always stood in the vesti-bule right inside the front door and greeted everyone as they passed by." Another swipe with the cloth. "Everybody loved him."

"He must have been a good man."

Her eyes widening, she put a finger to her lips and looking left then right to make sure no one was listening, she beckoned me closer. "That's the secret," she whispered. "Don't tell anyone. Nobody can know. He was bad, very, very bad."

"Mother!"

Verna and I whirled around.

"Roger dear," she cooed. "What are you doing here?"

"Looking for you." He nodded at me, a polite boy, well brought up. "Miss Ingersoll, thank you for looking after Mother, but I'm here now. Please feel free to leave."

Should I? He seemed calm enough, in control. But was *she*?

"I was telling Miss Ingersoll about your father," she said, "how he…how he…" The buffing cloth floated to the floor.

"I've told you over and over again, those stories are lies, Mother. Filthy lies." Roger's eyes met mine. "Mother's very upset right now. Please leave us. I'll take care of her."

"I know you will." I knew no such thing. For some reason, he didn't want me to hear what Verna was ready to spill, but though uneasy, I smiled and left without another word.

I didn't go far. Overhead the organ had started up again, its music coming through the floorboards like it was coming from heaven…or some place high up. At the foot of the stairs, I took off my spike heels and tiptoed barefoot back to the wall outside the kitchen.

"You have to get yourself in hand, Mother," Roger was saying. "Lashing out will do no good."

"You should know. Look where it landed you."

"Let that be your lesson." His voice more sad than angry.

"*My* lesson? I learned my lesson years ago. One lie at a time. I knew your father went to *that* house. He told me so, bold as brass. To minister to the poor souls, he said. And I *believed* him."

"Don't give in to bad thoughts. Put them out of your mind. That's what they told me at the hospital. Going over and over things keeps all the hurt alive."

"I did bury the hurt." Her voice icy calm. "Until the Petty woman came flaunting up the aisle like she had every right to be there. And after what she did? Seducing a man of the cloth."

"Don't say that, Mother. It makes me crazy. Father never had anything to do with those women. Nothing. He *wouldn't*."

"He *did*, I tell you, he did. Ask Reba." A sucked-in breath. "Oh, I forgot, you can't. Just as well. She was getting ready to talk to the police, had the town sheriff sniffing around, asking for old records and such."

A sudden draft chilled my bare feet. I hadn't heard a door open and the draft was soon cut off, but someone had snuck in. Footsteps, quiet and quick, were coming along a back-entry way. I hadn't spotted a rear door yet, but I wasn't surprised there was one. Fire codes demanded several entrances to a multi-use building like this.

On an impulse, shoes in hand, I darted into the storage room and closed the door. Filled with folding tables and chairs and cleaning supplies, the room had a stuffy, unused odor I hoped wouldn't make me sneeze. When the urge faded, I pressed my ear to the door but couldn't hear a thing from the kitchen, only the tail end of a hymn floating down from the church proper.

By now, Joanne must be feeling deserted in that

empty pew and worried about her grandmother. Maybe dashing into this storage room wasn't such a hot idea. Those footsteps might have been from the custodian or one of the church ladies coming to use the bathroom. Feeling brave, I slipped on my heels, opened the door a slit and peeked out but didn't see anyone. I tiptoed into the assembly hall and listened. Voices were coming from the kitchen. I moved in closer, flattening up against the wall outside the open kitchen door.

"I figured I'd find you here. Wipin' something' down. Always wipin' somethin' down." *That voice. I knew him. It was Carl Huggins.* "Why did ya go mouthin' off up there? You got the whole town talkin'. You might as well of hung a sign on her. That what you want? Why didn't you let her say her piece and leave quiet like? She left here once. She'd have done it again."

"She left because of you," Verna shot back. "She was scared of you. Well, she isn't scared now. That what's bothering you, Carl?"

"She had no reason to be scared of me. No more than of that husband of yours."

Verna drew in a breath so loud it sounded like a word.

"You can't talk to Mother that way," Roger said, not sounding too sure about it.

"No? Who's to stop me? You?" Carl broke out into an ugly laugh. It went on and on until, just like that, it was stopped dead by an ear-shattering crash. All went quiet. Good Lord, had one of those mammoth pots on the kitchen stove hit the floor?

From overhead, the heavy tread of many feet had replaced the music. The service must be over. Joanne would be frantic by now. I had to get upstairs to her.

No need to be reckless, though, so on tip-toes, bag slung over a shoulder, I sidled up to the kitchen door and risked a peek inside.

*Omigod.* Carl was out cold, flat on his back on the linoleum, a big ol' stainless pot sitting on the floor beside him. Roger, crouched by his side, was gently patting Carl's cheeks. I bet it had been a mighty long time since anybody had done that to him. Anyway, it didn't do a bit of good. Carl was a stone.

Roger looked up over a hunched shoulder at Verna. She was leaning against the stove and didn't appear to be the least bit frazzled at the sight of Carl stretched out by her feet.

"We have to get to a phone," Roger said. "He needs help."

I would have gone in then and there and called 911 on my cell, but Verna's next words stayed me.

"Not on your life." Without giving Carl so much as a glance, she reached down, picked up the pot and set it back on the stove. "The sexton will find him when he locks up."

"That might not be for an hour or more."

"You want to get put away for good?"

"Mother, you shouldn't have hit him. And now you just want to leave him here? That's not right."

"Was it right for him to barge in and give me what for?"

"Maybe not, but he was upset to see Juanita after so many years. Then you made it worse attacking her in front of everyone. You were wrong, Mother."

*Hmmph. Roger daring to defy his momma? Unbelievable.*

"You're talking wrong to *me*, son? To *me*? You

haven't got the right parent for that. Your daddy's the one who was wrong, having carnal relations with a trollop. And with others in that house, too. He's the one who was wrong."

"No! He never did, I tell you." Roger scrambled to his feet. "I'm going for help."

"You can't. They'll blame me, unless..." she stopped "...unless I tell them you hit him."

Halfway to the door, he came to a halt and, moving slow as a lazy cat, he turned back to face her. "Would you do that, Mother?"

"Only if I had to. I only do things when I have to. But sometimes no matter what you do, it isn't enough." Like a woman with a great weight pressing on her, she heaved a mighty sigh. "I took care of Reba's mouth and Darlene's too. And then look at what happened."

"Tell me," he said, pacing closer to her.

"The Ingersoll tart got the sheriff all riled up, and the two of them pried into matters that were none of their concern. If you ask me, they're the reason the Juanita hussy paraded herself in church today."

Roger waved a hand in the air like he was brushing away flies. "Never mind her. I want you to tell me about Reba and Darlene. What do you mean you took care of them? They're both dead."

"Of course, they are."

Roger's pacing stopped inches from her nose. "Did you kill them?"

I held my breath until she spoke.

"What I did was protect your father's name. And yours."

"Did you, or did you not, kill them?" He was in her

face now. "Tell me. For God's sake, tell me." His hands seized her shoulders and shook her. "Tell me."

"Yes, yes, yes!" she said, screaming like an animal caught in a trap.

"I know what happened to Darlene Petty. But what about your friend, Reba Knight?"

Roger's hands still clutched her shoulders, yet Verna shrugged. "She ate my brownies is all. She always was a glutton. Just like your father. Couldn't get enough of sweet stuff. I knew she'd gobble them down before anyone else had a taste."

"You *poisoned* her? And what of Father? Did you poison him too?"

I had to get out of there and find help fast. But how could I leave? Roger's hands had wrapped around Verna's throat. Lifting her until only the toes of her shoes touched the linoleum, he was squeezing with all his might.

I eased my bag to the floor and slipped out of my shoes. Then grabbing one of them, I raced into the kitchen and jammed the spike heel into Roger's back, pressing on it for all I was worth. "Let her go, or I'll shoot."

Gripped by rage, he paid me no mind.

"Let her go," I said. "Or I'll blow your spine in two."

He went to turn around.

I prodded harder. "No. Stay as you are. I'm waiting, but I won't for long."

As Verna's face went from red to purple, he loosened his fingers one by one, slid them over her shoulders and let his hands slip down to his sides. "I don't know what came over me," he murmured. "But I'm all right now."

*Really?* Well, I wasn't.

Neither was Verna. Freed from his grip, she stag-gered back and slowly, in a long, lingering slide, she slumped to the floor beside Carl and lay there, her knees wide apart, her skirt way too far north.

"Start walking," I said to Roger. Keeping the pres-sure on his back, I marched him out of the kitchen and over to the storage room. "Don't come out for ten min-utes. If I see you before then, I shoot. Got it?"

As threats go that was really lame, but it was all I could think of at the moment. Anyway, when he nod-ded, I laid a palm against his back and shoved, the sur-prise move sending him stumbling forward. I slammed the storage room door shut and grabbing a metal chair from the assembly hall, I jammed it under the door han-dle. It should hold for a few minutes, long enough for me to grab my other shoe and purse and run for help.

# FORTY-TWO

MATT WAS HALFWAY down the stairs and I was halfway up, when we slammed into each other.

"Whoa. What's your hurry?" he said, grabbing me before I toppled over.

Without bothering to ask what he was doing there, I pointed to the basement. "There's bodies all over the place down there."

*"What?"*

"Two people unconscious on the kitchen floor and a guy locked in a room."

"Wait up a minute. You're babbling."

"You got a gun on you?"

"Of course."

"Get it out. You may need it. I found the killer."

"You *what*?"

"Come on. There's no time to waste."

He put his hands on my shoulders, holding me on the stairs. "Who are these people, and where are they?"

"Verna and Roger Ledbetter and Carl Huggins. Two in the kitchen, one in the storage room."

He didn't move a muscle. "Explain."

Breathing fast, talking faster, I launched into what had happened. He listened all the way through and when I finished, he asked, "Did you see any weapons?"

"Guns and stuff? No, but I heard a crash. And now Verna's on the floor next to Carl."

Without asking me any more questions, he yanked his cell off his belt and called Zach. "Send an ambulance to Grace Church and get over here ASAP. I'll be in the basement."

"The back door is unlocked," I whispered.

He repeated that and signed off. We'd nearly reached the bottom of the stairs when up above, the alcove door opened and Joanne, cheeks tear-stained and pink with fevered worry, hurried down to us. "Oh, Honey, thank God the sheriff found you. I've been so worried. What's been keeping you? The cars are waiting. We're ready to leave for the cemetery."

"Go on without us," Matt said. "You explain, Honey." With that he headed down the rest of the stairs to the basement.

"Please go on ahead, Joanne. We'll catch up later," I promised.

She shook her head and started down the stairs after Matt. "No, something's wrong. What is it? Where's Roger? Where's Verna?"

"Well, Roger's in the storage room," I said.

A puzzled expression flitted across her face. "What's he doing in there?"

"I sort of locked him in."

*"Why?"*

I sighed. Too late for any way out but the truth. "He was strangling your grandmother."

The pink color drained out of Joanne's face. "Verna?" Her voice a whisper. "Is she...is she?"

"No, I don't think so. Matt called for an ambulance. It should be here any minute."

"Where is she?"

"On the kitchen floor. Next to Carl Huggins."

"Carl's there too? Where did he come from?" Not waiting for an answer, Joanne hustled down the remaining stairs. Nearly tripping in her haste, she grabbed the railing to keep from falling and I followed her into the basement.

Our hurried footsteps echoed in the empty space. Before we got to the kitchen, Roger pounded on the storage room door, hollering, "Let me out. Let me out."

Joanne went to free him, but before she could, Matt said, "Not yet. Let's deal with the injured first." He strode into the kitchen, took one step inside and swiveled back on his heel. "Honey, didn't you say Verna was in here?"

"Yes." I peered over his shoulder. Carl Huggins still lay on the floor, unconscious, but Verna was nowhere in sight.

"The back door," I said over Roger's pounding.

Matt nodded. "Probably. We know she didn't go up the stairs. As soon as Zach gets here, I'll have him search the basement, but she's most likely long gone." He knelt beside Carl and felt for a pulse. "He's alive, but Verna must have walloped him real good."

"Will you tell me what this is all about?" Joanne's jaw had taken on a firm look, meaning she wouldn't quit until she got answers. No doubt she'd make a real good digger when she got her anthro…anthro… whatever degree.

"Maybe Roger can help us find her." Matt hurried out to the assembly hall, lifted the metal chair out of the way and yanked open the storage room door.

Making no move to dash out, Roger stood in the

opening and stared straight ahead at Joanne. "My girl, my dear girl," he said. Blinking like he hadn't seen light in a very long while, he finally came forward one slow step at a time.

I sensed Matt tensing as Roger went over to Joanne. But making no hasty moves, Roger slowly put his arms around her and closing his eyes, he held her tight against him. And Joanne? Well, Joanne clung to him as if she had waited all her life for this moment. It lasted only a second or so before loosening his hold, but keeping her at arm's length, Roger peered into her eyes. "No matter what anyone tells you, I mean anyone, even my mother, you are mine, and you always have been. Everything else is a lie. Do you understand me?"

Unsure, like sun on a rainy day, she nodded anyway.

"You are my daughter, and I am your father. Whatever happens next, you are all that matters to me."

His hands fell to his sides, and like a man too tired to keep on his feet, he sagged onto the metal chair Matt had pushed out of the way.

Joanne's puzzled look quickly turned to alarm. She glanced over at Matt. "Please tell me what's wrong."

Before he could, the alcove door opened and heavy footsteps pounded down the stairs. The limo driver, out of breath from hurrying, spotted Joanne right off and blurted, "Miss Petty, the funeral director is beside himself." He paused to catch a breath. "You must come along. Your mother has to be put to rest."

"I'm sorry, it's just that…" Words failing her, Joanne bent over Roger and kissed his cheek. "Take care of them both," she said to Matt and me before hurrying up the stairs with the driver.

A siren in the distance screamed louder and louder

then screeched to a halt. Moments later, the rear basement door opened, letting in Deputy Zach and two paramedics.

"Over here, in the kitchen," Matt called. As the paramedics hurried in to Carl, he said to Zach, "Verna Ledbetter confessed to killing Darlene Petty. She's gone missing. Search the whole downstairs area. I don't think she's armed, but watch yourself."

Zach took off, and Matt approached Roger who, still seated on the metal chair, was staring down at his hands. "Mr. Ledbetter?"

Roger's head rose slowly, and he looked up at Matt with tired eyes.

"Did you, or did you not, assault your mother?"

"I did. I tried to choke her."

"Then I have to take you in," Matt said gently enough.

Roger shrugged and held out both hands. "I'm guilty. Cuff me."

With a few smooth moves, Matt did. "I'll put you in the cruiser for now until I can get you to the station. You can contact a lawyer from there."

"I don't want a lawyer. I don't want anything."

Matt eyed me over Roger's head, his glance saying this wasn't going to be good. No, how could it be?

With Matt's hand on Roger's elbow, they marched out the rear door together. It slammed shut, and they were gone. I wandered into the kitchen and stood in a corner, not wanting to get in the way. The paramedics were bent over Carl who was still stretched out on the linoleum with his eyes closed. The medic with Rick embroidered on his shirt pocket glanced up when I walked in.

"We can't revive him. He may be hemorrhaging

internally. We're taking him to county hospital for a brain scan."

I nodded, staying in the corner while the two men lifted Carl onto a stretcher, covered him with a thin, white blanket and wheeled him out the back way.

After everyone left, a gloomy pall settled over the church basement. Clouds had replaced the sun, and the gray light filtering in through the high, narrow windows seemed sparse and spooky. No need to linger down here. I'd get my coat from the pew and walk up Sugar Street for my car. What a day this had been. More than anything, I yearned to go home and climb into bed with the comforter over me and the phone off, but it wasn't about to happen. Past noon already and no work done, no calls answered, no showings to potential buyers, nothing achieved but sorrow.

Despite everything, I needed to put my mind to business, but it was hard what with worrying where Verna had disappeared to and wondering, once the funeral ended, who Joanne would contact for the answers she needed. Matt? Roger? Me?

If she wanted to talk to me, that would be just fine. I could tell her what I'd seen and heard and offer the comfort of friendship, but for official answers and results, she'd need to talk to the law. In the meantime, I'd better get cracking. I had a realty agency to run.

At the top of the stairs, I pushed open the alcove door and walked into the empty church. Quiet, now, smelling of candle wax and wilted flowers and grief, it wasn't much more cheerful than the basement, especially with the sun hidden behind those storm clouds.

My trench coat was in the front pew, right where I'd left it. As I bent over to pick it up, a slight noise behind me made the hair on my nape rise up. I whirled around, and my heart nearly stopped. "Verna! What on earth are you doing here?"

"You don't think I have the right?"

I grabbed my coat and clutched it to my chest. "No, no, I just wondered. You disappearing like you did and all."

"This is my house." She pointed a finger at me. "And this is my pew. Get out of it, trash."

The hair on my neck had settled down, but my dander sure shot up. "You talking to me, woman?" Nuts or not, seventy something or not, she had no cause to speak to me that way. I squared my shoulders. "I'm here to stay. I'm planning on doing some praying for our departed sister Darlene. Remember her, Darlene Petty?" Still clutching the coat to my chest, like it was a shield or something, I ventured a step closer to Verna, figuring it might cause her to move out of the pew and into the aisle. No such luck. "Darlene was a godly woman, Verna. Why did you hate her so?"

Verna sighed. One of those sighs you bring up from the soles of your feet. "I didn't hate her, just her questions. She threatened everything."

"What do you mean by everything?" I stood still, willing her to go on.

"She'd been out to visit Reba Knight at the courthouse, nosing around about her daughter's birth certificate. Well, whatever Reba said set this Darlene on a witch hunt. She came by my house the day you had that open house...cars up and down the street, parked all over the place."

"Go on," I urged. "Darlene?"

"Darlene?" Verna's brows beetled for a second as if

she'd forgotten the name and then she shrugged. "Oh, that one. She wondered what I knew about Joanne's birth. Said she was determined to get at the truth. Claimed it was general knowledge my husband used to minister to those girls at the Moose and what did I know about that? As if I'd tell her. As if I'd ever tell anybody." She stopped short, remembering. Her shoulders in her heavy winter coat sagged. "It doesn't matter anymore."

"Why not?" I asked, actually wanting to know.

"Because the ledger is gone."

"You *knew* about it?"

Verna nodded, once. "The reverend confessed to me one night before, before…said it was only a matter of time and everyone in town would know. Carl Huggins and his daddy were threatening to expose him."

*Keep her talking. She's got me trapped in this pew.*

"Why?" Though that was an easy guess.

"Greed. Filthy lucre. The root of all evil. Or so the Bible says." She wrung her hands twisting them over and over as if trying to wring out her demons. "I don't want to quarrel with the Lord, but what about lust?" She raised her eyes to the vaulted ceiling and hollered, 'What about lust, Lord?'" She waited for a long, tense moment, but when the Lord didn't holler back, her glance came down to earth, and her voice dropped to a whisper. "I ask Him the same thing night after night. He's never given me an answer. Never once." Her eyes narrowed into slits. "So I had to stamp it out alone. I had to. You can understand, can't you?" She moved deeper into the pew, closer to me. I backed up a step. "He'll forgive me, don't you think?" she asked, or pleaded, I couldn't be sure which.

She leaned in, waiting for an answer, her eyes glittering. That's when, like a fool, I took a chance, a terrible, terrible chance. "For killing Darlene and Reba, maybe He will forgive you. But what about your husband? A man you took a vow to love and honor? For killing him, the Lord might not be so forgiving."

Her mouth slipping open, Verna stared at me for a moment before throwing her head back and busting into a full-throated belly laugh. In the empty church, it rang on and on, bouncing off the high, vaulted ceiling, off the stone walls, off the tall windows.

Finally, gasping and red-faced, she wound down, like a toy top that couldn't spin any more. "As if...as if the likes of you know what the Lord is thinking."

"And you *do*, Verna?" I wasn't about to laugh and I wasn't about to cry, but my heart was pounding so hard and heavy, I could *hear* it.

She stepped even nearer, squeezing me in a vise with no way out. Unless I could snooker her into letting me leave. Fat chance of that happening, but I had to try. I threw my shoulders back and lowered my voice. "Move out of the way, Verna, I have to go to work."

"That's too bad." With a smile as innocent as an angel's, she reached into her coat pocket and yanked out a knife.

A shocked breath caught in my throat. "Where did you get that?" I asked, my tough guy voice fading to a whisper.

"In the kitchen, of course. From the locked drawer." She sighed a put-upon sigh. "I was the pastor's wife. I have keys to everything. People forget that. But they won't forget this."

She lunged, the knife pointed at my throat. Without

thinking, I flung the only weapon I had, my trench coat. It landed over her head and shoulders. From under the fabric, she jabbed the knife left and right, searching for me, desperate to slice me, but the blade hit nothing except cloth. With her free hand scrabbling at the material, she struggled to fling off the coat, but the blade had slashed the fabric and the hilt was hung up in the opening.

As she yanked and tugged, fighting to get loose, I slid the handbag from my shoulder and lifted it overhead. Using every ounce of my strength, I flung it free. It arced through the air, came down like a rock and—*pow*—caught Verna square in the chest. Thanks to my cell phone, keys, compact and the bottle of water I hadn't had a chance to sip, she staggered back, banging into the pew upright.

Her arms working like crazy, she finally wrestled my trench coat off her head and tossed it aside. It dropped, clattering, to the church floor.

*Aah. No belt buckle made that loud noise. She had thrown away the baby with the bath water.*

She heard it too. I could tell she had. Though her hair was wild and so were her eyes, certainty had fled from her face. She was scared, and she wasn't the only one. I needed to call for help, and fast, but how to keep her from killing me first? There was no way out but to use what the good Lord had given me for a weapon. Lowering my head like a battering ram, I made a mad dash across the small space that separated us and caught her right in the gut.

With an "oof" she collapsed into the aisle. Not giving her a chance to scramble to her feet, I fell on top of her, but I wouldn't be there for long. A beefy woman,

she was wriggling under me like a bag full of snakes.
I needed something to tie her up with. *Fast*. I glanced
frantically around. *Something. Anything*.

Inches away, stood the round table that had held
Darlene's ashes. The funeral urn and the ring of pink
roses that surrounded it were gone, but the long white
cloth was still draped over the tabletop.

I yanked my skirt up to my thighs, clasped my knees
around Verna's middle—not easy what with her thrash-
ing away like mad—reached for the cloth and pulled
it free.

"Give me your hands, Verna."

No response.

"Give me your hands or I'll smash your head against
the stone floor."

I wouldn't have, of course, but it sounded good.

Her fingers bent like claws, she scrabbled for my face,
desperate to get to my eyes. I grabbed her right hand and
twisted. "Give me the other one or I'll break your wrist."

She shook her head, flinging it from side to side, setting her gray curls to trembling. I couldn't let that ol'
lady hair-do make me go soft. I twisted her wrist some
more. She yelped and stuck out both hands. I quickly
bound them together and double-knotted the cloth. I
swear she was ready to spit in my face but couldn't
summon the saliva. Now for her feet.

The trench coat lay nearby where she had tossed it.
Now if I could get hold of it…still gripping Verna in
a thigh lock, I stretched out my left leg and snared the
coat with my heel. Inch by inch, I tugged it closer until
I could grab it. I pulled the knife out of the fabric and
flung it across the church where it landed with a thud.
Then I slipped the belt out of the loops.

Sensing what I was about to do, Verna was mighty fidgety. I'd better hurry. For an ol' lady, an ol' murderer, she had a lot of energy left to do more harm, and I wasn't about to let that happen.

I bent over, so near to her face, her hot breath fanned my cheek. "Just so's you'll know, Verna, I'll knock you out if I have to. Don't make me have to."

Her eyes, like two drops of acid, burned holes in mine. She'd kill me if she could. *Not now, Verna. Not when I have so much to live for.*

Quick as a shot, before she could react or try to sit up, I slid down her body, and swinging my legs to one side, I swiveled around, still holding her down, still sitting on her, but now facing her feet. While I wiggled around, she was straining under me like mad, and I knew if I lifted my weight off her, she'd kick my teeth out.

Working fast, I slipped the belt under her ankles, cinched it tight and knotted it. When I had her trussed up like a Thanksgiving turkey, I climbed off her, collapsed on the aisle floor and caught a few deep breaths. My thighs, my arms, my whole body aching, I finally managed to sit up and glance over at my prisoner who was lying in the aisle without moving. Like air from a leaky tire, the fight had oozed out of her. From all but her eyes, anyway. They stared up at me filled with poison…or were those tears?

# FORTY-THREE

IT'S A GOOD thing Kelsey Davis from the *Star* had his
fancy camera back, for he sure put it to good use the
day of the funeral and for the whole next week.

Like nothing else had happened in the world, the Eureka Falls newspaper spared little space for anything
but Darlene Petty's funeral, the events leading up to it
and the events following it.

"Look at this." I held up the whole second page for
Matt to see. "All pictures."

The church inside and out; Joanne at the gravesite,
going into the jail to see Roger, going into the mental
hospital to visit Verna; a photo of Darlene as a young
college grad; one of a teenage Juanita, even one of me
sitting on my trashed trench coat in the aisle of Grace
Church.

And then there was page one. For days, it ate up the
story, every day revealing details about a different person involved in the deaths. Actually, everyone and anyone involved in the scandal that had exploded over the
town: Verna, Roger, Joanne, Darlene, Reba and people
from the past too; the Reverend Ledbetter and how he
had ministered to the fallen. Carl Huggins (and his recent brain surgery, prognosis guarded); Kenny Knight
who, after the Petty funeral and all that had gone on

that day, intended to put his wife to rest with a small, private service. The date to be announced. There were even a couple of paragraphs about Andy Ballou and how he was counsel to both Darlene and her daughter, as well as a brief mention of Andy's friendship with another murder victim, Carmen DeLuca who had run a Ponzi scheme that bilked her clients—many of them Eureka Falls citizens—of their life savings.

I read about Andy without getting the least bit upset, so I guess I had turned a page. While charm was a great thing in a man, it wasn't everything. Working with Andy sure had taught me that.

Looking mighty comfy snuggled on my sofa with Jake by his side, Matt took the paper and read through it then folded it and put it aside. "Too bad Kelsey needs a tragedy to get a good story. The town could use a happy tale about now."

I edged Jake over a bit and sank down next to Matt. "Well, everything's not bad. Joanne's back at college. She'll finish her degree in three more months and get on with her life knowing her beloved momma received justice at the end. That will never be enough satisfaction, but it's some."

Matt nodded. "At least for the first time in his life, Roger's free from Verna's meddling."

"Right. As for Verna, well, I guess the mental hospital is where she needs to be. And then there's Juanita. She doesn't have to hide in the shadows any more, afraid of the past."

"Exactly. She and Dr. Hightower can put it behind them. They've definitely decided not to sue Tim O'Toole for embezzlement. Which means business as usual for the Toole Shed. So you can add Tim to your happiness list. That sticks in my craw, but we'll keep an eye on him. Any deviations, the law will be all over him like ants at a picnic."

"Lovely." I sat patting Jake till he purred like a kitten. "The only one I can't figure, Matt, is Carl Huggins. Why did he come into the church basement and lay into Verna the way he did?"

Matt gave me the cocked eyebrow stare. "A smart girl like you missed that?"

I shrugged. "Guess so."

"He was in love with Juanita. Had been for years. When he tried to pressure her into running away from the Moose with him, he had her so scared she did run away, but alone. Guess he never got over it."

"No, from what's happened, it doesn't seem so, but I never would have guessed."

"Not surprising. He's a pretty secretive guy. Tim O'Toole, however, was well aware of Carl's feelings. When Juanita asked Tim to help her escape, he did…he and the reverend. That's how Tim knew of her whereabouts and could blackmail her."

"The creep."

"Agreed."

I leaned back and rested my head on the sofa cushion. "Do you think folks will ever forget all this and look on the Moose as just another house?"

Matt stretched out his chunky legs, lifting his feet in their thick, white socks onto the coffee table. "It'll take a while. Years, maybe, and it will depend on a number of things."

"Such as?"

"How it looks for one. Painting the outside white was a good start."

"Um-hum." With its fresh coat of paint and new roof, the house already looked different from the dingy brown pile it had been for years. And once the shutters were painted and put back up and the front door refinished, the house would really shine. Come spring, I'd tend to the scruffy lawn and the weedy brick walk.

Inside, major progress had been made too. The electric wiring was completed right down to the front door chimes. The heating and cooling system should be finished no later than next week.

First thing in the morning I was meeting with Dexter from Peerless Painters. I had a dream plan in mind and wanted to share it with him—white ceilings and white woodwork throughout, dark, stained floors and doors, and a whisper gray paint on the walls.

"Matt, what's that expression for a clean slate?"

*"Tabula rosa."*

"That's the look I'm after. Then over time, when I can afford furniture and paintings, they'll really shine against that pale background. So for now, only the kitchen and bathrooms need to be made livable."

"Speaking of which…" Matt reached into his shirt pocket and pulled out an envelope. "To Honey" was written on the front in big bold letters. He handed it to me. "For you. A little gift. Some men bring a girl red roses, and I'll do that too. But first I wanted you to have this."

I sat there not moving, just staring at the envelope, wondering what on earth—

"Go on. Open it."

I did and let out a scream that sent Jake scrambling off the sofa. "Omigod! Matt Rameros, this is so wonderful. Thank you. Thank you!" I flung my arms around him, hugging him tight, squeezing the air right out of him. "You shouldn't have. You shouldn't have. But I'm so glad you did." I waved the gift card at Jake. "Look at this boy. We're going to have—" I scanned the card "—a brand-new stainless-steel refrigerator, a stove, a dishwasher, a disposal and…and a micro. I can't hardly believe it, Matt." I flopped onto the sofa cushions to catch my breath and come back down to earth, which I did with a thump. Gently, I tucked the card back into his shirt pocket. "Your gift is beyond wonderful, Matt, but I can't accept it. It's too much. Much too much."

"What if I insist?"

"But why would you? It will cost you thousands. Thousands." I glanced up into his smiling face. "Why?" I repeated softly.

"Why is a rhetorical question, Honey."

"Whatever that means. Just tell me."

"I love you, Honey Ingersoll." He stopped, gulped in a big swig of air and aimed those happy eyes at mine. "Will you marry me?"

"Of course."

His jaw dropped, his arms fell to his sides and, stunned, he sat up straight as a poker. "That's it? *Yes?* After keeping me guessing for months. Make that years. It's *yes*." He grinned, ear to ear as if the wait no longer mattered any more. "You're sure?"

"Yes," I said, my heart doing backflips of joy.

"Omigod."

We stopped talking for a wonderful little while, until he stopped kissing me to murmur, "When?"

"Whenever you say, Matt Rameros. Soon would be good. In fact, soon would be great. But first, want to help me pick out some cabinets and countertops and tile and stuff to go with the appliances?"

Matt's head jerked back. "That's a surprise."

"Why?"

"You've seen my house. I got the distinct impression you didn't care for the, ah, décor."

"To be honest, I didn't, not really, all those colors in those small rooms. But your mom had some beautiful, big furniture. I loved the dining room pieces."

"What about my bed?" The eyebrow arch again.

"Marvelous." Marvelous was one of my favorite new words, and I used it whenever I could.

"Marvelous, huh?"

"Yes. Effective too. Very effective."

"Oh?" He swung his feet off the coffee table and turned to face me, an unasked question creasing his brow.

I smiled at him, at his big dark eyes, his wide white smile, at the dimple in his cheek that appeared when he laughed, though he wasn't laughing just then. "What do you mean effective, Honey? What are you getting at?"

"What I'm trying to say is it takes a lot to turn a house into a home."

He nodded, all serious of a sudden. "I agree."

"And you've helped me do that."

"All I did was scrape off some wallpaper."

I shook my head. "You've done much more than that. Even more than the appliances. But still there's a lot left to do. For what I have in mind, it's going to take a family, a happy family. You know the kind with the patter of little feet who'll put their own stamp on it. Make the house their own."

"Go on." A little half smile was starting up on his face as if he knew where I was heading. Did he?

I scrunched down into the sofa cushions, set my bare feet up on the coffee table and took a deep breath. "The day when we stopped off at your house? After you took a shower and found me in your bedroom?" He went kind of quiet beside me. "Have you forgotten?"

"Never. How could I forget that afternoon?" He lowered his legs to the floor and turned to take me in his arms. "I'll remember it forever."

I knew he meant what he said, for as he leaned over to kiss me, the twinkle in his eyes could have lit up the sky.

"Well, I'm happy to hear that you remember it, because I have something important to tell you. You need to know the certificate for the refrigerator, the stove, the dishwasher and the micro isn't the only gift you've given me."

And then I told him what it was, but not until after he kissed me.

\* \* \* \* \*

# AND ONE MORE THING...

A WHOLE YEAR LATER, it's still a mystery to me why no one ever saw any beauty in the Moose. Of course, in recent years, it had slipped from shabby to seedy, I'll give you that. And its history didn't help folks warm up to it, either. But like people sometimes do, if they're loved long enough and deep enough, the Moose has blossomed into a brand new, happy future.

Matt and I are Mr. and Mrs. now, and live in the Moose with Matty—Matilda Rose Rameros. She's six months old and has big brown eyes, curly dark hair and the names of both her grandmas. Matilda for Matt's mom and Rose for mine.

In case you're wondering, Matt has remained sheriff of Eureka Falls, a town he's proud to say has had little to no crime lately. And I've kept on running the real estate agency, these days with Matty's help. A while ago, to celebrate our new life together, Matt and I held a big housewarming party. The baby loved it—the people, the excitement, the attention. We lit the fireplaces, set candles around and piped music through our stereo system. With all that and our friends, plus a dining room table groaning with food, the three of us had ourselves a day to remember. While you'll probably think I'm foolish, I believe the old place understood when all afternoon long folks kept saying how the Moose had been transformed. That's what they said, over and over, transformed. A fancy term for changed, and the truth, for the Moose surely has changed, in more ways than one.

So no matter what you may have heard, I can tell you with no word of a lie, that an old rundown house, a house that once, like the Moose, harbored sorrow and death, can be brought back to life and become what it was always destined to be—a family's happy home.